FIVE
4ths of July

FIVE
4ths of July

PAT RACCIO HUGHES

VIKING

An Imprint of Penguin Group (USA) Inc.

VIKING

Published by Penguin Group

Penguin Young Readers Group, 345 Hudson Street, New York, New York 10014, U.S.A.

Penguin Group (Canada), 90 Eglinton Avenue East, Suite 700, Toronto, Ontario, Canada M4P 2Y3
(a division of Pearson Penguin Canada Inc.)

Penguin Books Ltd, 80 Strand, London WC2R 0RL, England

Penguin Ireland, 25 St Stephen's Green, Dublin 2, Ireland (a division of Penguin Books Ltd)

Penguin Group (Australia), 250 Camberwell Road, Camberwell, Victoria 3124, Australia
(a division of Pearson Australia Group Pty Ltd)

Penguin Books India Pvt Ltd, 11 Community Centre, Panchsheel Park, New Delhi – 110 017, India

Penguin Group (NZ), 67 Apollo Drive, Rosedale, North Shore 0632, New Zealand
(a division of Pearson New Zealand Ltd.)

Penguin Books (South Africa) (Pty) Ltd, 24 Sturdee Avenue, Rosebank, Johannesburg 2196, South Africa

Penguin Books Ltd, Registered Offices: 80 Strand, London WC2R 0RL, England

First published in 2011 by Viking, a division of Penguin Young Readers Group

3 5 7 9 10 8 6 4 2

LIBRARY OF CONGRESS CATALOGING-IN-PUBLICATION DATA
Hughes, Pat (Patrice Raccio)
Five 4ths of July / by Pat Raccio Hughes.
p. cm.
Summary: On July 4th, 1777, fourteen-year-old Jake Mallory and his friends are celebrating
their new nation's independence, but over the next four years Jake finds himself in increasingly
adventurous circumstances as he battles British forces, barely survives captivity on a prison ship,
and finally returns home to Connecticut, war-torn and weary, but hopeful for America's future.
ISBN 978-0-670-01207-7 (hardcover)
[1. Adventure and adventurers—Fiction. 2. Connecticut—History—Revolution, 1775–1783—Fiction.
3. United States—History—Revolution, 1775–1783—Fiction.] I. Title. II. Title: Five fourths of July.
PZ7.H87374Fi 2011
[Fic]—dc22
2010049521

Printed in U.S.A.
Book design by Sam Kim
Set in Granjon

For my parents,

Pasquale Raccio, who instilled a love of literature,

and

Gloria Cuticelli Raccio, who encouraged reading and never censored.

FIVE
4ths of July

Boy

July 4, 1777

JAKE MALLERY STOOD on the raft's edge, looking toward the shore.

On the red rocks of Five Mile Point, his friend Tim cupped his hands around his mouth and called, "Are you ready!"

Jake bent his knees, leaning forward.

Beside him, in the same position, Caleb said, "Are *you* ready, Mal?"

"Ready to crush you," Jake replied.

"Take your mark!" Tim shouted.

"Ready for defeat, I meant," Caleb said breezily.

"Not much chance of—"

"Go!"

Just before Jake hit the chill water of Long Island Sound, he heard a splash. Blast! Caleb had got the jump, and Jake had only himself to blame.

Staying submerged, he stretched his arms ahead of him, then

pushed the water behind, again and again. He always swam underwater when racing; it left his opponent guessing. Jake could hold his breath longer than any boy he'd ever met, and nobody had beaten him in years.

But now . . . right now his reign was as shaky as old King George's. *Stretch. Push. Concentrate.*

A few rods from the jutting red rocks of Five Mile Point, Jake surfaced with a gasp. He could feel Caleb near—so near, he dared not waste a moment to look.

Their friends were cheering and yelling:

"Come on, Caleb!"

"Get him, Cay, get him!"

"Almost there, Caleb!"

But Jake heard Tim's voice above the others: "Swim, Mal, swim! Come on, Mal! *Swim!*"

When Jake felt a tug on his shirt, he recognized defeat's desperate grasp. He kicked Caleb away and, with a final frantic burst of speed, slapped his hand on warm rock.

"Victorious yet again!" Tim declared as Dan placed a bare foot on Jake's head and pushed him under.

Jake came up laughing. Standing in the chest-deep water, he stretched his arms to the sky. "Who's next?"

"I was counting on you to beat him for us all, Cay," Gideon said with good nature.

"Keep counting, old boy." Jake hauled himself onto the red rocks and shook the water out of his hair. "He couldn't beat me even with his cheating!"

"What cheating?" Caleb protested.

"First he distracts me from the starting call, and then he holds my shirt."

"I did no such things."

"And he compounds his sins with lies," Jake said as Caleb laughed in admission.

"He's like a cormorant," Caleb complained to the others. "He dives down and stays under so long, the surface shows no trace of him."

"Yes—and you never know where he'll pop up next," Gideon added.

"Dan?" Jake asked. "Want to go again?"

Dan waved him away. "I'm tired, Mal."

"Tired of losing all the time?"

"Have you some sort of devil's pact with Poseidon, Mallery?" Caleb asked, climbing out of the water.

"Cheer up, lads," Jake said. "I've a surprise for you."

Dan's grin was suspicious. "What sort of surprise?"

"One guaranteed to soothe the sting of defeat." Jake pulled on his breeches, letting his wet shirt hang out to dry. "Come on, Timo—go with me."

"I think I get the gist of this," Caleb muttered.

Jake lowered himself into his white-pine dugout canoe. "I only hope you dirty sons of Rebels brought your knives, for I don't intend to do all the work."

"Where *is* the surprise, Mal?" Gideon asked.

"Just up near the ferry landing."

"Just!" Dan hooted. "That'll take ages!"

"Daniel, I believe that's called 'looking a gift horse in the mouth.'" Jake steadied the canoe against the rocks so that Tim could get in easily.

Tim was terrified of the water. He was ashamed of that fact—how many coast boys feared the sea?—but he couldn't help it. When he was little, he'd nearly drowned after a fall from his father's clamming wharf. Ever since, he would wade only up to his knees and went in no boat but Jake's dugout. They pushed and paddled away from the Point, then Jake set his sail to tack into the harbor. There was a stiff breeze; they'd be back in no time.

Summer days on Connecticut's coast were often hot and humid, with a gray blanket of sky keeping the sun in bed till noon. But this morning, light sparkled and shimmered on the water's choppy surface, and a few picturesque white clouds were tossed across a bright blue firmament.

"'Tis a portent!" Tim called over the noise of the flogging sail.

Jake gave him a questioning look.

Tim raised both arms to the sky, grinning broadly. "For the first anniversary of our independence!"

Jake shook his head, twisting his mouth in an expression of cynicism. "First and last!"

Tim laughed. "You'll see." He stretched out in the bottom of the boat with his head upon the bow, eyes closed and a blissful look on his face.

As they sailed past the new fort at Black Rock, Jake gave a

friendly salute to Jeddy Thompson, the militia sentinel on duty. But to Tim he said, "Ridiculous place for a fort."

"Are you still on that?" Tim answered lazily.

"They should have built it at the Point. Having a fort within the harbor is—"

"—like inviting the British into the parlor, instead of turning them away at the doorstep," Tim finished, mimicking Jake to perfection.

Jake laughed, then fell silent.

Today the entire coast was on high alert for a British attack. Some said the British wanted to cut short any celebration of the new nation's first year. Others said it would be revenge for Patriot raids on Long Island.

But Jake was sure that if the attack came at New Haven, it would be because of Benedict Arnold. For New Haven was Arnold's home, and he had proved himself to be the Patriots' fiercest fighter.

When Jake let down his sail, Tim sat up cautiously. Jake handed him a paddle, pointing toward the rocky shoreline. "See the rope?"

Tim nodded, and they headed for the spot where a rope rose from the water and was looped around a rock. Jake let the dugout bump the shore, then scrambled onto the rocks. He grabbed hold of the rope and hauled a dripping bushel of oysters to the surface.

"This is the work of your evil genius," Tim said, grinning. He held the dugout against the rocks as Jake lowered the oysters.

But as soon as the bushel was in the boat, a shrill voice came: "Timothy Morris! What in heaven's name are you up to?"

Jake knew before he looked up: Servant Girl. What was *she* doing here?

"Good morning, Hannah," Tim said sheepishly. "We, uh—"

"You told your mother you were going to watch your friends swim races!"

"And I did, but, um—"

"Must you answer to a bonded servant, Tim?" Jake asked, trying to sound good-natured.

Hannah pointed at the oysters. "*That* is illegal, and you both know it. The taking of oysters from May through August is allowed only in cases of sickness and necessity," she recited primly, as if reading from a broadside.

"Well, then, we qualify," Jake said. "On the grounds of necessity."

"And *what* is your need?" she asked, folding her arms.

"We need them for our celebration," Jake replied, and Tim laughed.

"Tim, you should not allow yourself to be led astray by *him*," Hannah lectured. "Your father sits on the committee to enforce the laws against poaching—"

"He needs *you* to tell him that?" Jake interrupted.

"—and there's a good reason for those regulations. If everyone were to take oysters throughout the summer—"

Jake raised his voice to top hers: "Yes, Servant Girl, I believe we *all* know the reason for the law."

"But it's just one bushel, Hannah," Tim said in a supplicating tone.

"If everyone were to take just one bushel—"

"For God's sake, man!" Jake blurted. "Will you sit there and let this . . . *chattel* browbeat you? Tell her to mind her business and go back to the kitchen where she belongs!"

Hannah's face turned scarlet, and she spoke to Tim in a measured manner: "Tell your *friend* it just so happens I've been given a holiday, as well. It is not *my* fault that a morning walk has uncovered malfeasance, and—"

"Malfeasance!" Jake wasn't sure what it meant, but it had *mal* in it so it couldn't be anything good. "Oh, Tim, this *is* rich! Malfeasance! Who's been teaching the wench such big words?"

"Release those oysters," she said to Tim, "or I'll tell your father, and you'll both be punished."

Jake fixed cold eyes on her. "If I'd a servant like you, *she'd* be punished—with a whip."

"Mal," Tim said wearily. "Hannah . . ."

"If she tells your father, what will your sisters say about that?" Jake asked, then watched her blanch. "Ah! *There* we go. Now, let's settle this amicably, shall we? Servant Girl, be on your way. Tim, our feast awaits." He got back into the dugout and launched it with a paddle against a rock.

"You won't tell, Hannah, will you?" Tim pleaded.

"No. For *your* sake, Tim." She began walking along the rocks, to be able to keep up the harangue as the boat drifted away. "But he is a bad influence on you. You're much too good for the likes of him. He—"

To drown her out, Jake began to sing:

> *"And there was Captain Washington*
> *With gentlefolks about him.*
> *They say he's grown so 'tarnal proud*
> *He will not ride without 'em!*
> *Yankee Doodle, keep it up!*
> *Yankee Doodle dandy . . ."*

When he looked back, Hannah was staring after them, hands on hips. Jake turned his attention to Tim. "How *can* you let her speak to you that way! A *servant*!"

Tim let his hand dangle in the water. "I think of Hannah more as a sister than a servant."

"As if you need another sister. Watch out, or they'll all turn you into a milksop. And that one . . ." He jerked a thumb in Hannah's direction. "What right has she—"

"Ahh!" With playful exasperation, Tim skimmed a handful of the Sound into Jake's face. "She's harmless, Mal. You make too much of her. Besides, she's had a hard life. Would it kill you to be a bit kinder to her?"

"I don't consider living in the Morris home to be much of a hardship," Jake said.

"I meant her childhood. Before she came to us."

"She's had time enough to get over that. The girl needs to

learn her place. When I have servants, they'll know their place."

But Tim's placid expression showed he was done with the subject.

Tim had been Jake's boon companion since dame school days. Different as they were, people often could not believe they were friends. But Jake liked Tim's calm affability; he thought it would be tiresome to go around with someone as tempestuous as himself. And he knew Tim found in him the adventure and exuberance lacking at home, for Tim was the only boy following six sisters, and his parents were doting but elderly.

Tim's father was Captain Amos Morris, who had served in the French War nearly twenty years ago. Jake's own father had been a soldier under him, which was difficult for Jake to imagine—he couldn't see his father, fond as he was at giving orders, ever taking them from anyone else. Captain Morris was too old now for active service, but he was called a militia captain out of respect. He also served as a town selectman and was on the Committee of Inspections, helping Governor Trumbull with military matters. The Morrises had plenty of money and kept four Negro slaves on the farm as well as Servant Girl in the house. Compared to Jake, Tim led a life of leisure; his only responsibilities were to study with his tutor and help tend his family's saltworks on the beach.

Back at the Point, Jake held the boat steady again so Tim could climb out, then passed the bushel up to him.

"Ah, here's a fine breakfast!" Caleb said.

Tim turned the oysters onto the rocks; each boy took out his knife and set to work. Jake had had the most experience and deftly opened several before most of his friends did one.

"I propose a toast!" Dan said, holding an oyster as if it were a glass of claret.

Everyone followed suit.

"To the first of an eternity of Independence Days," Dan announced loftily.

"To Independence!" Gideon echoed.

"To the Fourth of July!" Tim said.

"Hear, hear!" Caleb said.

They all turned expectantly to Jake. "All right, all right," he said, rolling his eyes.

After slurping down their oysters, they tossed the shells into the Sound, then busied themselves with opening, and eating, as they talked.

"Have you *no* faith, Mal?" asked Dan. He would have been with the Continentals already, but his father said he was too young.

"Not none, but not much," Jake admitted. "Maybe if we had a few more officers like Benedict Arnold."

"Arnold, Arnold! Does he know how to say anything else?" Caleb asked.

"Yes: 'The fort should have been built at the Point,'" Tim said drily, and everyone laughed.

"Well, who else is there?" Jake asked. "Arnold is the only one with any sand."

"It's too bad we lost Wooster," Dan said. "He was a good man." General Wooster, also from New Haven, had been killed just a couple of months ago when he and Arnold attacked the British at Ridgefield.

"A good man," Jake agreed. "But too soft on the Loyalists for my liking. Arnold, though—he's gone after them right from the start."

"Care to enlighten those of us who haven't been here from the start?" asked Gideon. His family were Patriots from Long Island; they had been forced out nearly a year ago, right after the battle that gave England possession of their home. They'd fled with nothing but the clothes they were wearing, crossing the Sound to take refuge with family in East Haven—fourteen people crammed into one small house.

"Arnold has always refused to tolerate Tories," Jake explained. "He'd march to their doors in the middle of the night, rough them up, and fire their homes. Soon afterward, the Tories would decide New Haven did not quite suit them any longer.

"*That's* how to deal with the so-called Loyalists, as far as I'm concerned." Jake sang:

> "*The Tories with their brats and wives*
> *Have fled to save their wretched lives.*"

"That's funny," Gideon said, but he was not smiling. "When we were leaving Long Island, the same song was sung to us. Only it was *Rebels* instead of *Tories*. And most likely, the Loyalist Refugees that Arnold chased from here are living in *my* house right now."

Gideon's manner was so resigned, so sad, that Jake regretted his words. "Never mind, Gid." Jake gave his arm a gentle punch. "I babble too much."

"We'll allow you to babble at will, for such a breakfast." Tim reached for another oyster.

"Sheer nectar," Dan said.

"'Tis," Gideon agreed, nodding.

"A bit too salty," Caleb just had to say. "Where did you float them, Mal?"

"I had to float them in the harbor," Jake said defensively, "or take the chance of my father finding out. I notice the brine didn't stop *you* from eating a dozen."

"Or more," Caleb added, grabbing another.

"You're lucky to have them at all," Jake said. "Tim's indentured girl caught us hauling them out. 'Timothy Morris! Release those oysters this moment!'" he mocked in a high, haughty tone.

His friends laughed.

"That girl has ideas above her station, Tim," Caleb cautioned.

"Caleb! We *agree* on something?" Jake said.

"Hannah can be . . . a bit officious," Tim agreed. "But she's not had an easy start to life. And she's actually not at all difficult to wheedle—except when Mal's around."

"Hear him defend her," Jake said. "Careful, Tim, or we might start to wonder about your intentions."

"Never mind, we all know who Tim's got his eye on," Dan teased.

"And she on him," Gideon added.

Tim's face reddened, and he looked down, grinning shyly.

"Well, no doubt Sarah is the prettiest girl in town," Jake admitted. "But she is *so* proper. Personally, I prefer girls a bit more"—he held up an open oyster—"salty."

His friends began to snicker, watching him expectantly.

With somber pomposity, Jake pronounced: "I know not what girls other men take, but as for me"—he tipped the oyster toward his mouth—"give me Lydia, or give me Beth!"

As he made a show of curling his tongue inside the shell to slurp out the meat, his friends shouted and laughed.

EVERYONE CALLED HIM Mal—the bad one. He'd been Mal for so long, he'd forgotten who started it, or when. He didn't care for the name, but he'd never said so. His parents called him by his full Christian name—Jacob—but he didn't like that any better. It sounded so biblical, so sternly Puritan. Those days were past. Jake was what he liked to be called, and how he always introduced himself. But within days any newcomer learned he was Mal.

After the oyster breakfast, he went home to relieve his brother Ethan, who was thirteen, of ferry duty. Their father had the charter for the lower ferry, running across East River to the peninsula called the Neck, then across Mill River to New Haven. The family also farmed, and gathered oysters; Jake's father had set himself up pretty nicely in the oyster business, taking and barreling oysters and selling them to customers inland.

Of the family's three occupations, oystering was Jake's favorite;

the mollusks were so plentiful here that he need only stand in his boat in shallow water and rake them up. But until September, he was stuck with farming and ferrying.

Now he sat on the landing, dangling his feet in the water, looking across the harbor at General Arnold's estate. There was another reason to admire the man: he was rich. Very rich. The proof was in the grand brick house with marble pillars, the vast grounds that looked like a palace garden. Once Jake had counted ninety-four fruit trees—apple, plum, cherry, and pear. And he'd often watched Arnold's splendid coach come and go, pulled by four white horses.

Before the war, Arnold had been a successful merchant with a store near the waterfront. But he was among the first to join the New Haven militia and was quickly elected captain. When word reached New Haven of the battles at Lexington and Concord, Arnold announced he would march his regiment up to Massachusetts immediately. The New Haven town meeting counseled caution, but Arnold shouted, *Damn the town meeting! None but Almighty God shall prevent my marching!* Then he demanded the keys to the powder house, to get the ammunition he needed for the march. *No*, said the selectmen. *Well*, said Arnold, *I shall wait five minutes for you to change your minds; if you don't, I shall break the door down.* The selectmen gave him the keys. . . .

Suddenly, Jake jumped up: a man was standing on the New Haven landing, watching him, apparently waiting to cross. And Jake had been lounging there, daydreaming like a child, his toes in the water. But was the fool blind? Why had he not rung the big cast-iron bell, to call attention to himself?

Embarrassed, Jake leapt onto the ferry and pushed off with his pole.

The ferry was a scow about thirty feet in length, with a ramp on each end and overhead cables to keep it on course. Now it was low tide, so he simply poled across; at high tide, he used the sweep oar. When he reached Mill River's west bank, he tethered the ferry and lowered the ramp. The man was dressed like a sea captain, with gold braiding on his blue coat, and he stepped toward the ferry with the rolling walk of a man who spent most of his time at sea.

"You're meant to ring the bell, sir," Jake said in greeting.

"I am aware of that fact," the man replied agreeably. "But I was amusing myself with the pleasing sight of a young boy engrossed in a daydream."

"I doubt my father would be similarly entertained," Jake answered, and the man laughed.

"Your father—that would be Isaac Mallery?"

"Yes. Do you know him?"

"I am on my way to see him. We're very old friends, but we haven't met in years. When last I visited, I seem to remember one boy about six years, another in a pudding cap, and a third still a babe in arms."

"I suppose I'd have been wearing the pudding," Jake said. "I'm the middle son."

"And you are—?"

"Jake, sir."

"Well, it is a pleasure to make your acquaintance."

"Thank you, sir. I'll return the compliment if you tell me who you are."

The man laughed heartily and clapped Jake on the back so hard, the boy nearly lost his footing. "You don't stand on ceremony, lad, do you?"

"That's amongst my many faults."

"I'm Captain Harden, Jake. Before the war, I sailed merchant ships. Now—"

Whirling to face him, Jake finished: "A privateering man?"

Captain Harden began chuckling again.

"Was that you coming into port last night?" Jake said excitedly, pointing across toward the long wharf. "The *Scorpion*?"

The captain nodded.

"I couldn't help but notice her, sir. When privateers come into New Haven they're usually pretty battered. But she was perfect, and so graceful. Have you been in any battles, Captain? Taken any prizes?"

"Ah, it sounds like quite the way to spend a war, does it?" Captain Harden said. "Out on the high seas, capturing and plundering enemy ships, getting rich off the bounty."

"Yes, sir!"

"Well, I'll tell you, Jake. When we docked at Groton, my cabin boy said, 'Captain, I thought it would be all adventure and excitement. But it's been mostly privation, hard work, and spewing with seasickness. I'll not go out with you again.'"

The captain was short one cabin boy! Jake's heart began pounding with anticipation. A cabin boy on a privateer—now *that* was true freedom! But would the captain have him? Would his father allow it? "I'm not afraid of hard work," he said, poling harder to demonstrate. "And I'd take my chances on adventure or the lack."

The captain didn't respond; when Jake turned, he found the man examining him critically, from head to toe. Jake felt his face burning.

"How old are you?"

"I'll be fifteen in two months and one week."

"Have you ever been to sea?"

"No, sir, but I long to."

The captain laughed. "A true boy of the coast . . . I imagine your arms are rather strong, from doing this work."

Jake grinned. "No boy can beat me at swimming. I think it's because none of them powers a ferry."

As the ferry approached the landing, Jake poled it flush, secured it to the pilings, and let down the ramp.

"I like the cut of your jib, Jake," Captain Harden said. "So, if you are serious, I'll broach the subject with your father."

"I am shockingly serious, sir," Jake replied with mock solemnity. "I am most amazingly, keenly serious."

The captain laughed again, but Jake's joking demeanor belied his anxiety. Going to sea on a privateer! He couldn't wait to tell his friends. They would all be mowing their salt meadows as he sailed away. He imagined himself at the captain's right hand behind the ship's wheel, ready to serve during a broadside-to-broadside battle with a British man-of-war. . . .

"I'll choose my time carefully," the captain said. "Your father can be"—he seemed to ponder, choosing his words—"a bit prickly."

Now Jake laughed. "That's one way of putting it."

"Come, Jake. Walk me up to the house."

Jake leapt onto the dock, but at that moment the old miller, Mr. Rowe, came hobbling down the ferry path. Jake pretended not to see him.

But Mr. Rowe called out, "Boy! You there, Mal!"

The captain looked around, as if wondering where this Mal was.

"Yes, sir," Jake said wearily.

"Take me across!" the old man barked. "And no dillydallying like last time, or your father will hear of it!"

"Mal?" Captain Harden said quizzically.

"That's how I'm called," Jake admitted.

"Because he's a bad one!" Mr. Rowe tottered onto the ferry. "Bad through and through!"

Shut your gob, old man, Jake wanted to say, *you'll ruin my chances.*

But the captain only laughed. "To that, sir, I would reply that 'good boy' is a contradictory term. Do you not think? Or has time stolen memories of your own youth?"

Mr. Rowe grumbled as Jake raised the ramp.

"I'll see you again shortly, Jake," Captain Harden said, heading toward the house.

"Yes, sir," Jake said with a grin, touching his hat.

Just as he was poling away from the dock, Isaac Pardee ran down the path, leaping over the ramp and onto the ferry with a thud. Isaac was two years older than Jake; his family had the charter for the upper ferry, a couple of miles north. The Pardee ferry was horse drawn and went only to the Neck and back.

"Patronizing the competition, are you?" Jake said.

"Yours is more convenient for my purpose."

"You mean the purpose of avoiding working on your own?" Jake asked, and he and Isaac laughed.

"You useless boy! Can't you propel this tub any faster?" Mr. Rowe croaked.

Isaac came right up beside Jake to ask quietly, "Is he still angry about the mill wheel incident?"

"Or the skunk incident. Or perhaps the fire." Jake pretended to puzzle over the matter. "Or wait—maybe it was the rum incident."

Isaac was laughing all the while.

"Use the oar, boy! More work, less mirth!" Mr. Rowe barked. "I am in a hurry!"

But Jake ignored him and crossed at his own pace.

APPROACHING THE LANDING on his return, Jake saw his father and Captain Harden sauntering down the path. Ethan tore past them and waved to Jake from the dock, hollering, "Mal! Mal! I'm going with Father to see a privateer!"

I'm going? *I'm* going? Jake's stomach began churning. He tried to remain calm as he secured the ferry. When he lifted his head, all three were waiting on the dock. "Sir, may I come along?" Jake asked.

In a clipped tone, his father replied, "Of course not. It is your turn to tend the ferry."

"But, Father—can't Asa spell me? I really want to see Captain Harden's ship. Please, Father?" He hated prostrating himself, but begging was Father's favorite language.

"No, Jacob. You spent the morning with your friends. Now it is time to pay the piper." Father stepped onto the ferry. "Take us across."

"I'm sorry, Mal," Ethan murmured. "I'll tell you all about it."

But Captain Harden was speaking quietly to Father, who pondered, then turned to Jake and said, "All right, then, run up to the house and find your brother. If he agrees, you may come. But hurry."

Jake broke into a run, calling over his shoulder, "Thank you, Father!" But he was laughing as he raced up the path, because he knew what would happen next: Asa would protest vehemently, then capitulate. He had always been a strict brother, but he'd mellowed considerably since his stint with the Continental army last year. Asa had fought with Washington in the Battle of Brooklyn, experiencing horrors he wouldn't even speak of. Asa said it was only by God's grace that Washington had been able to evacuate his troops from the city and avoid surrender, execution, and the end of the Rebellion. When Asa's six-month term was up, he had left the Continentals and joined the militia here at home. What had happened at New York could easily happen at New Haven, he said. Best to defend your own home and state instead of other people's.

Asa was heading from the stable to the house when Jake caught up with him, calling his name. "Oh, no," Asa said, holding up his palms. "I know just what you're about to ask, and the answer is no."

"Please, Asa?"

"No, Mal! I slaved all morning while you were with your friends, and Father's just had me currying his horse, and now I intend to clean myself up and call on Polly."

"But is she expecting you, Ase?" Jake persisted, dogging his steps.

"Not exactly, but—"

"Can't you delay it, only for an hour or so? I'll pay you back the time."

"Not a chance, Mal!"

"Name your terms, brother." Jake folded his hands in prayer. "Anything. I'll do anything."

Finally Asa stopped and looked at him. "'Tis *that* important for you to go and look at a ship?"

"A privateer," Jake said with reverence.

"This whole country has gone privateering mad," Asa grumbled.

"Please, Asa?"

Asa pointed a finger in Jake's face and said sternly, "You'll do my morning chores for a week and let me sleep till breakfast."

"Yes, yes!" Jake turned on his heel. "Hurry, Father's waiting!"

When they ran to the landing and hopped on board, Captain Harden said, "Ah, excellent!"

And Father said, "So he got you again, Asa?"

"Yes, Father."

"You're too soft, son," Father said affectionately.

"He'll pay," Asa answered. "Starting *now*." He picked up the pole and thrust it at Jake.

Captain Harden caught Jake's eye and winked their secret.

WHEN THEY REACHED the Water Street landing, Jake's father told him to check for letters at the tavern, then meet them at Arnold's store.

"*Arnold's* store, sir?" Jake said dubiously.

Captain Harden grinned, nudging Father's elbow. "The boy knows his sire, eh, Mallery?"

"Don't question your elders," Father said to Jake as he walked away.

Liberty Tavern was just beside the ferry landing; any post for the east shore was left there until someone picked it up and brought it across the rivers. Generally that someone was a Mallery, as carrying letters was part of the ferry operator's job. But anyone from the east shore might stop for the post, and today Mr. Chandler, Dan's father, was standing at the small table where the mail was left.

"Good day, sir," Jake said

Mr. Chandler jumped and clapped a hand to his heart. "Mal!" He gave Jake a wan smile. "You startled me. I was deep in thought, reading this"—he waved a letter—"from my sister. She lives near the New York border. They're having a hard time of it with the blasted Tories." He shook his head, tucking the letter into his waistcoat pocket.

"Oh, I'm . . . uh . . . sorry about that, sir," Jake said.

"Never mind, lad, I should complain to adults, not boys." Mr. Chandler stepped away from the table. "How did the swimming races go this morning?"

Jake shrugged and grinned in response.

"Beat them all again, did you, son? Dan said he thought Caleb had a chance against you this time!"

"A chance, perhaps," Jake said. "But not a very good one."

Mr. Chandler laughed. "Are you going to the bonfire tonight?"

"Yes, sir."

"Good fun, good fun," Mr. Chandler said, patting his shoulder. "Happy Fourth to you, son!" he called on his way out.

"Same to you, sir."

Jake picked up the rest of the letters and headed for Arnold's store. He wondered how it would be to have a father like Dan's, who actually talked with you about things, even things like swimming races and bonfires. Jake's father never talked to him about anything. Mr. Chandler had called him *son*. His own father never called him *son*. And Mr. Chandler was such a jolly, friendly soul; Jake's father was always dour and scowling.

There stood the proof, right outside Arnold's store: Father frowning and gesticulating as he spoke. Captain Harden was laughing in response, a parcel tucked under his arm, a pipe in his mouth. How did Father get to be friends with a man as easygoing as Captain Harden?

As Jake approached, he learned the reason for Father's pique: the subject was Benedict Arnold, whom Father despised.

"But Mallery, you've got to give the man his due," Captain Harden was saying. "He quite literally built an entire navy on the shores of Lake Champlain, in the bitter cold."

"No one's disputing his bravery," Father replied. "But he's arrogant and self-serving."

"Does it matter, if he wins us the war?" Captain Harden said.

"No, of course not. But he's too hotheaded, and he always wants to be in charge. We heard he nearly came to blows with Ethan Allen up there, over who would be in command."

"He's fearless in battle," Jake dared to put in. "Did you hear what happened at Ridgefield, Captain? Back in April?"

"Be quiet, Jacob," Father said, waving a dismissive hand. Then, to Harden: "This one has mouth enough for two sets of teeth."

"Oh, come, Mallery, boys love stories of war!" Captain Harden replied. "Tell it, Jake."

Jake hesitated, throwing a quick look at his father before continuing: "Well, the Brits attacked our arsenal in Danbury, then burned the town. Arnold and Wooster were too late to stop them, but Arnold wouldn't let them get away without a fight. We had only three hundred men, and the British two *thousand*, but Arnold carried on. His horse was shot nine times, and fell right on top of him." Jake spoke more and more quickly as he got further into the story. He knew his father would put an end to it any moment now. "Then a Tory stood over him with a bayonet and said, 'You are my prisoner!' And Arnold said, 'Not yet!' Somehow he managed to pull out his pistol, kill the Tory, and escape. He—"

"All right, Jacob, that is quite enough," Father finally said. "Walk with your brother, please."

Ethan had emerged from the store with a small parcel, and now the four of them proceeded in pairs, the younger behind the older.

"Sounds as though your boy is a bit more enamored of Arnold than you are, Mallery."

"That is because he gets all his information from broadsides and ballads," Father said. "And because he doesn't know the man personally."

Jake knew better than to respond, but he was quietly fuming. He had that story from Caleb, who had it straight from his cousin, who had been in the battle and witnessed it with his own eyes.

Ethan unwrapped his new book and started reading as he walked. How could he read when there were so many interesting things and people to look at? The long wharf was lined with stores: grain and lumber dealers, sailmakers, merchants of all sorts. There was a ropewalk and a printer, taverns and inns. Before the war, the port shipped grains and flax; it brought in rum, sugar, molasses, coffee, and cocoa from the West Indies. Now the ships in the harbor were either idle or serving as privateers.

As the *Scorpion* came into view, Jake nudged Ethan with

his elbow. "Shut that stupid book," he muttered. "There is the *Scorpion*."

Ethan slapped the book closed and looked around. "Which one?"

"There," Captain Harden said, pointing.

"The brigantine?" Ethan said.

Before the captain could answer, Jake blurted, "She's a snow." He felt his father's eyes upon him; his face grew hot as he added quickly, "Is she not, Captain?"

"She is, Jake. But how did you know the difference?"

"Well, sir, I saw her under sail. She has the same square sails as a brig, but she carries a small trysail abaft the mainmast. The boom was set from that, with the luff of the trysail hooped to it."

"Impressive," the captain said, nodding.

But Father made a little snorting sound. "If the boy paid as much mind to his chores as he does to every ship sailing into the harbor, things would run much more smoothly at my place, Harden."

"Come now, Mallery—you can't blame a coast boy for dreaming of ships," the captain said in a jovial tone.

That's where you're mistaken, Captain, Jake wanted to say. *My good sire can blame this coast boy for just about anything.*

"How many in your crew, sir?" Ethan asked as they ascended the gangway.

"Twelve, at last count," the captain said. "But we'll not catch a glimpse of a single one." He brought his fist to his chin and gave his wrist a sharp twist, signaling to Father that the crew were on shore, drinking.

Jake counted five gun ports cut in the *Scorpion*'s larboard side; she would have an equal number on her starboard. "Ten six-pounders, sir?" he asked.

"That's right, Jake," Captain Harden said.

"What is a six-pounder, sir?" Ethan asked.

"A six-pound cannon," the captain explained patiently.

"Why is it called a six-pounder, Captain? That can't be the weight of it."

Jake wilted with embarrassment: and *this* was the brilliant son Father had earmarked for Yale!

"No, it is the weight of its cannonballs," Captain Harden said.

Father chuckled, clasping the back of Ethan's neck. "This one prefers the classics of ancient Greece to the trappings of modern war, Harden," he said. "He passed his entrance examination, and he'll be at the college in fall."

"Well, that's fine, Ethan, fine."

"Thank you, sir," Ethan said, then: "Have you been in any battles, Captain? Taken any prizes?"

Jake knew the quick change of subject was for his sake, and he was grateful to his brother.

"Not thus far," Captain Harden said. "The shipping lanes are jammed with vessels hunting for prey. I'll have to go a bit farther afield to track down a real prize. In three days, if I'm able to pull a crew together, I'll sail for the West Indies."

The West Indies! Jake could barely contain his excitement; his mouth felt dry, his palms damp. When would Captain Harden get around to asking Father? Surely Father would say yes—to him, Jake was far more worry than worth.

"Go ahead, boys, have the run of her." The captain swept out his arm. "Climb the rigging if you like. She's a sturdy lass—you won't hurt her!"

"Come on, Mal!" Ethan thrust his book into Father's hands and took off running.

Jake followed, anxiously—but at a dignified walk until he was out of sight of the men. Then he bolted, overtaking Ethan on his way to the nearest gun.

They ran out the cannon and pored over the accoutrements: worms and rammers, sponges, breechings, ladles, gun tackles. There were swivels and blunderbusses and ammunition, hand grenades, powder flasks and . . .

"What's this?" Ethan asked, picking up a small earthen jar.

"Ahhh . . ." Jake took it from him, turning it in his hands. "I've never seen one, but I think that's a stink pot."

"A *what*?"

"A stink pot. They take rotting fish and saltpeter and brimstone, stir it all together, pour it into these jars, and put in a wick. Just before boarding the enemy ship, they light the wick and"—he picked it up and faked a throw—"down the hatchway. The odor is so vile, the enemy pours out onto the deck . . . capture completed."

"Mal . . . how do you *know* so much?" Ethan asked in wonder.

"We all know what we're interested in knowing, I suppose," Jake said. Then, giving Ethan's ear a painful tweak, he jumped up. "Race you to the quarterdeck!"

They ran, shoes noisily slapping the deck. Jake reached the

quarterdeck ladder first, but Ethan grabbed him by the shirt and pulled him down. They collapsed in a heap, losing their breath to laughter.

At last they reached their destination and stood side by side at the ship's wheel. Jake felt awestruck, and by the silence he knew Ethan did, too. As the ship bobbed gently, the wood creaked and groaned. It was a comforting sound, a sound Jake loved.

"You be the captain," Ethan offered in a hushed tone. "I'll be your crew."

"I'm too old to play pretend," Jake said, but he was longing to do just that.

"Oh, come on, Mal! When will we ever have the run of a privateer again?"

You, never, Jake thought, gripping the warm wood of the gleaming wheel. *But I . . .*

"Please?" Ethan asked. "I'll not speak a word of it to anyone. And Father and the captain must be in his quarters—" He swept out an arm to show that no one was in sight.

"All right then, men." Jake threw back his shoulders. "Stand to your guns!"

"Aye, Captain!" They scrambled to the gun deck, and Ethan rushed to the nearest cannon.

"Make ready for the first broadside!" Jake strode along the deck. "Unstop the touchhole! Ram home wad and cartridge! Run out the guns!"

Ethan mimicked following each order.

"Aim your gun and fire!"

Ethan made an explosive sound. "We hit her, Captain!"

"Fine, boys! Load again! Hot shot and straight!"

"She's swinging about!" Ethan cried.

"Don't let her get away! Tack ship and give her another broadside!"

Ethan thundered again.

"Luff up under her lee!" Jake ordered. "We'll close and board!" Then in his own voice he said, "Now you're the British captain."

"No, let *me* be the American captain now."

"We'll have another battle," Jake promised. "Then *I'll* be the British."

"All right."

Jake pretended he was shouting into a trumpet—but not too loudly, in case someone might hear. "Haul down your colors!"

"Never, you Rebel dog!" Ethan replied.

"Have you not had enough? Strike, you damned rascal, or I shall blast that tub into tinder sticks, so help me God!"

"Strike colors!" Ethan ordered his imaginary crew in resigned tones.

"Boarding party!" Jake called. "Hoist out the boat, and let's examine our prize!"

In another battle, Jake imagined himself as a British powder monkey, running up and down the line, heroically delivering gunpowder in the nick of time to beleaguered gun crews before being obliterated by a Patriot broadside.

The third and last battle ended with Ethan, as a British gunner, falling dead on the blood-slicked deck after being run through by Jake, the Patriot crewman. Resurrecting himself, Ethan sat bolt upright. "Oh, Mal, wouldn't it be exciting?"

Jake couldn't withhold his secret any longer. "Ethan—I've something to tell you. But only if you promise not to say a word until the matter is settled."

"I promise. What is it?"

"Captain Harden has asked me to be his cabin boy."

Ethan blinked. "*You*, Mal?"

"Yes. He is probably talking to Father about it right now. So . . . you attend your classes"—he bumped Ethan's head with the heel of his hand—"and I'll tend the *Scorpion*'s glasses."

Ethan didn't seem the least bit excited or impressed. "But, Mal . . . do you really think Father will let you go?"

"Why wouldn't he?"

"Mmm . . . it does seem . . . a bit . . . dangerous," Ethan ventured. "And you're not yet fifteen."

"I'm well aware of my age, *little* brother," Jake answered. "Besides, boys go to sea at ten, eleven years old."

"Generally those are very poor boys, though, Mal," Ethan said, as if explaining to a tot. "Widows' sons . . . apprentices."

"That's the way in peacetime. This is war, if you hadn't noticed. And as Father is such a staunch Patriot, he should not mind sacrificing one of his sons for the cause. Especially *this* son."

"That isn't so, Mal. Father's very fond of you," Ethan said with unconvincing earnestness.

Jake made a noise of disbelief.

"He is," Ethan continued as they ambled toward the stern. "He only wishes you'd behave better."

"Like you and Asa?" Jake leaned over the taffrail and spit into the water. "I'll never truckle to him as you two do. Not to him, nor any man."

Ethan sighed. "Let's not fall out over it, Mal. I hope Father lets you go with Captain Harden, if it suits you."

They stood in silence for a moment, then Jake said: "Spit on the third beat." He demonstrated by tapping the taffrail. "See who hits the water first."

"All right," Ethan said, grinning.

In the midst of the game, Father hailed them from directly below.

"Best not stand *there*, old daddy," Jake muttered, and they both laughed.

"Coming, Father!" Ethan called.

When they reached the deck, Jake gave Captain Harden a questioning look; he answered with a slight but pleasant nod.

Jake felt his heart would burst from his chest. He couldn't wait to tell his friends—he was going on a privateer! While they carried on with their humdrum lives, he would be at Captain Harden's side on the high seas, making himself useful to the cause—and taking his share of the captured bounty, of course.

"I understand you wish to go to sea, Jacob," Father said.

"Yes, Father. I've wanted that as long as I can remember."

"I told Captain Harden I shall have to think the matter over, and I'll send my answer tomorrow."

Jake's spirits plunged, but he said nothing. If Father perceived even a hint of impudence, he would say no. But what could there be to think over? One troublesome boy out of the way—where was the problem? Father was just being his usual disagreeable self, to keep Jake miserable as long as possible.

But Jake decided not to let him. When it was time to bid good-bye to Captain Harden, he did so politely and cheerfully, and resolved to wait for Father to bring up the subject.

THE NEW HOLIDAY notwithstanding, Father expected the whole family at the supper table. In addition to Jake, his brothers, and his parents, there were his sisters—Lorana, who was ten, and Mercy, eight.

The girls served the meal that had been prepared by Sally, their Negro woman; she'd been given the night off to visit her husband and son. Sally was the family's only servant. Years ago, they'd had an indentured man, but he left for the frontier when his term was up. With three boys coming of age, Father had felt no need to replace him. Father had acquired Sally a few years ago, only because Mother had begun to lose her health. Sally's husband and son lived on the next farm, Uncle Luddington's.

All through supper, Jake anticipated Father's decision in agony. He wanted the answer before going to meet his friends. When bonfires lit the beaches, he longed to point across the harbor at the graceful *Scorpion* and say, *See that snow-rigged privateer, lads? She'll soon be my home!*

But when the meal was over, Father only stood up, asked the

boys about their plans for the evening, and warned them to return home when the clock struck eleven.

Jake could bear it no longer. He got to his feet, swallowed hard, and said, "Father?"

His father turned with a peremptory stare.

"I beg your pardon," Jake stammered. "But have you considered . . . decided . . . about Captain Harden's proposal?"

Father blinked, and said slowly, "Surely you are not serious?"

"I—I'm . . . yes, sir, I am."

"Well, it's out of the question, Jacob," Father said, seeming almost amused.

Now Mother asked, "What proposal?"

Blast the man! He had not even mentioned it to Mother! Jake's face burned with anger and humiliation. "You *said* you would think it over. You said you would send your response tomorrow."

"And my response will be no," Father said coldly. "How could you think it would be otherwise?"

The rest of the family sat still and silent as Indians—except for Mother, who repeated, "Pray, husband . . . what proposal?"

"Harden is looking for a cabin boy, my dear. And this foolish lad seems to have entertained the notion that I would allow him to go!"

"I entertained the notion, Mother, because my father allowed me to believe it would be entertained," Jake said evenly.

"Jacob," Mother said with quiet disapproval.

"You have a responsibility to this family and this town." Father's voice was growing louder. "Washington deprives Connecticut of troops—all he thinks of is the Highlands, the Highlands. We must keep every man and boy in case we are attacked."

"Sixteen is the age for militia service," Jake replied. "Let me go until then!"

"No. You are needed at home. With Ethan at college, we will all be working much harder this fall."

"All but *him*, of course," Jake said, casting a scornful glance at Ethan.

"Jacob, shut your mouth," Father warned.

"Why did you say you would think it over?" Jake shot back. "Why would you raise my hopes when you had no intention of letting me go?"

Now Father slammed his fist on the table. "Do not presume to question me, you young dog! If there were no need for you at home, I still would not allow it! What could it profit you, except in the pocketbook? What would you learn except to be more profane and ungodly than you are at present?"

Jake turned away fast, looking out the window. *I'll run away*, he thought. *I don't need his blessing.*

"You'll stay on this farm and sacrifice for this family and this state," his father continued, "not seek personal gain on a privateer! And if you go without permission, do not attempt to return home and enjoy the freedom *we* will win for you in your absence!"

Jake whirled around, protesting, "You would disown—"

"Not another word!" Father roared.

"*Jacob,*" Mother repeated, more emphatically this time.

"Mother, I—"

She shook her head, tightly pursing her lips.

Jake gripped the windowsill, staring down to the river. Sacrifice for this family. Yes, work like a dog while Prince Ethan trotted off to Yale. Personal gain. As if that were the only reason for privateering! It was the privateers who would win this war. Father was just too stubborn to acknowledge it.

Was Father serious about never allowing him to come home? Did Jake really want to test him? What if he ran away with Captain Harden and learned, like the last cabin boy, that he didn't care for the privateering life after all? Would he come crawling back to East Haven, only to be turned away?

The ferry bell rang. Jake took the spyglass from the sill and looked through it: Servant Girl! The thrill of cruelty rose in his throat, and he rushed out of the house and down the path.

When Hannah saw him, she quickly turned to face the water.

"Well, well, well. Where do you think *you're* going?" Jake asked.

She spoke in a clipped tone: "Take me to the Water Street landing, please."

"Not so fast. What if you are a runaway?"

"You know very well that I am no such thing. Please take me across."

He held out his hand. "Have you three pence?"

"You're to put it on my master's bill."

"Oh—have you a pass from your master, then?"

"I have leave from my master and mistress to spend the night with a friend."

Jake allowed her to board and guided the ferry from the dock before asking, "Spend the *night*? With a *friend*? What sort of friend, Servant Girl? Are you planning to do Lord-knows-what, Lord-knows-where?"

He knew his father would have beaten the daylights out of him for such remarks. He knew it was low to take out his bitterness and anger on Servant Girl. And yet . . . he couldn't help but feel a perverse satisfaction.

Hannah ignored him with a solemn dignity he could not bear. So as he briskly poled, he began to sing:

> *"An old woman all clothed in gray*
> *Had a daughter both charming and young*
> *Whom Roger deluded away*
> *With his false-flattering tongue.*
> *With him she so often had lain*
> *Abroad in the meadows and fields*
> *Till her belly grew up to her chin*
> *And her spirits fell down to her heels."*

Without even turning in his direction, Hannah said quietly, "For years, and for reasons I cannot ascertain, you have made it your business to torment and insult me whenever we meet. But I am neither afraid of nor intimidated by you, *Mister* Mallery. You may call me names and make insinuations and sing lewd songs, but keep in mind that such behavior does not befit the gentleman I'm certain your good mother hopes you will one day become."

For a moment, Jake was struck dumb; then he collected himself and replied, "You had best keep your opinions of me and all other *free* persons to yourself, Servant Girl."

But she continued with grave self-assurance: "Tim thinks so highly of you, and I so highly of him, that I can't help but believe there must be *some* good in you. I'm simply at a loss to imagine what."

His anger nearly boiled over, but another emotion held his tongue: shame. Because she was right. He was behaving abominably. And his quarrel with Father was no excuse.

Jake threw all his strength and fury into rowing the ferry, so as to get her off it faster. What was there about this indentured orphan that brought out such ugliness in him? Her pride, for one thing, he decided. She was too proud by half for a bound servant. And then there was her way of speaking—*ascertain*, *insinuations*. Who had taught her such words? They sounded ridiculous from a girl of her station.

He stole a glance at her. She stood very straight, looking toward the shore, both hands gripping the edge formed by the upraised ramp. What was she doing all prinked up in clothing cast off by Tim's sisters? She ought to be in her apron at this hour, cleaning the kitchen.

At the landing he allowed the ferry to bump the dock hard; she stumbled.

"Pardon *me*, your ladyship," Jake said.

She made no reply and stepped off the ferry with her nose in the air. *Someone*, Jake thought, *ought to cut this pretender down to size*. He only regretted that, for the sake of his friendship with Tim, he could not be the one to do it.

BONFIRES BLAZED ON both sides of the harbor. Boats glittered with candle lanterns and oil lamps, and lights glowed in New Haven's waterside taverns.

But as Jake paddled his dugout to meet his friends on the beach, he was not feeling very festive. The night had been tainted not only by his father's refusal, but also by the cruel and dismissive manner of it. Father had tantalized him with the lie of indecision, then casually dashed his hopes, as if Jake had had no right to them in the first place.

We'll all be working much harder this fall . . . When Jake had returned from crossing Servant Girl, Ethan was waiting at the landing with apologies for his unwitting part in Father's decision. Jake had refused to speak to him.

Would Ethan ever be called upon to sacrifice for his family and his state? Not bloody likely. Father favored Ethan—and Asa—in everything. *Only sometimes he wishes you'd behave better.* Well, let him go ahead and wish. Let him wish as much as Jake wished to go with Captain Harden and the *Scorpion*.

"What's wrong?" Tim asked the moment he saw Jake.

At once Jake poured out the story of Captain Harden's offer, the visit to the *Scorpion*, and Father's refusal. "And he says if I run off with Harden, I can't come back," he finished. "I should just go, but I haven't the nerve."

"No, you're right not to go without permission." Tim clapped him on the back. "But I'm sorry, Mal. It would have been just the thing for you, I know."

Jake nodded.

"Anyway, you can't leave now, just when I've decided to let you teach me how to swim."

Jake's eyebrows shot up. "Really? You'll try?"

"Yes, and who better to teach me? You're a first-rate swimmer. You're my dearest friend. And you won't laugh at me when I fail."

"Pardon me, correction, I most certainly will," Jake said solemnly, and Tim kicked sand at him, laughing. "What made you decide, Timo?"

Tim shrugged. "Independence day. This morning in your dugout, I thought, *I'll* never be free as long as I fear the water."

"Good man," Jake said, shaking his hand. Knowing he would be helping Tim made staying more palatable, but still. . . . He looked across the harbor at the *Scorpion*.

Tim gestured toward the Sound. "The ocean's gateway, Mal. You'll have plenty more chances to—"

He was interrupted by shouting and cheering; they turned to see Caleb, Dan, and Gideon with a group of older boys, all carrying torches in a procession that included a ridiculous red-robed effigy of King George, an enormous golden crown perched on his fat head. Jeddy Thompson was holding the king, and right beside him was Isaac Pardee, hoisting a stuffed likeness of a rattlesnake tacked to a long pole. Along the snake's curves were painted the words: DON'T TREAD ON ME.

Jake and Tim fell in with the loud parade, which led to a bon-fire being tended by a crowd of their friends, neighbors, cousins.

As cannon boomed and the band played "Yankee Doodle," the snake and the king began to fight. First the king dominated, beating the snake nearly to the ground as the crowd shouted dis-approval. But the snake fought its way back, striking again and again until it pushed His Highness directly into the fire.

Looking at the happy, hopeful faces all around him, Jake set his cynicism aside. Perhaps the new country would, one day, be free of the king—just as he, in a few years, would be free of his father.

He joined in the wild cheering as the king was engulfed in flames.

Rebel

July 4, 1778

TIM TOSSED A SHELL into the water and reached for another oyster. "Eventually, you'll have to admit you were wrong, Mal."

"You'd sooner find a priceless pearl in a Sound oyster," Caleb replied, and everyone laughed.

"In this case, I'd gladly admit my error," Jake said. "But I've yet to see how we can win this war."

His friends pelted him with jeers and oyster shells.

"Always looking on the dark side, Mallery," Dan said. "Last August, you stood with those who predicted New England would be cut off from the other colonies by the end of autumn. It didn't happen, nor is it likely to."

"Only because the Brits have turned their efforts elsewhere," Jake said.

But Dan continued: "Now we've chased them from Philadelphia, and—"

"Oh, we've *chased* them, have we?" Jake cut in. "For God's

sake, man! You know as well as I that they left Philadelphia for their own reasons—not from fear of us."

"Still, we've got our capital back," Dan persisted.

"With *your* General Arnold commanding," Caleb pointed out. "That should be a bright spot on your dreary little landscape."

Jake shook his head. "Lads, lads, lads. You've all succumbed to the comforting pabulum your fathers feed you. But the facts of the matter are these." He ticked them off on his fingers: "The Continental currency is worthless—we might as well use it for bum fodder. Our state is practically bankrupt. We've declared all Tories dead and have taken their property, yet they still find ways to help the enemy. And our prisoners die in festering prisons, with Washington unable or unwilling to do anything about it. Add to that—"

"The French have joined our cause," Dan interrupted angrily.

"Joined our *cause*?" Jake repeated. "Oh, I think not, Dan. The French have joined us, yes, but only because they believe it will benefit *them* eventually. What nation fights unselfishly for another's freedom?"

"I don't care why they're in it, as long as they're in it," Caleb said. "And the Regulars did not leave Philadelphia 'for their own reasons,' Mal. They ran because they were afraid the French would blockade them. With France's power behind us, we'll beat the British in no time."

"You're a fool if you think it," Jake snapped. "Listen: just a few years ago, we hated France as much as England does, and chased them off our continent. Some of your fathers fought the

French War right beside mine, and we've all heard them curse the French and their popish ways. But now—we've *invited* them back! We've joined forces with France against our mother country! That can only make England more determined to crush us—and hang our leaders."

Not one boy replied.

Jake formed a whole oyster of two empty half-shells and held it in his outstretched palm. "Has any of you ever watched a starfish devour an oyster?"

Again, no answer.

"The starfish wraps its arms around the oyster"—Jake closed his fingers over the shell—"and begins to try to pull the shell apart. Strong as the oyster's muscle is, 'tis no match for the powerful suction of the starfish's arms. It takes ages, but eventually the starfish wins. The exhausted oyster has no choice but to succumb. Its shell slowly opens"—he demonstrated—"and the starfish sucks out the meat. *That* is the fate Britain has planned for us Patriots."

"Perhaps you needn't call yourself a Patriot, spouting such Tory garbage," Dan fumed.

But Jake only shrugged. "I'm a Tory because I choose reality over fantasy?"

Gideon was the only one who had not said a word the whole time, but now he quietly spoke up. "Perhaps you're right, Mal—things don't look good for our side. But if we don't win this war, I may never see my home again. And what about the rest of you? Will the Tories take your homes, too, and turn us all out onto the frontier to be slaughtered by Indians? Or worse—make us work for them, slaves of a different sort?" He shook his head. "I won't believe it. If the British lose, they can pack up and go home, no harm done. If we lose, we lose *all*. So we've no choice, we—" His voice failed him, and he put his head down, scraping at a rock with an oyster shell.

Then Caleb and Dan gave Jake hard, accusing stares, and Tim just sat there looking so glum and reproachful that Jake knew he had to back down.

"You're right, Gid," he said. "Of course you are, and I apologize. And when we're on this spot fifty years from now, sharing the Annual Illegal Oyster Breakfast with our grandsons, you may all remind me of what a jackass I was on the second anniversary of independence."

"Fifty years from now, I imagine you'll *still* be a jackass," Caleb grumbled, and they all laughed.

Jake nodded. "All right, all right. That may be so. But I'm the jackass who taught our Timothy to swim."

"What?"

"*Did* you?"

"Really, Tim?"

Tim's grin was both proud and bashful. "I'm not very good. But I'm coming along. I can keep myself afloat, at least. . . ."

"He can do more than that. Ready to show them, Tim?"

Tim shrugged. "All right."

Jake lowered himself into his dugout. Tim followed, looking confident, but when Jake paddled away from the rocks into the calm water of the cove, Tim said, "I'm nervous."

"Just remember two things: one, you *can* do it, and, two, if you have any trouble, I'll be right alongside and I'll haul you into the boat with no ill effects."

"Except perhaps on my pride."

"Back to point one, then." Jake shrugged. "You can do it."

"This is far enough."

Jake kept paddling. "Nonsense. We're about one rod from shore. A pudding head could swim *this* distance. You'll be laughed out of town."

"All right, then . . . now. *Now*, Mal, this is far enough!" Tim said, sounding panicked.

Jake stopped. "I'm right beside you. Remember, you need only put out your hand and grab onto the dugout. Just as we've been doing."

"All right." Tim's breathing was fast and shallow.

"I won't let you drown, Tim. I swear it."

Without another word, Tim pitched himself over the side and made for shore as their friends hollered encouragement from the rocks. Jake kept his eyes fixed on Tim, paddling alongside him, saying, "Brilliant! . . . You're doing fine! . . . Keep going . . ."

But after a while, Tim began to falter. "Stop flailing," Jake advised. "You're halfway there . . ."

"I can't," Tim sputtered, reaching for the dugout.

"You can." Jake scooted the boat away from his grasp.

"Mal!"

"I won't let you drown, Tim! Keep going! Stop flailing!"

Tim did as he was told, regained his rhythm, and easily made it to shore. As their friends cheered, he pulled himself onto the rocks. The others slapped his back and rubbed his hair.

"Amazing!"

"You did it!"

"Good on you, Tim!"

"Ahem," Jake said. "No praise for the teacher?"

"The teacher is adept enough at puffing himself up," Caleb said, "and needs no further inflation from us."

Jake laughed with them, but Tim came to his defense: "I must tell you, Mal's a tearing fine teacher."

"*Thank* you, Timo."

"And far more patient than I'd ever have believed possible," Tim finished, and they all laughed again.

Now a group of four boys, all bound servants and apprentices, approached. One was Noah, who had recently moved to East Haven to be the cooper's apprentice. He stopped before Jake and said, "I hear you are the champion swimmer."

"You hear well."

"Will you race me, then?" The words were amiable, not defiant, and spoken with a friendly smile.

Jake gave him a skeptical look. "You're from Mount Carmel, are you not?"

"Yes."

"And you challenge a coast boy to a swimming race?" Jake asked, grinning.

Noah shrugged. "In Mount Carmel, we have a thing called a pond. Perhaps you've heard of it: water, surrounded by land. Quite fit for swimming."

The others laughed—Jake's friends as well as Noah's.

Jake nodded slowly, grinned slyly. "All right, then. Let's go." He stripped off his breeches and jumped in; Noah followed.

"Ready?" Tim called when they were standing on the raft.

Jake shook his head and pointed to Noah's friends, indicating that one of them should call start.

"Take your mark . . . ready . . . go!" the boy shouted, and they dove.

It was no contest—embarrassing, really. Jake quickly realized he wouldn't even have to strain himself, and still, by the time Noah reached the rocks, Jake was already sitting on them, drinking cider from the jug Tim had brought.

"You're good," Noah said, heaving himself out of the water.

"I know." Jake handed him the jug.

Noah took a drink and tried to return it, but Jake signaled that he should pass it to his friends.

"I'm joining your militia today," Noah said proudly. "Are you all in?"

"The four of us are." A sweep of Caleb's hand indicated himself, Gideon, Tim, and Dan. Then he jerked his thumb at Jake. "He's holding out."

"You don't want to join?" Noah asked Jake.

In truth, Jake was ready to join . . . but not today. Because it was the 4th, the muster would be carried out with more pomp and parading than usual, more people watching. And there he would be, the fumbling new recruit. It would be humiliating. But he wasn't about to admit that. He only shrugged and said, "I'm in no rush to play soldier."

"Oh, we're *playing* soldier, are we?" Caleb shot back. "You're the one who said you didn't want to join the Continentals because you'd rather stay and defend your home. Now the local militia are 'playing soldier'! Which is it, Mal?"

"Service is required at sixteen. I've two months before my birthday; I'll join then."

"Well, *I* joined the moment my father allowed it," Caleb said haughtily.

"Bully for you, Cay! You get the Patriot prize."

"I am not asking for the Patriot prize. I'm asking for every man and boy to be ready to defend our town in case of attack."

"If we are attacked, I shall pick up a gun and shoot. I can hit a duck on the wing; I imagine I can hit something much larger in red."

Now Tim caught Jake's eye and inclined his head toward the apprentices, who just sat, looking embarrassed to be witness to the quarrel.

Jake rose and stretched. "Well, anyway. Apprentices may have a holiday, but this slave must get home. If I'm not prompt for my turn at the ferry, my father will draw and quarter me."

"*You* are the ferryman's son?" Noah seemed to look at him with new eyes.

"Yes."

"The upper or lower ferry?"

"Lower. Why?" Jake asked suspiciously.

"Oh, nothing, nothing." Noah got to his feet; his friends followed suit. "Well . . . perhaps I'll beat you next year."

"Don't count on it, pond boy," Jake said, and with those words he got the last laugh.

THERE WAS BARELY any wind, so Jake paddled more than sailed back to the ferry landing. General Arnold's Water Street house stood empty now, and New Haven was a duller place without him. It had been quite a year for Arnold: before Washington gave him Philadelphia, Arnold had been responsible for the extraordinary victory in the Battle of Saratoga, against old Johnny Burgoyne's troops. Arnold's own commander, General Gates, had been fainthearted—as always—while Arnold fought like a demon, urging his own men to keep fighting, to push forward. *If the day is long enough, we'll have them all in hell before night!* Arnold shouted in battle.

But he had been badly wounded, nearly losing his leg. Close to six thousand British were captured, including eight generals. The prisoners were marched from Saratoga all the way to Boston, where they were paraded through the streets. Jake would have given a great deal to see that spectacle.

Arnold himself had been unable to enjoy it, for he was forced to spend the winter and spring recuperating until finally, on May first, he'd arrived home to New Haven. The town had welcomed him with a parade of his Second Company, Governor's Foot Guard, in full dress uniform, a band, and a thirteen-gun salute. Jake had pushed to the front of the crowd to shake the general's hand and walked about in a cloud the rest of the day. His friends laughed, but Jake didn't care. He had touched the Hero of Saratoga. That was all that mattered. . . .

Jake tied the dugout and walked up the path, singing:

"Six hours the battle lasted, each heart was true as gold,
The British fought like lions, and we like Yankees bold;
The leaves with blood were crimson,
Then brave Arnold did cry—
''Tis diamond now cut diamond!
We'll beat them boys or die!'"

When he reached the house, still humming, Father and Asa were beside the barn, cleaning and oiling their muskets. "Ah!" Father said, getting to his feet. "*There* is our newest minuteman!"

Jake turned to see who was behind him.

"You, Jacob!" This was puzzling; Father seemed almost happy, approaching Jake with a musket in his hands. "I've decided you will muster with us today." He held the weapon out to Jake.

Jake stepped back, holding his hands behind him. "I . . . I'm not yet sixteen," he stammered.

Father waved a hand. "You'll be sixteen soon enough; no one is seeking out the birth records. I've already told Lieutenant Bishop you'll be in the ranks."

"But I—" He hesitated. Admit to Father that he was embarrassed by his inexperience? "No," he said firmly. "I'll join when I'm sixteen, and not a day before."

Asa kept his head down, pretending not even to hear, oiling his musket with tremendous concentration.

"You'll join when *I* say you'll join," Father said. "And there's no better day for it than the anniversary of our independence."

At that, Jake took a mad freak in his head—there was no other explanation for it. Slowly and coolly, he said, "The only independence I care for, sir, is freedom from the tyranny of *you*."

Now Asa sat straight up, his mouth flying open.

The next thing Jake knew, he was flat on the ground—and Father, who had hit him quite handily in the head with the musket stock, stood looming over him.

"How dare you speak to me in such a manner?" Father gave him several more whacks about the shoulders, this time with the gun's butt. Shielding his head with his arms, Jake felt a sharp crack on his elbow. "Insolent brat! You have your brains in your breeches!" Father roared. Two more blows, these in the ribs; Jake couldn't help but curl his knees toward his chest. "Now get to your feet!" As if it would help the process along, Father applied a swift kick to his posterior.

Jake had been beaten before, but never in such spectacular fashion. He slowly raised himself to his elbow and felt the sticky sensation of blood dripping from his head. Almost overcome by dizziness, he struggled to his feet and looked—manfully, he believed—into his sire's eyes.

Father, however, perceived it quite differently. "You dare yet to show me that defiant stare?" Then again Jake found himself sprawled on the ground, head throbbing anew.

"No son of mine will be taken for a Tory or a coward!" Father shouted. "Report to Lieutenant Bishop at one o'clock sharp! He will instruct you as a new recruit before the muster." With that, he stomped away, calling, "Asa! You may tend to your brother!"

Asa jumped up and rushed to him.

"I need no tending," Jake snapped, waving him off.

Asa watched as Jake sat up, then stood. "Why do you do these things, Mal?"

"Why do *you* sit by and meekly watch?" Jake replied.

"Because I've no quarrel with it. If you were my son, I'd cudgel you, too!"

"Well, then, your sons will hate you as much as I hate him."

"Mal!" Asa caught him by the arm. "Don't speak so!"

Jake pulled away and walked to the house.

"OUCH!" SEATED ON a kitchen chair, he drew back from his mother's ministrations. She was applying hot balsam; it stung even worse than the wound. "Mother—I don't need that."

"Hush," Mother said. "It will stop the bleeding."

"I want it to bleed," Jake replied. "When I go down to the ferry, I want the blood to pool at my feet, and then everyone will say, 'Pray, Mal, what's happened to you?' and I'll say, 'Oh, nothing of significance—my good sire beat me to a pulp with a musket.'"

"Hush," Mother repeated. "Each time you move, it bleeds more freely."

As she continued to tend the cut, Jake sneaked a look at her pale, drawn face. During the winter, she had been unwell again; the newborn boy died, and Mother was taken with childbed fever. Since Lorana's birth, there had been four more children; Mercy was the only one yet alive.

Mother considered herself blessed to have five robust children.

But this last lying-in had taken a hard toll on her health—and her spirits. Now she said in a low, grave tone, "Jacob, you must beg your father's pardon."

"I beg *his* pardon! Mother, I think he ought to beg *my* pardon for—"

She interrupted quietly: "Jacob. Own your fault."

He gave a deep sigh.

"My son, recite the Fifth Commandment."

"Mother, I know the—"

"Jacob."

He said in a monotone: "Honor thy father and thy mother, that thy days may be long upon the land which the Lord thy God giveth thee."

"You are a good son to me," she said, her eyes searching his. "But you do not keep the Fifth Commandment as regards your father."

"Mother, he—"

"It is sinful. It is shameful, Jacob. It hurts my heart."

"But he—"

"Hush." She placed her hand on his shoulder. "Whether you feel wronged . . . it does not signify. You must show your father respect, Jacob. I cannot love a son who refuses to honor his father."

Jake was silent.

"Go and lie on your bed awhile. You must be fit to take your place at muster."

"Yes, Mother." But as he got to his feet, his father entered the house. Mother urged Jake with a nod; he turned. "Father." He made a deferential, but not obsequious, bow, and forced himself to say: "I beg your pardon for my behavior."

He could feel his father's cold gaze but took care not to meet it: he had no desire to be flattened again.

"One o'clock, on the green," Father said at last. "And don't forget your weapon. Now, I heard your mother tell you to go upstairs."

Jake climbed the ladder and stumbled into his bed.

"Jacob! Come down!" his mother called from the bottom of the ladder.

Now what? he thought. *Lie down or come down, which is it?* "Make up your mind," he mumbled.

"Jacob, are you up? It is time for the muster."

He had already been asleep? He could scarcely believe it. "Coming," he answered. "Thank you, Mother." He raised himself by degrees; his head ached horribly, and he wanted nothing more than to shut his eyes again. But there would be nothing worse—nothing—than to have to take to his bed because of his father's beating. He drew a deep breath, steadied himself, and climbed down the ladder.

He had not yet reached the green when the clock struck one, and when he arrived Noah and two other recruits were already standing at attention. Lieutenant Bishop told Jake to fall in, which meant "go stand with the others"—but of course it wouldn't do to simply say so.

"I thought you were not yet joining," Noah mumbled.

"My sire had another opinion," Jake replied.

Lieutenant Bishop taught them how to carry themselves: the position of a soldier without arms; the facings of right, left, and about-face; the common step and the quick step; the march by files.

It seemed so strange, to be strutting like a soldier . . . it felt just like playing on the *Scorpion*, pretending to be something he was not. He could not get the hang of any of this, and Lieutenant Bishop singled him out for correction any number of times: *Bring your foot back to position without stamping, Mallery! Keep your shoulders square to the front! Don't lean so, Mallery, preserve a proper balance!*

When they were sufficiently hot and exhausted and Jake sufficiently discouraged, the lieutenant said they could rest; then he issued ammunition and cartridge boxes. Now *this* would be the fun part—learning to shoot the ancient Queen Anne musket, which was much different from his father's fowling piece.

But the *Manual of Arms* turned out to be as foolish as the prancing and marching: *Step back six inches to the rear with the right foot, bring the left toe to the front, whilst at the same time the butt end of the firelock must be brought to an equal height with your shoulder, placing the left hand upon the swell and the forefinger of the right hand before the trigger, sinking the muzzle a little . . .* And that was only the command for "present arms." It all seemed ridiculous—more like learning how to dance than how to go to war. In the heat of battle, would a soldier really load and fire with all this fuss?

At last Lieutenant Bishop allowed them to be at ease, and the rest of the militia began to arrive, along with the many who had come to watch the muster. His friends were surprised to find him among the recruits, and some of the older boys had a go at him:

"Mal's joining us today?" Jeddy Thompson asked.

"Oh, that's rich!" said James Chidsey, who was the brother of Asa's intended, Polly.

"Do you know how to hold such a musket, Mal?" Jake's cousin Nathan Luddington said.

"'Tisn't a fowler, you know," Jeddy said.

"Perhaps he thinks it is a ferry pole," Isaac Pardee said.

"Well, 'tis nearly as long as my pole," Jake said with great solemnity, leading to much mirth. "But *this* pole"—he examined it, feigning confusion—"which end goes in?"

"Whoooaaaa!" Their voices rose in a crescendo.

"The water! I meant the water!" Jake protested, and they all laughed some more.

Lieutenant Bishop gave the order to fall in, and the group dispersed.

Tim stayed to ask, "What happened to your head?"

"Only this musket applied to my skull." Jake shrugged. "A mere trifle, compared to the welts you can*not* see."

Tim frowned. "What happened?"

"Let's just say that my father demanded I join today. And I took issue."

"But why?"

"I don't care to have my course set for me," Jake said. "And I think a split head is a small price, considering how others are paying for this so-called freedom."

Tim grinned, shaking his head. "But clearly you are *not* free to set your own course. Because here you are."

"Then in the same conciliatory spirit I showed at breakfast, I shall say only that I am like my country." Jake shouldered his musket and winked. "Not free *yet*."

He tried to copy the others' moves as they responded to Lieutenant Bishop's orders, but he fumbled awkwardly with his weapon. Lydia, Beth, and the girls giggled behind their hands while the younger boys laughed openly and heartily.

Then what could he do? Show the whole town how ashamed he felt, how angry and indignant? No. He would not give anyone, especially his father, that satisfaction. So instead he made sport of the drill—tripping, stumbling, holding the musket wrong, all behind the backs of the officers and the adults in the front ranks.

At one turn he came nearly face-to-face with Servant Girl, who stood with a group of apprentices and servants. Her expression was peculiar—a sort of amused indulgence, as if he were a small, naughty child.

Jake quickly turned away.

He and Hannah had been operating under an unspoken truce ever since the evening on the ferry, one year ago. They had even been quite civil to each other at times—for Tim's sake. But if she dared to start acting high and mighty with Jake again, he'd haul up his colors and start firing broadsides.

When the muster was finally over, Jake breathed relief. If

forced to admit the truth, he would have to say that he was proud to belong. He was now a part of this thing; he belonged to the Revolution, just like thousands of other American men. Just like Arnold.

But as he walked off the green with his musket on his shoulder, the thought occurred to him: now that he was in it, he had better start believing it.

JAKE PUT ON white stockings and nankeen breeches, olive green waistcoat and a brown coat, lapelled to match the waistcoat. The coat and waistcoat were handed down from Asa; not such finery as Tim wore, but new to Jake, and, he thought, rather sharp.

He tied his neckcloth securely, his hair loosely—attempting to cover the gash on his forehead. He buckled his shoes and breeches. Just for the occasion, he'd been saving red and blue bird feathers; he pinned one of each onto his hat, then took the measure of himself in the looking glass.

"Pretty, ain't he?" he asked, and his image laughed back.

To avoid the possibility of a confrontation with Father, he slipped out through the kitchen, went to the barn for his horse, then made his escape up the ferry road. Any moment now, he expected to hear one of his sisters calling, *Mal! Papa says you must come back!* When it didn't happen by the time he reached the cove road, he dug in his heels and rode at a gallop the two miles to Tim's house, savoring the exhilaration of escape.

His head still ached, his shoulder was stiff, and the ride made his ribs hurt ferociously. But plenty of rum punch would cure those ills soon enough . . . as would the attentions of Miss Lydia Woodward, whose favor he expected to gain tonight.

Frolics at the Morris home were festive affairs, with good food, music, and drink. When Jake dismounted, Pomp, the Negro groom, was in the yard with his little boy, who took the reins. Being served by others always felt strange to Jake—especially when the chore was something that, at home, was his own responsibility.

In the front hall, the family was welcoming guests. Four of Tim's sisters descended upon Jake like locusts.

"Oh, look! Here's our Mal!"

"Is it, indeed?"

"This magnificent creature looks *nothing* like Mal!"

"Ladies." Jake removed his hat and made an extravagant bow.

"When did *he* become so refined, sisters?"

"Hmmm, it must have been . . . yesterday!" All four dissolved into giggles.

"My dear ladies, if you are quite finished, I'll see about getting myself some punch."

But the sisters began to circle him. "Not so fast!"

"Yes, let us have a look at you!"

"What a fine figure he cuts!"

"He thinks himself a flash lad."

"Neatly buckled, knee and shoe."

One of them took his hat and held it up. "And see his feathers! Shall we call him macaroni?"

"Surely he did not tie his own neckcloth!"

"All that's missing is powder in his hair!"

"You don't suppose this pup's got his eye on a young lady, do you, sisters?"

"Now, now, girls, are you making sport of our Mal?" Captain Morris approached and gave Jake's shoulder an amiable squeeze.

The bad shoulder. Jake kept himself from wincing. "Good evening, sir. I've grown accustomed to your daughters' teasing, though fortunately I do not have to bear it very often. I admit, I don't know how Tim keeps his good humor."

"The boy is sure to make some woman a fine husband," Captain Morris said to Jake, behind his hand. "He'll be so relieved to have only *one* female to cope with, he'll treat his wife like gold!"

Jake laughed with him.

"Oh, what *did* you say, Papa?"

"You are not teasing about us, are you?"

Captain Morris winked at Jake and took his leave.

"Mother, Papa is telling jokes against his own daughters!"

"Good evening, Mrs. Morris," Jake said with a bow as Tim's mother came forward. She looked elegant in her summer gown, jewels around her plump neck, her hair piled fashionably high. With a pang, Jake thought of his own mother—so weary and plain and thin.

"Dear Mal!" Mrs. Morris reached for his hand. "I trust your parents are well?"

"Yes, thank you, ma'am."

"I cannot say I was surprised to hear the marriage banns for Asa and Polly."

"No, I don't imagine it came as a shock to anyone."

"And how is Ethan faring at the college?"

"Judging by the brief and infrequent nature of his visits to the east shore, I'd say he's faring quite well," Jake said, not without bitterness. "I imagine college life is far more agreeable than the tedium of tending ferries and haying salt meadows."

At that, Mrs. Morris seemed flustered, stumped for a response.

Jake regretted divulging his emotions; quickly he added, "Of course, knowing Ethan, I'm sure he spends far more time reading than socializing. It would be just the opposite with me, so Father has undoubtedly sent the right son to Yale."

Then all was well again, and Mrs. Morris laughed merrily. "Oh Mal, you *are* a delight! Go into the dining room and take some refreshment!"

"Thank you, ma'am." He moved on as she turned to the next guest.

"Well, you look none the worse for wear," Tim said, coming to Jake's side as he was ladling a cup of rum punch.

"Any lingering effects from *my* good sire's handiwork will be erased by *your* good sire's rum," Jake replied. "And by the sight of the fair Miss Woodward. Is she here?"

"She is, and she's brought her visiting cousin. Come and be introduced."

Jake gulped down the punch and followed Tim to the parlor. As they approached the two girls, Jake feasted his eyes on Lydia.

She wore a purple-and-white-striped gown, and her blonde hair was piled up, with tendrils curling down to frame her delicate face. A sort of glittering ornament in her hair set off the sparkle in her blue eyes.

"Good evening, Mal." She offered her hand; he took it gently in his, raised it to his lips dramatically. "This is Mr. Mallery," she told her pretty cousin. "Mal, I'd like to present my cousin, Miss Margaret Woodward."

"Delighted to make your acquaintance, Miss Woodward," Jake said with a slight bow. "I am *Jake* Mallery."

"How do you do, Jake," she said warmly. "Please call me Margaret."

"You must be wary of Mr. Mallery, Margaret," Sarah warned, joining their group.

"Yes," Lydia agreed. "We call him *Mal* for good reason."

"Because he is a perfect horror!" Sarah finished, and they laughed.

"Good evening to you, too, Miss Sarah," Jake said pointedly. "Miss Margaret, I assure you my reputation is entirely undeserved."

"Then pray, how did you earn your name?" she asked.

"'Tis an abbreviation of my surname; nothing more."

"Ha!" Lydia said to Jake's face, then turned to her cousin: "He was given the name at dame school, by the mistress who knew the French language. She called him *le mal garçon*. Do you not recall, Mal?"

"Miss Margaret, this is sheer fancy on your cousin's part."

"He is a wild, noisy mortal who torments old millers and young girls alike," Lydia informed Margaret while looking coyly at Jake.

"Give one example, please, if you are to accuse." Clasping his hands behind his back, Jake rocked on his heels.

"I'll give several, without even having to think. First, there was the time you stole the rum from Mr. Rowe."

"Mmmm . . . that was more of a permanent borrowing."

"And how about when you dove under the ferry and left Mrs. Chidsey alone, thinking you had drowned? The poor woman went into palpitations."

"Youthful antics gone awry," Jake explained.

"And what do you call the time you jumped off the Morrises' stable roof and landed on Tim, causing a dislocation of his shoulder?"

"I call it ancient history! We were six years old!"

As they were all laughing, Gideon joined the group. Lydia introduced him to Margaret, who quickly gave him her full attention. Tim already had Sarah's, so Jake was left with no option other than the one he would have chosen.

"Now, Lyd, I have been wondering—what is this made of?" He used the question as an opportunity to touch her hair ornament.

"Marcasite and pearls," she replied.

"Very becoming."

She made a fetching little curtsy and favored him with a smile that made his face burn.

He stepped closer to her and said, "Lyd, I must warn you, I

am determined to have you alone as my dance partner tonight."

"Such a gallant proposal!" She laughed. "Shall I have any say in the matter?"

"None whatever. I'll allow no other boy to come near. Unless there is a minuet. You don't think they'll have a minuet, do you? I loathe that dance."

"I *adore* the minuet, Mal," she replied. "I think it the most refined of all the dances."

"Refined? Phhh." He waved a hand. "It always appears to me that minuet dancers are in some sort of gastric distress."

"Mal!"

"'Tis only true. They never look at all happy, and dancing should make people happy. Give me a jig or a reel any time—or contra dancing. I *know* you like contra dances, Lyd."

"Yes, but I shall have to carefully consider whether I want to join one with a boy whose father had to beat him to make him join the militia," Lydia said, arching her eyebrows.

Jake was taken aback, but he quickly replied, "Ah, I put forth that story myself, just for devilment, and now you use it against me!"

"Well, you certainly did not *look* as though you wanted to be drilling."

"The only reason I did not want to drill was that my father forced me into it."

"I call that a poor reason."

Her haughty tone set Jake's teeth on edge. "Do you believe in blind compliance, Miss Lydia?" he asked coolly.

"I don't believe a child should defy his parent."

"Then you are no friend of the Patriots."

She bristled. "How dare you say it!"

"Aren't we colonies defiant children toward Mother England? Isn't that why they call us Rebels?"

"That is different. England is a bad mother."

"And perhaps mine is a bad father—how would *you* know?"

"Well, I shall have to carefully consider whether I'll dance with such a Rebel as you, Mal. There are so many brave boys in town who are quite *willing* to join the militia to defend us." Half turning from him, she took Margaret's arm. "Excuse me, gentlemen—I must introduce Margaret to Caleb and Dan."

Jake was stunned—and unsure whether he was more furious or hurt. Did she really think he was a coward? And was this now the common opinion? Had he been a fool to make such a show of his ignorance at muster? To tell what had happened between his father and him? Perhaps he should have just shut his mouth. But that was the hardest task anyone could set for him, or he for himself.

Still—Lydia would not even listen to his explanation. She'd taken the first opportunity to dismiss him out of hand, as though she *wanted* to think badly of him. Now there she was, giggling and batting her eyes at Caleb.

"What's wrong?" Tim asked, coming to his side. "You were so cheerful when you arrived."

"I've been spurned, Timo." Jake glared across the room at Lydia. "And for no good reason."

Tim laughed. "Women need no reason, good or bad, to refuse

some poor swain, Mal. They do it simply on a whim. That's one thing I've learned from living with so many sisters."

"At first she was friendly enough, even flirting with me. And then—I'm not *brave*, she says. Just because I wouldn't join the militia on a moment's notice with no—" He cut himself off.

"Never mind, Mal." Tim clapped him on the back. "There are other girls."

Just then came the call to supper. Upstairs, at one end of the ballroom, a vast table was laid with an extravagant and colorful feast of meat and fowl, fish and turtle, puddings and sweetmeats. There were trifles and jellies, creams and custards, whipped syllabubs and floating islands.

But Jake couldn't eat much; Lydia now seemed to have an entire regiment of boys attending to her every need, and it nauseated him. Liquid refreshment was the only thing that helped settle his stomach.

"Perhaps this is her way of being coquettish," Tim suggested. "Why don't you make *her* jealous? Ignore her. Dance with other girls."

Gamely, Jake took the advice. But every time he sneaked a glance at Lydia, she was happily dancing with Caleb or Gideon or some older boy until Jake was nearly blind with rage.

At last he decided to go downstairs and join the group singing liberty songs—and toasting the Revolution—in the parlor. After he'd been there awhile, Tim came in and took him aside, saying, "Mal—are you drunk?"

"*Me?* Of course not!"

"Yes, you are. I think you'd best—"

"Have another? Don't mind if I do." Jake went back to the sideboard with Tim trailing him, and quickly drank off a draught of rum.

"I doubt that making an inebriated fool of yourself will help endear you to Lydia," Tim said.

Jake only turned away and joined in the song:

> *"Come all you brave soldiers, both valiant and free*
> *It's for Independence we all now agree,*
> *Let us gird on our swords, and prepare to defend*
> *Our liberty, property, ourselves and our friends."*

"Say, Mal." Joining the group, Caleb nudged Jake's hurt shoulder. "Do you think if you sing loud enough, we'll believe you want to fight?"

Jake swung around, grabbing the front of Caleb's coat. "Let's go outside and we'll see who wants to fight."

The room fell silent.

"Steady, steady!" Caleb held up his hands as Tim wedged himself between them. "I was *joking*, Mal!"

"Well, I don't find it humorous to be called a coward." Jake's words sounded slurry in his own ears. "I'll fight you—or you—or *any* of you." The sweep of his arm took in the whole room.

"Come, Mal." Tim was tugging at his arm. "Come away."

"Yes, you crack brain, do shut up," Caleb said lightly. The tension broke, and the song resumed:

"And now, brave Americans, since it is so,
That we are independent, we'll have them to know
That united we are, and united we'll be,
And from all British tyrants we'll ever be free!"

Jake started toward the door.

"Where are you going?" Tim asked fretfully.

"To use the necessary, Mother, if that is permissible. And I'll need no one to hold my skirts, thank you," he added as Tim, laughing, waved him off.

Then there was Lydia, lurking in the front hall. She seized his arm cheerfully as he tried to pass. "*There* you are, bad Mal. They are playing the contra dances now, and I believe you promised me."

"That is odd, Miss Woodward," Jake replied. "*I* believe you refused me." He extricated his arm and went outdoors. "Rotten wench," he muttered, stomping toward the backyard. First she wouldn't even bother to hear his reasons or learn his thoughts— only reject him for a coward. But then she'd simper and coo after hearing him offer to fight!

Just as he reached the necessary house, its door flew open, smacking him right in the very spot where his head had been split. "Aaah!" he cried out, stumbling backward, covering the throbbing wound.

"Oh!" the perpetrator exclaimed. "Oh, I beg your pardon!"

Servant Girl!

"You clumsy thing!" Jake snapped. "What *is* your rush, are we under attack?"

"No, I . . . are you hurt?"

In response he showed both hand and head, covered in blood.

She drew a sharp breath. "Oh! I was in a hurry, I . . . please, come into the kitchen and let me tend to it."

"I'm not sure I trust you," he said peevishly. But he followed along.

In the lighted kitchen, the blood must have looked even more impressive; she yelped at the sight of him. Then she bit her lip and looked so upset that Jake decided to admit the truth. "It is not all your doing." He sank into a chair. "I had the cut already. You only opened it again."

"Oh," she said with a relieved sigh. She wet a cloth in the basin and squeezed out the excess water. Approaching, she asked, "May I—?"

"Be my guest."

Gently she wiped the blood, taking care to stay on the edges of the cut. "'Tis bleeding rather freely," she said. "When were you injured?"

"Just this noon."

"Was it tended?"

"With hot balsam."

"*Well* then." Her tone was disapproving. "Perhaps it is best that it was reopened."

"Really?" He shook his head, smirking. "I thank you, good doctor, for that professional assessment. I like how you turn your careless act into a noble deed."

"Hot balsam often ulcerates the wound," she said primly.

"Common sticking plaster is the thing for a cut like this. But hold the rag to it, to stanch the bleeding first. It should take only a minute or two."

"How about getting me a draught of rum while I wait?"

"Never mind that. You appear to have had quite enough of spirituous liquors."

Up close, Jake thought, she really was not a bad-looking girl. Or maybe that was the spirituous liquors' opinion. "What *were* you in such a hurry over?" he asked.

"That is my business."

He grinned. "Generally, it is on the way *to* the necessary that one feels the need for urgency."

Sighing, she shook her head. "You *must* run your mouth, mustn't you?" She glanced toward the door. "Is it simply that you love the sound of your voice?"

"Have you got a swain coming to see you?" he asked.

She didn't answer.

"If so, I hope you don't trifle with his feelings the way *some* girls do to boys."

"*Some* girls have nothing better to do than trifle with boys' feelings," she shot back.

"Ah! Better than her betters, because she is a busy servant girl!" Jake instantly regretted the words. He meant them as a gentle tease, but he had no right to joke with her that way. And she could not but take it seriously, coming from him.

They fell silent; she went into the pantry and returned with the sticking plaster.

"You're right about this mouth of mine," Jake said quietly. "It flaps independent of my brain, much of the time. I apologize."

"And I apologize for hurting you." Stopping before him, she carefully lifted the rag from his cut.

"*Your* actions were unintentional," he said.

"And so, as you have admitted, were your words."

He tipped his head back to look up to her. She gave him a brief smile; he repaid it, then quickly cast his eyes down again. She began to plaster the cut.

"I thought the whole town had heard how my head got split," he said.

She made no reply.

"My father beat me with a musket because I wouldn't join the militia."

Still, not a sound.

"It isn't that I didn't want to join. Only . . . he took me by surprise. I don't like learning something at the last minute, then being expected to leap up and comply. My father would know that, if he ever paid the slightest attention. The man knows nothing of me, and he does not care to learn."

After a silence, Hannah said, "'Tis interesting, really. I've noticed it any number of times. Free people are forever telling servants the minutiae of their private lives. As if, somehow, the servants ought to feel sorry for them. And had the capacity— or the desire—to ameliorate their troubles. Why *do* you imagine that is so?"

Taken aback, Jake was momentarily stumped. But then he

said, "Well, I can't speak for others, but I suppose my excuse tonight is spirituous liquors."

Then for the first time, he heard her laugh. The sound surprised him, for it was light and lilting when he would have expected bitter and harsh.

"There," she said. "You are all fixed."

"Thank you," he said, but did not make a move to stand.

She began cleaning around the kitchen; he watched until she asked, flustered, "Do you mean to just sit there and plague me?"

"Am I plaguing you?"

"No . . . not really . . . but . . ."

"Did you do all the cooking for this supper?"

"Mrs. Morris and the girls helped."

"I see." He looked around, pointedly surveying the mess. "And now, I suppose Mrs. Morris and the girls will help you clean up?"

"Now you *are* beginning to plague me."

"How was it that you came to live here?" he asked, then quickly added: "If you don't mind my asking."

"I *do* mind," she said, and turned from him. "So please—"

The door opened, and in walked the cooper's apprentice. Seeing Jake, he stammered, "Oh . . . I . . . um . . ."

"'Tis all right," Hannah told him. "I'm allowed to have friends in the kitchen."

Jake recalled Noah's words this morning: *You are the ferryman's son?* Of course, she had complained about him to her "friend."

"Evening, Noah," Jake said, giving him a sly grin.

"Evening, Mal," Noah mumbled sheepishly.

Jake turned to Hannah. "Did you hear that your fellow had the audacity to challenge *me* to a swimming contest this morning? And was quite soundly beaten?"

She looked at Noah.

"Did you not tell her, Noah?" Jake asked the apprentice, who just stood awkwardly.

"Noah hasn't the vast amounts of leisure time that you have, Mr. Mallery," she said. "To sit around people's kitchens prattling about nonsense."

The rebuke caused a quick, sharp ache in Jake's throat. He thought they had been conversing, but it turned out he was only "prattling about nonsense." And it wasn't as though his life was like Tim's. In fact he had remarkably little leisure time—as indentured to his father as she was to the Morrises, or Noah to the cooper.

Still, why should he care what she thought? And why did he feel embarrassed that she had said it in front of Noah? It was Noah who ought to feel embarrassed.

"If I were you, Noah, I'd caution my girl about her quick tongue," Jake told him. "Fellows might think you unable to defend yourself without the aid of a female." Before giving either one a chance to reply, he added, "Well, I'm sure you two would prefer to be alone, so I'll resume the task I was about to undertake when I was so rudely interrupted." Unsteady, a bit dizzy, he got to his feet and looked into Hannah's face. "Then I guess I'll find someone else to *prattle* to."

She turned her head fast—but not before he saw regret in her eyes.

As Jake headed for the door, he sang:

> *"'Tis of a young apprentice who went to court his dear*
> *The moon was shining brightly, the stars were twinkling*
> *   clear.*
> *When he went to her window to ease her of her pain,*
> *She quickly rose and let him in and went to bed again . . ."*

Noah might have been a bit slow to defend himself, but he protected Servant Girl's honor ferociously. Blocking the door, he took Jake by the arm. "Listen here. That is uncalled for, and—"

"Let him go, Noah," Hannah said, putting herself between them. "Please, don't allow him to cause us trouble."

"All right." Noah released him. "Only because you ask, Hannah. Besides—he's drunk, isn't he?"

"And *that* is the least of his woes," she replied.

They both laughed as Hannah shut the door behind Jake.

Returning to the party, he continued to avoid Lydia, but he stopped drinking rum. There was to be a ceremony at Black Rock, followed by fireworks over the harbor. When everyone began to leave the house, Lydia sidled up to Jake and said in a pouty tone, "Mal, *will* you stop being so cross?"

"I don't see why I should."

"Because it is ungentlemanly."

"That's never served me for a reason."

"Come, Mal," she cajoled. "It is dark, and if you don't let me lean on you I shall turn my ankle and it will be your fault."

At that he relented and held out his arm. Girls were

infuriating; he supposed he'd have to accept and cope with that fact. Lydia held on to him much tighter than she needed to, and as they walked his height allowed many an opportunity to steal a glance at her bosom. A hurt feeling or two seemed a small price to pay for such privileges.

Now that he was sobering up his head started aching again, but he was thinking more clearly. With a pang of shame, he remembered his song in the kitchen. Why hadn't he just exited on his line about finding someone else to prattle to? Then *he* would have been the injured party. Now she was free to think badly of him again. . . . But what did it matter? And why was he thinking of Servant Girl when he had this fair creature on his arm?

All at once there was a commotion on the road, a clatter of wagon and horses and shouting men. At first Jake thought they were celebrating, but as the chaos came closer, he recognized the angry sounds of a mob. East Haveners heading toward Black Rock hurried to the road to find out what was happening.

"Oh, Mal!" Lydia huddled against him. "I'm frightened!"

Jake could not even think of a witty reply.

Tim, with Sarah, came up close. "Someone's being run out of town," he predicted.

Now the mob came into view. Horses were drawn up, rearing; the wagon stopped, and everyone rushed to circle it, craning their necks to see who was inside.

Silas Field, the most radical of Patriots, hauled a tarred and feathered man to his feet. The odor of pine tar was strong; the sticky substance coated the man's naked body. But who was he?

His hands were bound behind him, and he hung his head. Goose feathers, affording him little modesty, stuck out at all angles. Despite the heat, the man was shivering; he looked like nothing so much as a ridiculous, quaking bird.

Silas crowed, "Fellow Patriots! I give you a rank Tory revealed! What shall we do with a man who distributes counterfeit money and signs his letters 'God save the King'?"

"Who is he?" someone called out.

"Why, do you not recognize him with all his pretty decorations?" Silas laughed harshly. "He is honored citizen Thomas Chandler!"

Dan's father!

"Oh!" Lydia gasped, covering her face.

"It can't be," Tim muttered.

"No! No!" Dan pushed to the front of the crowd.

"Son!" His voice quavering, Mr. Chandler reached toward Dan.

"Let him go!" Dan said, swinging a fist at Silas. "It is not true!"

Silas dodged the blow. "Not true, young dog? Your good sire has been under surveillance these four months, and he has been going out at all hours of the night, traveling west to meet with suspicious persons. This night he was discovered far from home, without a pass, so we have given him a patriotic escort back here to face his townsmen. Thomas Chandler, what say you to these charges?"

"I . . . I . . . demand a hearing before the Committee of Safety," Mr. Chandler croaked.

"Ah! Where is your Tory gasconading now? *You* demand a hearing from *our* Committee of Safety, as if you were one of us? Perhaps your king and his minions will save you from New-gate prison!"

"No!" Dan shouted, and as he tried to scramble up into the wagon, Silas knocked him to the ground.

"Now, listen here, Field!" Captain Morris pushed to the front. "This is not how it is to be done! We have laws to—"

"Laws?" Silas scoffed. "Don't speak to me of laws, sir! This damned traitor has scorned our republic and endangered our lives, and now you'll shelter him under *our* laws?"

"Yes!" Captain Morris replied. "And if you don't follow them, I'll see that *you* are arrested!"

But Captain Morris wielded no weapon, so Silas only shouted: "Out of my way, old man!"

From the north came more clattering of horses, and when those in the road stepped aside Jake saw his uncle Luddington, chairman of the local Committee of Safety. Behind him were Jake's father, Asa, his cousin Nathan, and two other men.

"Deliver him to me, Silas," Uncle Luddington said evenly, drawing his pistol.

"He signs his letters with 'God save the King'!" Silas sputtered in appeal to the crowd. "We suspicion him of passing counterfeit bills!"

Uncle Luddington cocked the pistol. "Now, Silas."

Silas dumped Mr. Chandler over the side of the wagon as though he were a sack of rye.

"If you have evidence, you had best hand it over." Uncle Luddington rode right up to the wagon and held out his hand.

Silas thrust a letter at him like a sulky child deprived of its candy. Then he pointed at Mr. Chandler, who was crouched in shame on the ground, trembling. "You may have been saved from hanging, you damned Tory scoundrel," he snarled. "But I'll see that you rot in the copper mines, you may count on it." With a signal to the wagon's driver, the horses were whipped up, people scurried out of the way, and Silas and his crowd were gone.

Uncle Luddington was frowning as he read the letter. All at once Jake remembered Mr. Chandler, standing in the tavern reading another letter, jumping with surprise when he realized Jake was there. His sister's family harassed by Tories . . . tucking the letter into his waistcoat. Had it all been a lie? Had Mr. Chandler been there to intercept someone else's letter? Now other scenes flashed through Jake's mind. Mr. Chandler, alone in a rowboat early one morning when Jake was oystering. And once when Jake had been in New Haven, he'd seen Mr. Chandler on the green, giving something to a man. He had thought nothing of it—why should he? But now it hit him . . . counterfeiting.

Quickly he turned toward Mr. Chandler; Dan was on his knees beside his father. "'Tis all lies, Father, is it not?" he begged. "Father, tell me this is not true."

Uncle Luddington folded the letter and tucked it into his waistcoat pocket. "You had better come along, Chandler," he said, his countenance very grave.

"No! Father, no!" Dan cried out. "It can't be—you can't be!"

But Dan's father could not even look at him. "Please . . . someone take the boy to his mother," he muttered.

Now Dan's demeanor was entirely transformed; wild-eyed, he yelled, "I am not a boy! I'm more a man than you are, sir! And I shall go to my mother myself, and learn if *she* knew that her husband is a traitor to his country! And if it is so, you may both go to the devil!"

He turned and ran; Caleb started after him, and they disappeared into the darkness.

The crowd was left in grim silence. Uncle Luddington and the others began to lead Mr. Chandler toward Black Rock.

When Jake's father spotted him, he said, "Fetch your horse and go home, Jacob."

Jake opened his mouth to protest, but shut it before a word could escape. He was weary, body and soul. The morning's oyster feast seemed many days past. He *wanted* to go home.

Back at the Morris house, he was on his horse and nearly at the road when Hannah entered the lane arm in arm with her apprentice.

"Good evening, Noah," Jake said, bringing the horse up.

"Good evening, Mal," was the solemn response.

"I hope you'll both accept my apologies for my behavior earlier." He tipped his hat. "Hannah."

She met his gaze, then quickly shifted her eyes.

ALONE IN THE stable, Jake reflected on the evening's events as he brushed his horse. What if he said nothing about the things he had seen, and Mr. Chandler was freed for lack of evidence? And what, then, if Mr. Chandler really was a Tory and went right back out and continued his activities? On the other hand, Jake didn't really have evidence, either—just observations. What if those observations really meant nothing at all? And Mr. Chandler was such a nice man, always so kind. What if Jake's words put him in prison when he was really innocent? When this was all over, Jake would still have to live in this community with the Chandlers.

Father entered and led his mare to her stall. "You may tend to this one, too, when you are done," he said gruffly.

"Yes, Father." *I should tell him*, Jake thought: *Father is the one to tell, he'll know what to do.*

"She's had a hard run tonight, so brush her well and make certain she has water."

"Yes, sir." Jake was still brushing his horse, trying to decide whether to speak, when he realized his father was standing there, staring at him. He looked up.

"Did you ever hear that boy express Tory sentiments?" Father asked, a deep frown creasing his face.

Jake couldn't help but smile. "No, sir."

"Please enlighten me as to the humor in the situation, Jacob."

"Only this, sir: of all my friends—of all the boys in town—Dan is the warmest Patriot."

"That is not humor, then—'tis irony."

"I believe it was you who said 'humor,' sir," Jake replied. "I merely smiled. Is one not meant to smile at irony?"

His father turned to leave.

"Father," Jake said quietly, and his sire stopped. "Do you think . . . could it be untrue? Why would Mr. Chandler sign his letters in such a way, when he must know that letters don't go safe? Is it possible that . . . he is a Patriot spy? Perhaps the letters are meant to trick the person to whom he is writing?"

"He confessed to us, Jacob. He is a king's man. And it is the counterfeiting that is the most grievous charge; the Tories are playing havoc with our economy. Chandler confessed to it all. He begged our protection for himself, and safe passage to Tory friends for his family."

"What will happen to him?" Jake asked, resuming brushing the horse.

"If he is lucky, he will end up in New-gate prison."

"And Dan?"

"He'll be carefully questioned. If he is a true Patriot, he'll be free to stay amongst us. God knows we need all the *fighting* men we can get, when we have boys around who must be forced into service."

Jake's anger burned his face, but he made no reply and continued with his chore. His father lingered, though he had no reason to stay. What was he waiting for? For Jake to prostrate himself, whining that he, too, was a good, brave Patriot lad?

At last Father left the stable, and Jake breathed a deep sigh of relief. It was sad, of course, sad and awful that Mr. Chandler was a Tory. But at least the truth was out, without Jake having to divulge what he knew. Father would have found a reason to fault him for it. *Why didn't you tell me before this? God only knows how many counterfeit bills he was able to pass because of you! Perhaps you are a Tory as well. Perhaps that is why you refused to join the militia. . . .*

Jake shook his head at his own stupidity. To think he had imagined confiding in his father. That was one mistake he would not make again.

Soldier

July 4-6, 1779

ALONE AT SUNRISE, Jake walked the highest rocks at Five Mile Point. He'd been here about an hour, judging from the tide. Today there would be no oyster breakfast; it was the Sabbath, so all 4th of July celebrations must wait until tomorrow.

Jake didn't care. He was not in a mood to celebrate anything.

Time for him to do chores . . . his *and* Ethan's *and* Asa's. Now that Asa and Polly had married and moved to the Mallerys' grant of land on the Neck, Jake was working harder than ever before. But he couldn't force his feet toward the dugout.

Facing west, he stared far into the Sound. Rumor had it that a British fleet under General Tryon's command was sailing from New York, headed for New London or Newport with malicious intent. Some said New Haven would be their target, but Jake didn't believe it. For three years now, there had been false rumors that the British were about to attack New Haven.

Still, if they came he was ready for them. He'd been drilling with his unit every Saturday and was confident of his musketry skills. The British could come, or pass by. He wasn't worried.

The only war he feared was the one in his heart.

Jake sighed heavily, turned slowly, and walked off the rocks. He kicked at the sand with every step across the beach. When he reached the path to Tim's house, he stopped. He frowned. Then he took a deep breath and started up the path, quietly, so as not to alert the Morrises' flock of geese. If they heard him coming, their honking would tell everyone in the house of his presence.

Entering the yard through the back gate, he kept to the shadows of the shrubbery as he made his way to the kitchen door. He ducked his head, squeezed his eyes shut, hesitated—and knocked.

Inside, he heard quick footsteps; then the door cracked. When Hannah saw him she tried to shut it again, but Jake wedged his foot in the narrow opening.

"Go away," she said.

"No."

"Stop it!" She tried to kick his foot away.

"I need to speak to you."

She stood still, listening.

Jake rested his head on the door and mumbled, "I've been in hell, Hannah."

She turned away; he slipped inside.

"They'll be up soon," she said, walking to the hearth. "You cannot stay."

He leaned back on the door to close it, then watched her tend to the breakfast she was cooking. The heat was suffocating. "Why did you run away?" he said at last.

"You know perfectly well."

"Why are you angry with me?"

She didn't reply.

"Is it all my fault?"

Whirling around, she confronted him with a defiant look. "Ask yourself this, Jake: would you even have attempted to take such liberties with a *free* girl?"

In two strides, he was right before her, and he seized both her hands. "Damn it, Hannah, how should I know?" His voice was a fierce whisper; his eyes searched hers. "I don't love any free girl. I love *you*!"

Her look of pain and confusion tugged at his heart; he pulled her to him and held her close.

"You cannot stay," she said softly. "Someone will see you."

"I don't care."

"Don't be a fool."

"I love you," he repeated, this time more deliberately. Cupping his hands around her face, he pressed his lips to hers. When she kissed him back, he felt blessedly relieved, ecstatic.

But her words belied her actions. "You must *go*," she insisted, pushing him toward the door.

"When can you meet me?"

"Four o'clock."

"If you're not there, I'll be back," he said, gently pinching her chin.

"I'll *be* there, Jake. But really, you *must* go. And listen"—she looked down, blushing, tenderly adjusting his neckcloth—"don't stare at me during meeting. It's sinful."

With mock solemnity, he pressed his fist to his chest and said, "I shall be the very image of holiness."

She looked as though she wanted to smile. "Oh, Jake. Don't make light." She fiddled with the buttons of his waistcoat. "I *am* troubled," she added in a whisper.

"There's no need," he said. "Meet me at four."

She walked him to the door and allowed one more quick kiss before pushing him out.

Jack ran back to the beach feeling as though a cannonball had been lifted from his chest. Everything would be all right, he was sure of that now. He had seen it in her eyes.

Paddling home, he reflected on how they had come to this. Of course it had started with the simple but intimate act of her plastering his cut. For weeks afterward, he had imagined her touch, the fingers rough from work, yet gentle. Her blithe, confident manner, her spirited laugh. The way she'd managed to politely shame him with her keen observations about free people and servants.

He had thought about that for a long time.

And he had thought about her and Noah. What was between them? Noah seemed like a good fellow, but he was nowhere near as smart and sharp as Hannah. What could she see in him?

Jake had found himself reliving, again and again, every moment with her in the Morrises' kitchen. Why wouldn't she speak of her past? Had things happened that were too painful to recall? Or did she simply not care to talk about it with him because he had been so awful to her?

The next time he'd taken her across the river, he'd been uncharacteristically tongue-tied—so flustered, in fact, that he'd nearly reverted to insults. But instead he heard himself say, *I want to thank you again for fixing me up at the party.* And she replied, *I trust the cut is healed? Yes, entirely,* he said. Just before docking, he had tried once more: *Perhaps we could be more civil to each other from now on.* As soon as he'd spoken, he felt his face burning, and quickly added, *For Tim's sake, I mean.* As she stepped off the ferry she responded with a sly smile, *For Tim's sake, that would suit me quite nicely.*

Not long after, Lydia had complained to friends that she did not understand why Mal had cooled toward her. He couldn't admit to himself, let alone anyone else, that he had feelings for Hannah. He had tried to rekindle his ardor for Lydia, but all that burned was his jealousy whenever he saw Hannah with the cooper's apprentice.

Then two things happened: Noah went to the Continentals as a substitute for his master, and Jake's mother died.

He had been expecting it for so long—Mother had never thoroughly recovered from her last lying-in—but when the blow finally came, he was devastated. Bereft of the only parent who cared for him and ashamed that he hadn't honored her wishes about his father, he had fallen into a deep funk.

To make things worse, Father acted as though Mother's death

had been a mere inconvenience. For a time he had even sent Lorana and Mercy to stay with Asa and Polly—leaving Jake deprived of his sisters' sweet company, and alone with his sour father at table and in the fields.

Tim had tried to console him when he could, but Tim had precious little free time these days. His father had decided he should also go to Yale, so Tim had been spending long hours with his tutor, preparing for the entrance exam.

Jake's only pleasures had been oystering and drinking. In the evenings, he'd ferry himself across to New Haven and drown his sorrows in the Long Wharf taverns. Mornings, he would go out in his dugout to rake up oysters, then float them upriver in the freshwater till they were ready to be barreled.

One morning Hannah had been sitting on the rocks, looking out at the harbor, and he found himself paddling right to her. He just sat silent in the boat and she stayed silent on the rocks and after a while she said, *My parents came over from Ireland when I was little. They paid for our passage, but we were very poor. My father went to Pennsylvania, to look for farmland . . . we never heard from him again. Mother was sure he was killed. She knew he never would have abandoned us. . . . When I was eight years old, she died of a fever and I was put in the almshouse. Mrs. Morris came looking for a girl. She wanted someone older, but she took pity on me. She said, Hannah, will you work hard and be a good girl? I said I would, and she took me home.* Jake said, *I am sorry for you, Hannah.* She responded: *And I for you, Mal.*

With that came a sort of acknowledgment of their intention

to like each other. At first it was a simple exchange of greetings when they happened to meet. But very soon they were going out of their way to happen to meet.

She discovered reasons to visit the ferry landing: *Did you take Pomp's boy across earlier? He's nowhere to be found.* Jake found cause to stop in at her kitchen: *Could I have a bit of your sticking plaster? Lorana's cut her finger. . . .* Then they would talk for a while, and laugh, and shyly look away, and part with reluctance.

And on Sundays, Jake could not help but stare at her throughout meeting. She always looked especially nice there—gracefully simple, dignified, serene. He began to think about her all the time, and those thoughts were not always pure.

His father complained that Jake's work was even sloppier than usual, that he paid no attention to direction, that he was always distracted. *It is as though you've turned imbecile*, Father grumbled, and Jake replied, *Why Father, I thought you* always *believed me to be an imbecile!* But he'd said it with such good nature that Father was too flustered to chastise him.

Finally the day had come when Jake nerved himself to tell Hannah, as he poled the ferry with great concentration, that his feelings for her went beyond friendship, and that he absolutely must know if she felt the same way.

She tried to laugh off the question, but he demanded an answer. At last she said with great solemnity, *If you absolutely must know, yes, Mal, I do. But of course . . . only for Tim's sake.*

His heart plunged, then soared when he caught the gleam of mischief in her eyes. He was giddy with joy, felt he would have to shout it out or his lungs would burst. *I'll die if I don't kiss you soon,* he told her, and she said drily: *Oh my, how dramatic you are!*

They'd agreed to meet in the tall sea grass north of Black Rock; Jake had waited in indescribable anguish, and when at last he heard her rattling through the reeds he rushed to take her in his arms, murmuring such tender endearments that she laughed and said, *This is astonishing, Mal. I'd never have figured you for such a romantic! Are you playing with me? Are you about to cry out, Ha! Servant Girl, how could you think I cared for you?* At that Jake had felt deep sorrow and deeper emotion. Cupping her face in his hands, he looked into her sea green eyes and said, *Don't throw my vile past self up to me, Hannah.* And they had kissed. . . .

For three months now they had been stealing time together—in the reeds, in the salt grass meadows, wherever else they could arrange to meet. They began writing their thoughts and feelings to each other in between times, and before parting they often exchanged letters. Jake no longer felt the need to spend hours every night in the taverns. Recently he had asked Hannah to call him by his Christian name; she thought it charming that he had waited so long to make the request.

Then, just a few days ago, Jake had told her he wanted to stop hiding their attachment; but Hannah forbade him to speak of it to anyone. She still had nearly a year left to her indenture, and besides . . . what would his father say to love with a bonded servant? Jake said the man's opinion wasn't worth a Continental dollar. If Father didn't like it, that was too bad. Jake could find a way to make a living away from his father. He and Hannah would move far away from here. Then they would *both* be free. If only this war, and her indenture, would hurry up and end. Hannah said he must be patient, and he agreed to try.

But when it had come time to part, he could not tear himself away. He'd felt a sick panic at being separated from her; his kisses were more passionate, more desperate than ever before, and he drew her closer, touching her, pulling her down to lie with him. . . . She had not protested or resisted. But afterward, when he felt only blissful peace, she turned her face and, quickly adjusting her petticoats, got up and ran away.

His joy had melted into sorrow and shame: what had he done? How could something so pleasurable lead to such misery? And was it all his fault? No. . . . She didn't tell him to stop, they had both done it, together. So why had she run from him? He'd kept himself from calling out to her or following her. Someone might see.

This morning he could bear it no longer and finally walked up that path to confront her . . . and now all was right again. She would meet him later, and the day was bright and beautiful, and although it was the Sabbath it was still the 4th of July.

He thought of his friends last year, saying, *Eventually, you'll have to admit you were wrong, Mal.* Tomorrow when they celebrated together, he just might have to own his fault. Three years into this experiment of independence, and the tide was—perhaps—turning for the Patriot side. It was true Britain had captured two ports in Georgia, but it was also true that they'd only moved the war into the South because they'd been unable to conquer New England and the middle states. Jake had no personal knowledge of Southern men, but he'd heard they were fierce fighters, as dedicated to the cause as any New Englander.

And perhaps the latest news was the most hopeful: Spain also had declared war on England.

Maybe the oyster would best the starfish after all.

But there was one piece of the war that had been gnawing at Jake. Down in Philadelphia, Benedict Arnold was in trouble, accused of misusing government funds, mistreating militia-men, and "slighting Patriotic persons, while pandering to those of another character," according to a broadside. The implication was clear, but Jake had been so shocked by the phrase that he'd read it several times: Arnold, favoring Loyalists? Arnold, who had chased scores of Tories out of New Haven in fear of their lives? The broadside then went on to say that Arnold had *married* a Tory woman. It all seemed impossible.

Arnold had demanded a court-martial to clear his name, but just before the trial was to take place, Washington had it post-poned. No explanation, no new trial date. What a joke! They probably had no evidence against him, and that was why they couldn't go to trial. It was shameful for the new government to treat the greatest hero of the Revolution in such a manner. . . . If only they'd give Arnold his day in court, Jake knew he'd prove them all wrong, then go out and win the war for them.

Jake tied his dugout at the ferry landing and went up to the barn. He was turning out the horses and cows when Lorana came to feed the dung-hill fowl. "Papa's sharpening his tongue for you, Mal," she announced cheerfully.

"Nonsense, little sprite," Jake answered. "Our dear sire has only honeyed words for his favorite son. *You* know that."

She giggled, then mimicked their father's deep voice: "'Where is that numskull brother of yours now, daughter? The way he's always disappearing, I'll swear he's either spying for the British or he's got a sweetheart! And if he cares to keep his head, it had better be the latter!'"

Jake stared at his sister. "*Father* said that? Really?"

"Yes. *Have* you got a sweetheart, Mal? *Have* you?"

"None but you, Lor." He tugged at her pigtail.

She laughed, darting away. "Come, Mal. Breakfast will be ready!"

Jake headed for the house, amused and amazed. His father had actually thought about him long enough to spin a theory about his comings and goings!

"Where have you been?" Father grumbled when Jake came through the door.

"Just out walking, Father. Sorry to be late."

Sally set a plate of rye flapjacks before him.

"Thank you, Sally."

"Welcome," she replied. "Mercy, sit up straight!"

Jake winked at Mercy across the table.

"Did your wanderings take you beyond the harbor?" his father asked.

"As far as the Point."

"Any evidence of British ships?"

"Not that I could see, sir. But the horizon is thick with haze."

"Will the British attack us, Papa?" Mercy asked, her voice thin with worry.

"No one knows," he responded gruffly.

"They wouldn't dare," Jake said. He sang dramatically:

> *"Where'er they go, we shall oppose them,*
> *Sons of valor must be free.*
> *Should they touch at fair Rhode Island,*
> *There to combat with the brave,*
> *Driven from each dale and highland—"*

"Stop that!" Father said. "At the table! And on the Sabbath!"

"We sing at meeting on the Sabbath, Papa," Mercy said.

"That is different. Those are songs for God."

"Why are there no songs for Connecticut?" Lorana asked.

"'Tis rather hard to rhyme," Jake mused, and his sisters giggled.

"So is Massachusetts," their father grumbled. "That doesn't stop songs being made about *them*."

Massachusetts was a sore spot with Father; he thought the state received far more than its share of glory. At least Jake could agree with him on that one thing. Just because the Massachusetts men had thrown a little tea into the harbor—disguised as Indians, those chicken hearts!—and because the first shots of the war were fired there, the state and its men were hallowed all out of proportion. Did Massachusetts have a single general as brave as Arnold? Not likely. A hanged martyr such as Nathan Hale? Besides, it was Connecticut that was providing the new nation with everything it needed, from weapons to salted meat. Even Washington acknowledged that.

Would Connecticut forever have to exist in her neighbor's bloated shadow?

The door rattled, and in walked Ethan, looking quite the college dandy in a brocade waistcoat and neckcloth of yellow silk.

"Ethan!" Father nearly knocked his chair backward trying to get to him fast enough.

"Good morning, Father!"

Jake set his teeth and watched with grim fascination as Father gripped Ethan's shoulders, appraising him. And what was that peculiar thing Father was doing with his mouth? Smiling?

"You look fine, son, fine!" Father acted as though he hadn't seen Ethan in a year rather than only a month.

"Thank you, Father. It's good to be home." Lorana and Mercy went to him, too. "Who are these grown-up girls?" He embraced each one. "I've brought your favorite sweets from New Haven!"

The girls clapped their hands excitedly.

"You may have them tomorrow," Father added, passing Ethan a cup of small beer. "Now back to your seat, Lorana. Mercy, go and tell Sally to bring your brother some breakfast."

"Mal!" Standing at his side, Ethan thumped him on the back. "How are you, my good fellow?"

"Have you come to help us mow the salt meadow?" Jake asked. "We start day after tomorrow."

Ethan laughed, pulling up a chair. "I'd like to, brother, but I'm only here for the holiday."

"Naturally, *brother*," Jake muttered.

"Listen—" Ethan looked first at Father, then at Jake, and said in a conspiratorial tone, "Let me tell you the war news from New Haven. They say Tryon's fleet is sailing toward us, and we may be attacked."

"This will come as a shock to you, Ethan," Jake said. "But Yale and New Haven are not the center of the civilized world. We here in the backwater of East Haven have heard the same intelligence."

Ethan deflated like a sail out of wind. "Oh. Well . . . what do you think of it, then?" His eager eyes darted from Jake to their father.

"I give the notion no credence whatever," Father said. "The fleet is on its way to Rhode Island."

If Father had said "oysters have shells," Jake would have had no choice but to refute the claim. "Why, sir?" he asked. "Do you think New Haven is of so little consequence that the British would never bother with us?"

"I've no intention of debating the topic with a boy," Father said with a dismissive wave. "What are the *men* saying over at Yale, Ethan?"

"Well, Professor Stiles—"

"Peculiar, Ethan, is it not?" Jake interrupted. "He thinks me a man when it comes to work, but a child when it comes to discussion."

Ethan flushed, casting his eyes down.

Father slapped the table, startling the girls so that they yelped. "How dare you speak of me as if I am not present!" he roared at Jake.

"How, sir?" Jake got to his feet, pulling the napkin from his neck and flinging it onto the table. "You have ignored *my* presence all my life. Is it not fair play to repay you in kind?"

He headed for the door; Father scrambled to his feet, blocking the way, and seized Jake's arm.

"Leave go, sir," Jake said steadily. "I'll not stand your bullying any longer. For nearly two years, I've done the work of three men while your golden boy has been off enjoying himself at Yale. Yet you show me nothing but contempt. Then he dances in and—" Jake heard his voice falter, and stopped to gather himself. "Release me, Father," he said through clenched teeth, "or I shall not hold myself responsible for my actions."

Looking utterly stunned, Father did as he was bid. Jake gave the door a satisfying slam on his way out.

He went down to the ferry landing, got into his dugout, and paddled briskly toward the Point. . . . Keeping the Sabbath was a stupid old Puritan notion. As if God begrudged people what small pleasures this grim world afforded. What better way to honor the Sabbath than by enjoying God's creation, instead of sitting, stiff and stifling, inside a structure of man's making?

Besides—today was the 4th of July, not tomorrow. Jake looked down at his oyster rake; he would have his own celebration. The Point was deserted, and he was pouring sweat from paddling so hard in such heat. He stripped off shoes, stockings, and breeches, and dived into the Sound.

WILD ROSES GREW rampant in the scrub beyond the rocks and the beach; at this time of year, the bright pink flowers dotted the shoreline. Jake picked a bouquet while he waited. He'd been hatching his plan for hours and was ready to tell it to Hannah. When she rustled through the rushes, he held the flowers out to her.

"The whole town is talking," she said by way of greeting. "Why did you miss meeting?"

"Excuse me, madam." He took his hat in his hand. "I expected to meet my sweetheart, but it appears I've stumbled into dame school."

"Oh, Jake." She took the flowers and put her arms around him. "I heard Ethan tell Tim your dugout was gone. I was worried."

"I'm sorry." He kissed her nape, her dark hair; she was wearing it the way he liked best, plaited in one braid down her back.

"Ethan said you quarreled with your father."

"It's becoming a Fourth of July tradition." Plucking flowers from the bunch, he tucked them into her hair at various spots. "That looks alarmingly beautiful," he said, stepping back to admire the effect.

"Thank you." She blushed, still unaccustomed to his compliments, and said in a serious tone: "Now. Tell me what happened."

They sat in the reeds, holding each other. Jake related the scene in the kitchen, and he finished with: "And I've made a decision, Hannah. I won't go home again. In fact, I've come up with a plan. We'll run away."

"Run away!"

"Yes. Tonight. We'll go north—Vermont, or Maine. We'll get married."

She pushed him gently away. "I'll do no such thing, Jake.

Imagine me running away from the Morrises, after all they've done for me! And with less than a year before an *honorable* end to my indenture."

Jake did not respond.

"It concerns me when you're so rash, in speech and . . . in actions."

Her accusatory tone made him bristle, and he asked coolly, "What is that supposed to mean, Hannah?"

It was her turn for silence.

"Because it sounds like you've convinced yourself you bear no responsibility for what *we* did the other day."

"It cannot happen again," she said, low and solemn.

"That does not answer my question."

Tears spilled down her cheeks; she quickly brushed them away.

"Listen," he whispered near her ear. "I love you, Hannah. With all my heart."

"It was wrong."

"Who is to judge?"

"There are rules. Proper behavior is set by . . . by the church," she stammered. "The community."

"Do you think we are the only ones who—"

"I'll not do it again, Jake. If anyone were to find out . . . it would be *my* reputation ruined, not yours."

"We *are* going to be married," he said emphatically.

"Are we?" Her eyes searched his. "And what of your father? What will he say when you announce you have promised yourself to a bound servant?"

"Why should that matter? He stands for a republic where all men are created equal, does he not?"

"All *men*," she repeated. "Not women. And not servants, either—black *or* white."

"Those words sound pretty unpatriotic, my girl," he teased.

"Perhaps—but true."

"Hannah. I've told you. I care nothing for my father's opinion. If he won't accept you, I'm quite capable of striking out on my own." He scratched at his cheek, making a quizzical face. "And, well, if I'm not—you're capable enough for us both. Are you not?"

She gave him a rueful smile, shaking her head.

"When the time is right, I'll tell my father about us. Whether he chooses to accept it is nothing to me."

"You say that now, Jake. You've no idea what it is to live on your own, with no family."

He pressed his lips to her temple. "You'll be my family."

Cocking her head, she studied his face.

"What?" he asked.

"Sometimes, when I'm away from you, I *still* think you must be playing with me," she admitted. "That this will all turn out to be a cruel joke."

"You ought to know by now that I'm unskilled at pretense of any kind."

"But sometimes I ask myself, 'How can a boy who hated me so thoroughly now claim to love me?'"

Offended, Jake turned his face from hers. "Why do you

torment me with who I used to be, Hannah? Have I not told you, and shown you, often enough that I love you?"

She did not answer.

"The way I behaved in the past—I was a stupid child. And I didn't know you. Directly I began to know you, I stopped being hateful. Didn't I?"

Now she cupped her hand under his chin and turned his head so that he must look at her again.

"Haven't we spoken of this enough, Hannah?" he persisted. "How many more times must we have this conversation?"

"Never. Not ever again," she said softly, and for a time they sat in silence.

"I think we should tell Tim," Jake said at last. "It doesn't seem right, deceiving him. He still thinks we hate each other."

She nodded thoughtfully. "He'll be surprised, but—"

"To put it mildly."

"—he'll be pleased. Won't he?"

"I'm sure. . . . Still, I can't wait to see his face when I tell him."

"Don't tell him without me there!"

"I love your laughter." He kissed her just above the gathered neck of her shift. "So light and . . . oh, I don't know, imagine I said something wonderfully poetic."

She laughed still more and turned her mouth to his again.

"Don't you object to this, my little Puritan?" he teased after a while.

"Not in the least."

"Hannah, you're a wonderful girl," he said, overcome with emotion.

"And you, Jake . . . well, you just *might* become a wonderful boy, someday."

Seizing her, he began to tickle her; she wriggled away, stifling laughter. Then for a long time they sat, his arms about her and her head on his chest.

"You never said," he reminded her at last.

"Said what?"

"'Yes, Jake, I love you, too, and I will marry you just as soon as possible.'"

She drew back to look into his eyes. "Yes, Jake," she whispered. "Yes, and yes, and yes."

LET ETHAN DO the chores and tend the ferry; it only served him right. The evening was oppressively hot, without a breath of wind, and Jake was plagued by ravenous mosquitoes as he paddled home after dark. He had to keep stopping to scratch his head, his face, his hands. The day had been very long. Exhaustion threatened to overpower him, body and soul.

He hoped the rest of the family would be in bed. He didn't want to talk to anybody, explain his absence to Father, listen to Ethan's understanding apologies. He wanted only to eat something, then sleep. Tomorrow morning he'd do his chores and slip out early for the oyster breakfast. By the time he returned home, today would be forgotten.

But when the house came into view, there was a light in the parlor. His first thought was to sleep in the barn. . . . No, that would be childish. He would face his father, and the music.

Ethan's and Father's heads were turned toward the doorway,

anticipating his entrance. Ethan looked worried, Father stern. But his tone was quite civil as he said, "Please join us."

Jake removed his hat and sat on the edge of a chair, to indicate he would stay only as long as necessary.

Father said, "I was instructing Ethan as to the plan I wish him to carry out should there be an attack."

Was *that* all? Silently, Jake exhaled his relief. He'd thought Father was about to start spouting speeches and levying punishments.

"He's to put Sally and the girls in the wagon and start for your Aunt Grannis in Mount Carmel," Father continued. "I've already had Sally pack up the silver and other items of value."

Ethan began, "Mal, don't you think I'm old enough to—"

"Silence!" Father snapped.

Ethan sat back in his chair, fuming.

Jake kept a straight face, but . . . Father and Ethan at odds? This might start to get interesting! And didn't it just figure that Father wouldn't allow his college boy to fight. It was all right for Jake to be killed, but not the precious one.

"You, of course, will follow Lieutenant Bishop's orders," Father told Jake. "You and I are amongst the men designated to defend Black Rock."

You and I . . . men were the words that struck Jake first. He felt impressed with his own importance . . . until the words *defend Black Rock* sank in. Was this attack an actual possibility?

Jake said, "Do they really think—?"

"How can we know?" Father interrupted with worried

impatience. "How can we see what is in their dark hearts? 'Tis a fleet of forty-eight sail, we hear, commanded by Tryon with George Collier under him. Some say they intend to bypass us entirely and make land at New London. Others . . ." He got to his feet, walking quickly to the window that overlooked the harbor. "If they come, they'll seek out the homes of the ardent Patriots. Those of us who provision the army, who are Sons of Liberty— the British know just who we are, thanks to the wretched Tories. Well, if the house is to burn, so be it. We will rebuild."

"Why should I not come to the defense of my home, Father?" Ethan said passionately, leaning forward in his chair. "I'm nearly fifteen! Sally is perfectly capable of driving a wagon herself, and if the British attack, we will need every man and boy."

"All right, Ethan," Father said wearily. "Please yourself."

Ethan sat back, looking quite pleased *with* himself. "Thank you, Father."

Jake was disgusted: when had Father ever given in to *his* wishes that way? Then he caught himself and grinned, shaking his head. Not five minutes ago, he was angry because Father *wouldn't* let Ethan fight.

"If there is something amusing about the situation, please do share it with us," Father said. "I could use a bit of humor right now."

Jake cleared his throat. "No, sir. Nothing amusing at all."

"Then you boys should get some sleep. We'll soon enough know what is to transpire. If there are any new developments, the signal will be three shots fired from the cannon on Beacon Hill."

Father trudged off to his bedchamber.

"I'm starved," Jake announced, leaping to his feet.

Ethan followed him to the kitchen. "Where were you all day?"

"I was where I was." Jake took a chunk of corn bread from the bread box and began to eat.

"I wish you wouldn't be angry with me, Mal. 'Tisn't my fault . . . about Father and you. Is it?"

"No," Jake admitted, and sighed. "Sorry, Ethan."

"Father seemed quite remorseful. Even . . . sad."

"Really?" Jake took another piece of corn bread. "What did he say?"

"Well, nothing, actually. It was in his manner."

Jake just laughed under his breath. "I'm going to bed. I can scarcely keep my eyes open."

Ethan picked up the candle and again followed him, up the ladder to the loft. Jake peeked in on the sleeping girls. Mercy had her arms around Lorana's neck, her head on Lorana's shoulder; both looked serene and secure. What would tomorrow bring them?

When Jake had undressed and lay on the bed, he realized that his brother was, with methodical precision, removing his clothing and draping each piece on the chest of drawers.

Jake leaned up on his elbow. "What on earth are you doing?"

"If I'm to call myself a minuteman, I'd like to be worthy of the name." Ethan's tone was in manly earnest.

Jake burst out laughing.

"You *are* finding yourself rather droll tonight, aren't you?" Ethan said.

"Put out the candle and go to sleep, little minuteman." Jake was still chuckling as he turned to face the wall. Alone in his room at bedtime, this was usually his time for writing to Hannah. With Ethan here, and Jake so tired, he decided to leave it for tonight. But he surrendered his thoughts to her as he fell pleasurably asleep.

He awoke to the cannon's boom; the room was pitch-dark.

"What's happening, Mal?" Ethan's voice was high and anxious.

"Shhh." Jake sat up. "Listen."

But both girls cried out, "Mal! Mal!"

"Holy Ghost," he muttered, getting out of bed. "It's all right, girls," he called. "Hush—we need to listen for the—"

Then Sally was shouting from the bottom of the ladder. "Mal! Ethan! Bring those children to me!"

"Boys!" Father roared. "Dress yourselves!"

"If this is indeed the signal," Jake mused, "I'd certainly like to hear it."

A second cannon blast.

Ethan crashed to the floor.

"What was that!" Father cried out.

"Our minuteman, tripping over his shoes." Jake sat on the bed to pull on his stockings. "Are you hurt, little minuteman?"

"Stop calling me that!"

Jake got into his breeches and tied them at the knees, put on his shoes, and tied back his hair.

"I can't find my other stocking!" Ethan said.

Jake located the stocking and draped it over Ethan's head.

The cannon fired once more; Jake's heart sank.

"That was the signal," Lorana said as he entered the girls' room.

"All will be well," he told them. "But perhaps you ought to dress yourselves, just in case."

"Will the British kill us with bayonets?" Mercy asked.

"Even the British are not so evil as to kill little girls," Jake assured her.

"But they might kill *you*," Lorana said solemnly. "*You're* taking up arms."

"Thank you for pointing that out," Jake mumbled.

Sally came huffing up the ladder. "If you won't bring those children to me, I suppose I've got to bring myself to them. You'd better get down there—your brother's already gone off with my master's fowler."

"Yes, I'd best show him which end one shoots from," Jake said.

As he left the room, he heard Sally's soft laughter.

In the parlor, the candle burning on the mantel allowed Jake to see the time: half past ten? Surely that was not possible. It felt like hours had passed since he'd gone to bed at half past nine. Perhaps the clock had stopped—but no, the pendulum was still swinging.

Just as Jake joined Father and Ethan in the dooryard, horses' hooves thudded up the lane. Father raised his musket to his shoulder. "Who goes?"

"Friend, sir!" came Gideon's voice.

"What is the news?" Father asked, lowering the weapon.

"The fleet has passed Stratford."

"What are the orders?"

"Mal and Tim Morris are to join Sergeant Moulthrop at Five Mile Point, sir. You're to remain here for now. There are sentinels all along the coast. The signal will be three guns again if the British come to anchor; then you're to report to Black Rock."

"What is the time, Gid?" Jake asked.

"The time?" Gideon sounded puzzled. "About half past ten, I imagine," he said, and galloped away.

"How can it yet be so early?" Jake mumbled.

"Jacob, get your things," his father said. "Ethan, fetch your brother's horse."

In the house, Sally was chastising Mercy for crying, telling her to be a good, big girl. Jake lifted his sister into his arms, and she hugged his neck.

"I don't want to go to Aunt Grannis, Mal."

"Why ever not? You love Aunt Grannis."

"I want to stay here and have cakes and fireworks for the Fourth."

"Aunt Grannis bakes delicious cakes," he said. "And perhaps they'll have fireworks in Mount Carmel."

"Put that child down," Sally scolded. "She's too big for that."

Jake obeyed. "Be brave," he said, kissing both girls. To Lorana he murmured, "Be a good example to our sister."

"Yes, Mal."

He put the strap of his cartridge box over his head and under his right arm; the haversack went on the left side.

Sally, who had rushed outdoors with his canteen, returned

and handed it to him. "Water," she said. "That's all you need, you hear?"

Jake grinned. "Thank you, Sally." He slung the canteen strap over his head and under his left arm.

"Will there be shooting?" Mercy asked.

"I hope not."

"But if there is . . . you be brave, too."

He gave her a wink. "I'll try," he said, and left them.

JAKE IMAGINED CHAOS on the cove road. Surely he and his horse would be battling a wave of wagons driven by women and servants heading inland with the children, all in a panicked frenzy. Instead he found it eerily quiet, the only sound the thunder of his horse's hooves.

Perhaps the British had already landed and performed a stealthy house-to-house massacre, bayoneting civilians in their beds. . . . Their first likely target would have been the Morris house, closest to the Point. And whose chamber would they have reached first? Hannah's, just off the kitchen, its little window facing the dooryard—

Jake dug in his heels and bade his horse go faster.

When he arrived, he was relieved to see Tim and his father standing calmly at the front door. As Jake dismounted at the gate, they walked to greet him.

"Evening, sir," Jake said, nodding to Captain Morris.

"Have you any news, Mal?" the Captain asked.

"Just that the fleet has passed Stratford. Tim and I are to join those keeping watch on the beach."

"I'll get my gun," Tim said, and dashed up the walk.

"Why us? Why now?" Captain Morris mumbled, as if to himself.

Why anyone? Why any time? Jake thought. *'Tis war, old man. That's why.*

"I shall have Pomp's boy drive Mrs. Morris and the girls to Cheshire."

And Hannah, Jake thought. *Don't forget Hannah!*

"Pomp and my other men will guard the saltworks," he continued distractedly. "The enemy will want to destroy them."

There was no doubt of that: Captain Morris's salt was instrumental in preserving beef for the Continental army—and the British surely knew it.

Tim ran back down the walk, jamming his hat on his head.

Captain Morris put his arms about both their shoulders. "Look out for each other, boys."

"We will, sir," Tim said.

"I'll take your horse to Pomp, Mal," Captain Morris said.

"Thank you, sir."

"Bring news as soon as you know it. I'll wake Hannah later and have her cook breakfast."

At the mention of her name, Jake felt the blood rise to his face, and he was grateful for the concealing darkness.

". . . and tell Sergeant Moulthrop he may send the men up to eat here."

"Yes, Father."

"Thank you, sir," Jake managed to mumble while thinking most unthankful thoughts: *Hannah to cook for every man*

Moulthrop cares to send? Why doesn't Captain Morris wake his plump spoilt daughters and have them help her?

"Come on, Mal." Tim started down the beach path at a trot.

"Slow down. I swear you're worse than Ethan," Jake said, and as they walked he gave a theatrical account of his brother trying to prepare himself for battle in the requisite sixty seconds. By the time they approached the Point, Tim was bent over with laughter.

"Who's there?" Sergeant Moulthrop was standing sentinel, a torch planted in the dirt.

"Jake Mallery, with Tim Morris, sir."

"Good boys—you are the first, so go ahead and take the rocks."

"What shall we do, sir?" Tim asked.

"There's nothing we *can* do right now, except to keep our ears and eyes open. I expect we'll know their intentions at daybreak."

"Father will have our Hannah cook breakfast for those keeping watch," Tim said. "Do you really think there will be a battle, sir?"

Moulthrop heaved a sigh. "It does seem things are heading in that direction. So my suggestion is that if you boys can, spell each other and try to get some sleep. This day could be a very long one."

"Yes, sir," they said, and in silence they walked along the beach.

Father will have our Hannah cook breakfast . . . I'll wake Hannah later . . . As Jake climbed the rocks with Tim, he realized his jaw was clenched in anger. He was not even thinking about the possibility of participating in battle. It was only Hannah on his mind.

Two years ago, he was hurling insults about her on these very rocks. Even up to one year ago, he'd disrespected her, in front of Noah, with his crude song. And now . . . he heard slight in every mention of her by another. A sound escaped him—a noise of self-derision.

"What's funny?"

He longed to share his secret, but he had promised Hannah they'd tell Tim together. "Oh, I was just thinking . . . no oyster breakfast in the morning, eh?"

"No. But they'll keep. And I'll bet Hannah makes spider cake. When you taste it, you'll forget all about oysters."

"Hmm," was all Jake answered. Now he was thinking of Captain Morris waking Hannah, most likely with a startling rap on her door. How much more sweetly would Jake do the job himself, entering quietly, brushing a wisp of hair from her face and gently kissing her eyelids. He would wake her that way every day, when they were married. . . .

"Mal? Mal?"

"What?" he said sharply, and realized Tim had stopped several strides behind him.

"I said I think this is a good spot. The rocks are flat; we can take turns lying down."

"Oh. Sorry . . . yes."

They put their muskets down and sat facing the harbor. The third-quarter moon, still on the rise, gave a soft glow to the surrounding landscape. All was deceptively silent and peaceful.

"Look." Tim pointed out the mountains, red by day, that

were called East Rock and West Rock. "They're like twin sentinels, watching over us all. 'Come no farther, you damned British
scoundrels, we have guard over those who live here.'"

"Very poetic, Timo. If only mountains carried muskets." Jake
stretched out on the rocks.

"Mal?"

"Yes?"

"Are you scared?"

"Well, I imagine I might be if something were to actually *happen*. But right now. . . ." Jake covered his cartridge box with his
hat and used it as a pillow. "Mind if I sleep first?"

"Could you?" Tim asked. "Sleep, now?"

"Oh, just watch me. I'm so tired, I could sleep on a picket
fence."

"What was up with you, anyhow? Ethan said you ran off after
arguing with your father."

"Tim, can we discuss my trials and tribulations after I've had
a nap?" Without waiting for a reply, he said, "Thank you." Then
he placed an arm over his eyes and fell asleep almost at once.

AGAIN A CANNON blast shocked him awake, and he
vaulted upright, confused, disoriented, forgetting everything
until he saw Tim sitting beside him with his knees drawn up and
arms locked around them. Day was about to break.

"Why didn't you wake me?" Jake asked. "You'd no time to
rest."

For reply, Tim raised an arm slowly and pointed at the water.

There in the Sound were about twenty ships—men-of-war, transports, tenders, and more. The larger ones lay at anchor, not a mile from these rocks; the smaller vessels were sailing brazenly toward the harbor on the West Haven side.

"My God," Jake said.

The cannon boomed its second alarm; Tim raised his spyglass to his eye. "They've only been visible a few minutes." His voice was low and calm. "They'd extinguished all their lights so we couldn't know their intentions."

"Well, their intentions are quite clear now. Let's find Moulthrop." As Jake moved to get to his feet, Tim took hold of his sleeve, then handed him the spyglass. Jake looked; the men-of-war were putting out their boats, and red-coated Regulars poured into them like poisonous ants escaping a disturbed nest. When a boat was filled, it would push off—and begin rowing toward the west shore.

The west shore.

Not here.

Jake felt an initial rush of relief, closely followed by the realization that he'd no cause for such an emotion. "They'll go to New Haven by way of West Haven, most likely. We'll have to go across and help."

They gathered their things and ran back to the beach. As they leapt along the rocks Jake wondered if Tim was hoping what he was hoping: that perhaps they wouldn't have to fight after all. East Haveners should stay and protect East Haven, should they not? Surely there were enough New Haven men to defend that fair city. Let those self-satisfied Yale boys make themselves useful, for once. . . .

On the beach, a few other men were already gathered around Moulthrop. "I say we go across, Eli!" Silas Field was urging as Jake and Tim arrived.

"And leave East Haven defenseless?" Moulthrop replied.

"So we do nothing?"

"We wait," Moulthrop corrected. "I see no alternative. Just because they're landing men at West Haven does not mean they won't come here next. But we must await the lieutenant's orders." As he was speaking, a dozen more militiamen gathered around, including Caleb and Dan. "Does everyone know his post?"

All mumbled assent.

"Good. If you live near enough, I suggest you go home and eat your breakfast. Prepare your wives and children to flee. Bury your valuables, and pasture your stock lest the devils fire our barns. I'd like some volunteers amongst those of you with no wives or children to stay and haul the fieldpiece and ammunition cart to the beach. If they try to land, at least we'll give them a couple of good blasts."

Dan was the first to step forward. "I'll stay, sir."

"And I," Caleb added immediately.

"And I," Tim echoed.

Jake held back; surely three were enough to drag the fieldpiece from its shed at the Morrises' saltworks. He was dying to get back to the Morris house and see how Hannah was doing. The day was already unbearably hot—perhaps he could go to the kitchen under the guise of fetching cider for those doing the hard work?

Tim shattered his plans with an elbow to the ribs.

"Uh . . . yes. So will I," Jake mumbled.

"Good. Bring it down to the Point, and conceal it as best you can with brush. Then go and eat some breakfast at the Morrises'."

Damnation, Jake thought. He did not want Caleb and Dan going along to the Morrises'. It would be hard enough to talk to Hannah on her own with Tim there. *And* his sisters *and* his parents . . . everyone probably flying in ten directions. But for now he must put it out of his mind as they took care of this business of the fieldpiece.

It all seemed unreal, more like a play day when they were small, pretending they were in the French War and their beach was that of Lake Champlain as they battled French forces. . . . But this fieldpiece was no phantom, and it was remarkably obstinate when rolled onto the sand. The four of them tugged and cursed and sweated and laughed and loudly wished that they'd had the more pressing and less strenuous duty of attending to family matters.

Then there was an embarrassed silence as they became keenly aware of Dan's having no family matters. Soon after his capture, Dan's father had been sent to the New-gate prison and remained there to this day, as far as anyone knew. His mother had gone with the other children to the western part of the state, where the Loyalists were thick. Dan was staying with Caleb's family and had no contact with his own. If he longed for or worried about any of them, he never spoke a word of it.

With the fieldpiece in place, they started covering it with brush. "Where is Gid?" Jake asked, to change the topic.

"Still playing Paul Revere, I imagine," Caleb said, and they all laughed.

"Nearly got himself shot, clattering up to our house with no warning," Jake said.

"Your old daddy would shoot Washington himself just for the chance to fire his musket," Dan said, prompting more mirth.

When they finished the job, the British fleet still had not moved. No more boats could be seen taking soldiers to the west shore.

"This may yet come to nothing," Jake said.

"You don't really believe that, do you?" Caleb asked.

"I'm parched," Jake replied. "Let's go and get some cider at Tim's."

"Have you nothing in your canteen?" Tim asked.

"Nothing of any use. Sally filled it with *water*." He clutched at his throat, sticking out his tongue, and his friends laughed again.

"Dan and I will be along soon," Caleb said. "I want to stop at home first."

When Jake and Tim reached the Morris house, Tim's father was at the gate, looking as though he hadn't left the spot in all these hours.

"Let me have a word with you, son," he said wearily. "Mal, go on in and get some breakfast."

"Yes, sir," Jake said, but before he could head for the kitchen door, Tim caught him by the arm.

"Mal . . . don't start in. You know . . . with Hannah."

Jake could scarcely stop himself from laughing. "I shall try very hard to be good, Timo," he said solemnly. "For *your* sake."

"Thank you, Mal," Tim said in earnest, and Jake ran to the kitchen the second Tim's back was turned.

Hannah had been keeping watch; she threw open the door and, when he was inside, flung her arms about his neck, holding him close. "Oh, Jake!"

"I'd like the threat of battle every day, if this is the welcome it warrants. Come, give us a kiss before Tim gets here," he said, and she pressed her mouth to his.

"The captain is sending us to Cheshire," she said after a while.

"I know."

"I don't want to go . . . and leave you."

"No, you *will* go. Promise me."

"What if something—"

"*Promise*, Hannah. If there's a fight, I want to know you're out of harm's way."

"All right. I promise." She reached into her pocket and withdrew a letter; quickly, he stashed it in the pocket of his breeches.

"I didn't write," he mumbled. "I was so tired, and Ethan was home, and then the alarm—"

"'Tis all right." She brushed some loose strands of hair from his face; he kissed her again. "Here." She put him away firmly. "If anyone comes . . ."

"I don't care who knows."

"I do. Now sit at the table."

He obeyed, and she brought a pitcher of cider. Until then he had forgotten his desperate thirst; he gulped down a cupful. She stood beside him, alert to any approach, smoothing his shirt and his hair as he told her what was happening in the Sound.

"Do you think they'll come here?"

"'Tis anyone's guess." To put her at ease, he smiled slyly and said, "So where is this spider cake young Timothy is bragging about? As if you belonged to *him* and not *me?*"

"In less than a year's time, I'll belong to no man, woman, *or* boy," she replied. "And I'll thank you to remember that, Mr. Mallery." She gave his face a playful slap, then went to the yard to get the spider cakes from the outdoor oven.

Jake decided her letter would be safer tucked in his stocking, so he untied the knee of his breeches and slid the letter down his leg. Just as he finished retying, Tim came in through the pantry.

"My mother is distraught." Tim picked up the cup and gulped down the remaining cider, then poured himself more. "She's saying the British are sure to know our role and burn us out."

"My father says the same of us."

"If they make it as far as your house. But we're so close. . . ." Tim stood at the window, peering out toward the beach. When Hannah came in he said without turning: "Morning, Hannah."

"Good morning, Tim." She set the cakes on the table and cut one into wedges. The sight and scent made Jake realize how hungry he was, and he reached for a piece. "Careful—it is hot," she said.

He took a large bite anyway, and immediately the roof of his mouth was seared by something more like liquid than cake.

"Ahhh!" He reached for a drink, but none was at hand. "Blast, girl, are you trying to kill me?"

"Did I not just this moment say that it was hot?"

"You didn't say molten! What in the world *is* that?"

"Cream," she said. "I put cream on my spider cakes just before baking."

"That's what makes them so good," Tim added, still not turning from the window.

"That's also what makes them so dangerous." Jake ran his tongue over the sore ridges of his palate. "As Timothy has purloined the cup I was using, would you be so kind as to fetch me another?"

"How polite he is when he wants something," Hannah replied.

Knees bent, shoulders hunched, Tim was trying to see down the lane. "Can't you two keep from bickering, even now?" he asked with distracted impatience.

Jake signaled Hannah with a wink. "Come, Servant Girl," he said, standing. "Let us get another cup of cider."

"You may fetch your own cider, Mister Mallery," she replied.

Jake took Hannah by both hands and drew her close. For Tim's benefit, he shouted: "More cider, wench!"

"Mal!" Tim warned sharply—but when he turned around, they were kissing. Now they broke their embrace but stood close, Jake keeping an arm about her shoulders. Tim stared with bemused suspicion. "What are you doing?"

"Shall I explain, Timo?" Jake said. "You see, the boy and the girl touch their lips together and—"

Tim shook his head. "You two?"

Both nodded.

"You won't tell, Tim, will you?" Hannah said.

"*You* two?" Tim repeated.

"I've been wanting to tell you, but Hannah thought—"

"*You*, and *you*?" he interrupted, pointing to each in turn. "Are—?"

"—going to be married as soon as we can manage it," Jake finished.

"But don't say anything, Tim, please?" Hannah repeated. "I want to wait till I'm free before anybody—"

"You're having fun with me," Tim said accusingly.

"We are not," Jake answered, fixing his eyes on Tim's.

Tim turned to Hannah, baffled.

"We are not," she said, almost whispering.

"Oh." His gaze darted all over the room, as if watching scenes in his mind's eye. "Oh . . . so that's why you. . . ." Now he looked to Hannah, then Jake. "And the time that you. . . ."

"Yes," Jake said, grinning. "Whatever it is you're remembering, yes."

"But how did you . . . I mean why did you . . . I mean . . . you two *loathe* each other!" he blurted, and Jake and Hannah laughed.

"We thought we did," Hannah admitted. "But that was before we came to know each other."

"Well, where on earth was *I* while you were coming to know each other?"

Jake shrugged. "Studying?"

"How long have you been keeping this from me?"

FIVE 4THS OF JULY ★ 123

"A few months."

"Months!"

Jake shrugged again, guiltily, turning up his palms.

"How did it happen?" Tim asked.

"We're . . . not quite sure," Jake admitted.

"Well, perhaps you've always loved each other, but felt you should not," Tim offered. "Perhaps you were only pretending to hate each other."

Jake and Hannah appraised each other frankly, then shook their heads. "No," both said at once, and all three laughed.

Suddenly there were footsteps on the path, and Caleb's voice: "Tim! Mal!"

Tim dashed to the door and threw it open; leaning heavily against the jamb, Caleb choked out, "They're coming!"

"Who?"

"Who do you think, fool! The British!"

"Where?"

"Just behind me! They're marching up to the house!"

"This house?"

"Yes, this house! Come on!" And he was off again.

As Jake and Tim scrambled for their weapons, Tim said, "Are you scared *now*, Mal?"

"I'm sufficiently alarmed," Jake replied.

Hannah pushed them toward the door. "Go!"

Then it hit him: leave Hannah to the mercy of the British? "No." He stopped, resting the butt of his musket on the floor. "I'll stay with you."

"Jake! You must go! They'll kill you if they find you here!"

"*No.*"

"Tim!" Her voice was panicked, strangled. "Take him and go!"

"Come, Mal." Tim caught hold of his arm. "We'll be needed at Black Rock. Come, Hannah is right, they'll kill us here."

Jake shook his head, keeping his eyes on Hannah's.

"Please, Jake," she said tearfully. "*Please.*"

"Wait for me at the gate, Tim?" he asked.

"All right. But hurry."

When Tim was gone, Jake asked, "Are *you* afraid, Hannah?"

"Only for you."

"Don't worry about me. I'll be fine." Jake drew her to him and kissed her. Then, touching his forehead to hers, he said, "Now, when they get here? Don't wait for them to come in. Meet them on the doorstep. Then drop to your knees and shout at the top of your voice, 'Thank God you have come! God save the king!'"

She held him close, laughing and sobbing at the same time.

One of Tim's sisters called from the front of the house: "Hannah! Hannah!" She was growing closer. "They are here! Quick, we must go!"

"Coming!" Hannah called back.

But Jake couldn't bear to leave her. He could not move. Unable to speak, he ran his fingers over her face, her lips.

"Oh, Jake, don't." Her eyes searched his face. "I'll see you after a while."

He nodded, swallowing the lump in his throat.

There was a commotion of British soldiers in the front

dooryard. Jake looked at Hannah, whose eyes widened with fear for him as she whispered, "Go!"

He shouldered his musket and ran.

The Morrises' geese were honking madly, rushing about hysterically, and Jake heard a maniacal laughing, yelling sound escape him as he tore past Tim at the gate and they ran toward the beach.

"Damn them!" Jake shouted.

"We'll drive them out!" Tim answered.

And as Jake ran, he felt such a peculiar heightening of sensation—exhilaration and fear, excitement and terror, the things of love all mixed up with the things of war.

The thunder of guns began. From the fort? From the harbor? Not just a single boom, this time; no longer a warning. Blast followed blast: cannon shot, artillery fire, and then the crack of muskets.

The Regulars were here, and there was to be a battle, here in New Haven, in East Haven. They would be shooting their weapons, he and Tim, at real people, trying to take them down like deer in autumn, and the king's men would be attempting to deal them the same fate. Here on the beach, in the woods, in the places where they lived and worked, the king's men would try to subjugate them, just like Adams and Jefferson and Franklin had said. Now it was really happening, he would be fighting for all that was dear: for home, for Hannah, for family . . . for freedom.

They started up the hill that overlooked the harbor. Tim had always been the faster runner; Jake lagged slightly behind through the familiar woods, sun-dappled, thick with the summer scent of moist bark and hot loam.

When they reached the summit, they were greeted by a nightmare landscape: British ships in a thick line at the Point, discharging boats filled with the British Regulars in red coats, the hired Hessian soldiers in blue.

"God damn them!" Tim shouted, his voice trembling with emotion, and they both plunged down the hill.

The shortest way to Black Rock was across the beach, but without speaking they knew they would have to reach the fort via the woods. Zigzagging among the trees, leaping over rotting logs and tangled clumps of brush, Jake's steps matched the rhythm of the song going through his head, the same two lines over and over:

> *Where'er they go, we shall oppose them*
> *Sons of valor must be free . . .*

At last he and Tim got to the nail fence that led into the fort; they shoved their muskets beneath it, then scrambled over the top.

"Mal! Tim! Wait!"

The voice came from behind them, on the beach. They paused, and turned. . . . It was Isaac Pardee, running toward them with two others. Why was he stopping them?

"What?" Tim called back, annoyed by the delay.

A massive blast threw up sand and black smoke, just at the

spot where Isaac had been. When the smoke cleared, his headless body was crumpled on the beach.

"What was that? What was that?" Jake heard the shrill screams in his own voice as Tim grabbed him by the sleeve, tearing his shirt, yelling:

"Don't stop, don't look!"

"Did you see it? Did you see it? Is he dead?"

"Don't look!" Tim shouted back, making a dash for the ramparts. "Get in the fort!"

Still running, Jake caught sight of his father in the line of men along the ramparts—and to his own great surprise he threw himself down beside the old man and huddled against the breastwork.

"Load your weapon, son!" Father's voice was loud, but calm. "We're killing them as they land."

"I can't do this, I can't do this," Jake muttered. He squeezed his eyes shut, trying to obliterate the gory image of Isaac.

"Fire at will!" Lieutenant Bishop was yelling over the din.

"Load your weapon, Jacob."

"I don't know how, I don't remember. . . ."

"Yes, you do," was the grave reply. His father knelt, took aim, fired, took cover again. "Come, we'll do it together. . . . Half-cock firelock. Come."

Jake sat with his back against the breastwork, following Father's orders one at a time.

"Handle cartridge."

With trembling fingers, Jake opened his box, took out a cartridge, bit off the top, and covered it with his thumb.

"Prime," Father said.

Jake tried to shake the powder into the pan, but some spilled over. He rubbed his eyes with the back of his hand and choked out, "Isaac . . ."

"I saw," his father said. "Shut pan."

Jake shut the pan and turned his musket to the loading position, the muzzle nearly under his chin.

"Charge with cartridge," Father said.

Still holding the cartridge, Jake put it into the muzzle and shook the powder down the barrel.

"Draw rammer and ram down cartridge," Father said; Jake pulled out the rammer and jammed it down the muzzle. "Don't bother returning the rammer. You'll be using it again soon enough. Now, poise and cock firelock, and take aim." Father knelt in the ready position, pointing his musket's muzzle through a gap in the breastwork. He fired, and dropped back. "Now you, son."

Jake took a deep breath, rolled over on one knee, pointed his muzzle.

"Take aim," his father said.

Jake's fingers fumbled with the trigger.

"Steady, Jacob." Father touched his shoulder. "God nerves the soldier's hand."

Jake selected one of the British soldiers heading straight for the fort. He took aim; he fired. The soldier went down.

"I got him!" he yelled as he dropped back. "Did you see—"

"Quiet, son." Father's grim countenance did not change. As he knelt into position to fire again, he told Jake: "Again: half-cock."

Jake loaded, fired; loaded, fired. With every shot, he was faster, he grew more confident, and another song came into his head:

> See now, my laddies, 'tis nothing at all,
> But pull at the trigger and pop goes the ball!

The British seemed to multiply by the minute, landing in scores, marching up the beach, and now their ships were in the harbor, the guns run out, firing volley after volley.

The sounds of battle grew ever louder, ever closer. "Never mind the rammer!" his father shouted. "There's no time! Watch me!" When he had primed his musket and put the cartridge down the barrel, he struck the butt end of the musket hard on the ground, aimed, and fired.

Jake mimicked his motions.

"That's the way, son!" Father was loading again.

They got off a few more shots, but the British continued to advance in ridiculous numbers. Each time one fell, ten more took his place.

"Where are they all coming from?" Jake heard his own wild panic. "What shall we do?"

"Keep shooting," his father said steadily. "Wait for orders."

A cannonball hit the ramparts near them; they shielded their eyes from the spray of rock. Jake reached for another cartridge, but his fingers found nothing. He looked down at the box. Empty. "Father! I'm out!"

His father fumbled in his own cartridge box; withdrawing one of two remaining cartridges, he held it out. Jake was alarmed to see the old man's hand shaking.

"You, Mal!" Lieutenant Bishop shouted. "You're needed on the gun crew!"

Jake made a move toward the fort proper, but his father grabbed his shirt. "Your rammer!" Jake picked it up and slid it back into position, then ran along the ramparts and into the fort, leaping over dead and wounded neighbors, friends, relatives. . . . Who were they? No time to think about it. . . . But where was Tim?

Sergeant Moulthrop was the gun commander, but Jake saw that with so many artillerymen down, he was doing more than giving orders. At Jake's approach, he pointed at the ammunition box. "Run the rounds, Mal!"

Jake had had no gun crew training, but he knew it meant to bring the ammunition to the gunners.

"Advance round!" someone shouted.

Moulthrop pushed him in the direction of the voice. Jake grabbed a round of fixed shot from the box and ran to the south-facing cannon, the one pointed toward the open Sound. The gun was manned by Silas Field and Asa's brother-in-law, James—and writhing at their feet was Jeddy Thompson, his entire front covered in blood. He reached up, as if in supplication, but his eyes were empty. No one was paying him any mind.

Silas grabbed the round from Jake and loaded it into the cannon. Jake had never been so near to cannon fire. There was an eerie warning sound—*zzzzzzip!*—followed by a deafening bang. With the day so hot and still, the powder smoke hung over the fort, making it difficult to see anything—and making his eyes sting and tear. Instinctively, he rubbed at them, but his fingers were covered with gummy gunpowder, which only made his eyes hurt more.

"Advance round!" someone else shouted, and Jake ran back to the ammunition box, then headed for one of the two west-facing cannon.

"Advance round!"

"Faster, boys, faster!" Lieutenant Bishop yelled as he loaded his own musket. "Diamond cut diamond!"

We'll beat them boys or die . . . Jake dashed blindly back and forth, retrieving and delivering the rounds. Once, he got too close behind a cannon when it fired and was knocked to the ground by the gun's recoil.

"Stay back, Mal!" James warned.

When Jake scrambled to his feet, he realized one side of his shirt was blood-soaked. Was he wounded? Was he shot?

"Advance round!"

He felt of his flesh in the area where the blood was: no pain.

"Mal! Advance round!"

He ran to fetch another round.

Every time he looked up, the British on the beach were closer. Every time he looked around, more of the men in the fort were down. So he told himself not to look anymore, just run the rounds. See nothing but the ammunition box and the outstretched hands of the man awaiting his delivery. Hear nothing but the shouts to advance the round. Think nothing at all.

Next time he reached into the ammunition box, he saw that

there were only two rounds left. Running to deliver one, he told the gunners: "I'm out!"

"Advance round! Mal!"

He retrieved and delivered the final round.

"Advance round!"

Jake waited until Moulthrop had fired his piece before approaching. "Sir! We've no more ammunition!" His voice sounded oddly muffled in his ears.

"Mal! Advance!" one of the gunners shouted in a panic.

"Mal!" called another.

"I'm out!" He patted his shirt, as though he might, if he tried hard enough, find ammunition on his person. "I'm out!"

"Spike the guns! Abandon fort!" Lieutenant Bishop shouted. "Fall back to Beacon Hill!"

Jake lunged for his musket; the gunners were pounding iron rods into the touchholes of the cannon, so that the enemy would be unable to use them.

"Run, Mal!" Lieutenant Bishop yelled at him. "Abandon fort!"

"The wounded!" Jake replied.

"They cannot be helped! Run!"

Then Jake was running along the ramparts once again, with musket fire behind him and men collapsing in front of him, and he jumped the nail fence again, wildly trying to outpace death.

Suddenly he remembered his father. The old man couldn't run this fast, he could hardly run at all. Where was he? Jake stopped and pivoted, calling, "Father! Father!" In a blur of blood and gunpowder ash, men rushed past; none was his father.

Someone seized his arm and whirled him around. "Mal! Come

on!" Tim's shout brought Jake to himself, and he followed as Tim veered off toward the north.

"Beacon Hill!" Jake yelled. "We're supposed to meet at Beacon Hill!"

Waving Jake on, Tim did not change direction. At last under cover of the woods, they dove into a culvert and lay prone, still and silent, their faces pressed into the earth. For the first time, Jake noticed the bitter taste of gunpowder in his mouth. His eyes burned; his throat was parched from the powder and the smoke. He felt stunned, like the time he'd fallen from the top of Mr. Rowe's mill wheel and had just lain on the ground, unable to move, while his friends urged: *Hurry, Mal, hurry! He'll see you!*

After a while, Tim nudged him; Jake looked. Tim was leaning up on his elbow. His lips were moving, but Jake heard only a rushing noise, like the sound of fast-moving water. "What?" he asked, and Tim, looking alarmed, flattened himself again and furiously pressed his finger to his lips.

Jake squeezed his eyes shut, thinking, *I am asleep. I'm asleep and this is all a bad dream. . . . I'll wake up and it will be time to mow the salt meadow. All right, wake up . . . now.* But when he opened his eyes, he was yet lying in the woods covered with dirt and gunpowder residue, his shirt soaked with sweat and someone else's blood. The noise in his ears was quieting. Slowly he and Tim sat up and looked around. They were alone.

"Don't shout again," Tim whispered.

"I couldn't hear," Jake said. "From the cannon . . . I'm better now."

Tim's eyes fixed on Jake's shirt. "Whose blood?"

"I don't know. Jeddy's? I think he's dead." The outstretched hand, the vacant eyes . . . Jake flinched against the image, then said quickly, "Why did you come this way?"

"We were the last on the beach—did you not see that?"

"I was looking for my father."

"Last out, first shot. I thought if we separated from the rest, we'd have a better chance."

"Do you think my father got out?"

Tim furrowed his brow. "I don't know, Mal."

"Never mind," Jake said gruffly. "That old man will survive if the whole town perishes."

"What about us? What shall we do?"

Now Jake realized that every fiber of his clothing was soaked, stuck to every bit of his skin. His eyes still burned fiercely. "Is this not the hottest day of your life, Timo?"

"In every sense of the word," Tim said.

Jake removed the stopper from his canteen and took a drink. Then he poured some water on his shirtsleeve and rubbed at his eyes with it. "I'd say ammunition is our first concern. Any ideas?"

"Did they burn my house, Mal?" There was a hard new edge to Tim's voice. He turned his head in the direction of home. "Did those damned dogs burn my house?"

"Here." Jake offered the canteen; as Tim was drinking, Jake said, "I'm sure they're all right. Your mother and sisters and Hannah. Houses can be rebuilt."

Tim suddenly laughed. "You and Hannah. Are you sure you're not joking with me?"

"Tim." Jake eyed him with suspicion. "Are you well?"

For reply, Tim lay on his back and stared at the sky. After only a few seconds he bolted upright and said, "Let's go to my uncle Tuttle's. I know where he keeps his powder and balls, and we can fill our canteens."

Without another word, they set off. Tim's uncle lived just a few rods north, and they crept through the woods, through the Tuttles' salt meadow, and into the house. Guns at the ready, they called out for Tim's aunt and young cousins as they searched from room to room—the parlor, the bedchamber, up to the loft, back down to the dining room, and, finally, into the kitchen, where the first thing they did was get a drink of cider.

Tim said, "Look, Mal. Just as if they expected us."

Scattered across the table were a few formed cartridges, along with balls, dowels, pieces of paper, a ball of string, and a knife; on the floor was a powder keg. Tim's aunt and cousins had been making cartridges, God bless them, probably until the moment they fled. Jake and Tim split them, each taking six, fitting them into the slots of their cartridge boxes.

"Let's go." Jake headed for the door.

But Tim lingered at the table. "Mal . . . maybe we should make more. As long as we're here. . . ." He shrugged. "What is six car- tridges on such a day? Why go out only to run out of ammunition again?"

Jake looked around the peaceful kitchen. "It would only take a few minutes."

"Yes, and we deserve a bit of rest, don't we?"

Without another word, they sat at the table and began to work, quickly and quietly.

"It all seems impossible," Tim said after a time.

"I know."

"Did you kill any, Mal?"

"Yes."

"Good. So did I."

Jake said, "I wonder what Isaac was trying to tell us?"

"The sight of him . . . it keeps coming back to me."

"Don't let it," Jake advised.

"But I—"

"Stop," Jake interrupted. "Think of something else."

They continued in silence until Tim said, "You and Hannah . . . I can scarcely believe it."

"Nor did I, at first."

"How *did* it come about?"

"I'm not quite sure, really." He shrugged. "Cupid shot his arrows."

"Won't my parents be surprised. And my sisters!"

"Oh, your sisters are going to give me the devil," Jake said, and they laughed quietly.

They worked quickly as they talked; each completed cartridge went directly into a cartridge box.

"She calls you Jake?" Tim said.

"Yes."

"Why?"

Even as he felt his face flush, Jake thought, *How odd, to feel bashful on such a day.* "I asked her to," he muttered. "I prefer it."

"Hmm. You never said." Apparently after mulling the possibility, Tim announced: "No. It would seem wrong. You'll always be Mal to me."

"That's all right." Jake nodded toward the door. "Awfully quiet out there."

"Perhaps it's finished."

"If so, we're defeated," Jake said.

Just then the sounds of artillery shot came from the direction of Beacon Hill, followed by a few bursts of musket fire. Jake looked at Tim; they knew each other so well neither one had to say what both were thinking: *We could stay here for the rest of the battle. No one need ever know.*

"Could we live with it, though?" Jake said at last.

"But we *did* fight at the fort," Tim said. "Everyone saw us there."

Then the popping of musketry began in earnest and the decision was made. They jumped up, quickly stuffed the remaining supplies into their haversacks, shouldered their guns, and headed for the Tuttles' lane, which led to the cove road.

"Wait." Jake stopped, planting his feet.

"What is it?"

"If we go to the road—who knows what we'll be walking into? I say we keep to the woods and kill them from cover, as the Indians do."

Tim looked skeptical. "It seems cowardly."

"No. What's cowardly is landing thousands of armed soldiers

to attack a town that is practically without defenses. They must have known there were no Continentals in the area. That's why they decided to come now."

Tim nodded, pondering.

"Fighting them in the open is suicide—we saw that at the fort," Jake continued. "And if we are dead, we are useless to our home, our families, and our country."

"Listen to him speechify," Tim said. "All right, Patrick Henry, I am persuaded. Where to?"

"I think first we should head back toward the water, and try to see the state of things. If they are coming up into the harbor, we can shoot at them as they try to land. If not, we'll go back to the rock fence along the cove road and shoot at them from there."

"All right," Tim agreed, and they reversed direction and ran through the field and woods behind Tim's uncle's house. When the trees met the tall red rocks of a smaller cove north of the fort, they dropped to the ground and crawled on their bellies. Across the cove, they could see the British swarming the fort. Some were standing in a group on the beach, talking, with the relaxed air of victors. Jake and Tim heard voices, but only occasional words:

"House . . . lieutenant . . . boat . . . prisoner . . ."

At Tim's signal, Jake followed him to a different vantage point, and within moments they heard: " . . . advance guard to capture the ferry . . . meet in New Haven and burn the whole damned town."

Jake and Tim darted each other a look, then both turned in the opposite direction, snaked along for a few feet, got up and began to run, keeping their backs bent and their heads low.

New Haven was, of course, too far into the harbor for the British ships. In West Haven, the soldiers had only to march long enough to reach the town; but here on the east shore, they would have to capture a ferry to get their men to New Haven with ease.

And the first ferry in their line of march was the Mallerys'.

"Why didn't our officers think of this?" Jake wondered aloud.

"We haven't enough men," Tim replied. "They were hoping to stop them at the fort. They'd no idea how many the British were landing."

"It's Ethan up there alone," Jake panted as they ran.

"Gideon was to send word up the river," Tim said. "Perhaps the men have come from Mount Carmel and Cheshire."

"Even if so, why would they stop at the ferry?"

"The British advance guard must be ahead of us by now."

"Not necessarily. They're probably going by the cove road, and taking fire from our men. We'll take the shortcut through the salt marsh."

"The *salt* marsh!" Tim repeated, at his heels. "Mal—'tis impossible! We'll get bogged down!"

"I know a way. Come on!"

CONCEALED BY TALL reeds, they slogged through the muck of the salt marsh. They had fixed the straps of their cartridge boxes and haversacks high around their necks and held their muskets over their heads, anticipating a sudden step into deeper sludge.

"Perfect surrender pose," Tim grumbled.

"Good thing there's nobody around to capture us, then."

Their feet sucked up mud with every step. *Thhhhp. Thhhhp. Thhhhp.*

"We'll probably lose our shoes," Tim said.

"And our lives!" Jake said cheerfully.

"Thank you. Just the assurance I needed."

From the cove road, artillery and musket fire sounded continually. But it was behind them—had they gotten ahead of the enemy's northward push? Here the only noises were their sludgy steps and the rustling of reeds.

Jake would not let himself think of what might already have happened or what was to come. He trained his thoughts on the here and now: each step signified, every moment mattered. They had only to get through the salt marsh. Then they would consider their next move.

At last the marsh gave way to solid ground; the reeds ended; they could clearly see into the harbor. The British ships had not advanced and were no longer firing. Over on the West Haven side, plumes of black smoke wafted into the air.

"They're burning houses," Tim said solemnly.

Jake tugged at his sleeve. "Come, we must stay ahead of them. We've got to get to Ethan."

They started to run again, but Jake soon found himself slowing down. It was so hot; he was so weary; his musket felt heavier with each step. Now he realized Tim was not even keeping up with him. "Hurry, Timo."

"I know," Tim said. "I know." But he was barely able to speed up at all.

Jake halted, unstopped his canteen, and took a drink of tepid water. He shuddered at the taste, causing Tim to laugh.

"What'll we do when we get there?" Tim asked after drinking from his own canteen.

"Cut the cable and tow the ferry into Mr. Rowe's millrace. It won't be difficult, as the tide is coming in. Then we'll get back to the cove road, figure out where our men are, and rejoin them."

Tim grinned. "Who knew you'd be such a military tactician, Mal? You ought to join the Continentals after this. Perhaps you can serve under Arnold."

"Uh, thank you, but no—this one battle will be quite enough for me."

"Really, Mal?" They started off again, this time at a fast walk. "Because I was thinking I might."

"Join the Continentals?"

"Yes. And I thought we could go together."

Jake shook his head. "Timo—not for me. I'm willing to defend my home when I must. But when this battle is over, the first thing I'll do is kiss Hannah a thousand times. And then I intend to introduce her to my father and my brothers and sisters, and tell the entire town of—"

As he was speaking, they came into view of the ferry landing, stopped short—and stared.

The ferry was gone.

"Where is it?" Jake's eyes darted to the Neck, then to the New

Haven side of the harbor. No ferry. "Where in hell is the ferry?"

"Perhaps this is good," Tim said quickly. "Perhaps someone else had the same idea—to take the ferry upriver. Ethan, maybe."

"All right, all right—let's think." Pressing his hand to his forehead, he looked down . . . and a short distance away he saw, unmistakably, a broadside on the ground. "What's *that*?" Running to it, he bent and picked it up. It was titled:

ADDRESS TO THE INHABITANTS OF CONNECTICUT

"Tim—look!"

Tim rushed to his side, and Jake read aloud the first line: "'The ungenerous and unwanton insurrection against the sovereignty of Great Britain, into which this colony has been deluded by the artifices of designing men' . . ." Jake laughed bitterly. "Damned cretins."

"Who takes credit for this trash?" Tim said. Jake's eyes darted to the bottom of the page just as Tim read the words printed there: "'Given on board His Majesty's ship *Camilla*, on the Sound, July 4, 1779.'"

It was signed by George Collier and William Tryon.

"Tim! They are ahead of us!" Jake said in a fierce whisper, and immediately they retreated into the woods.

With their backs to the water and against a tree trunk, they looked at the broadside again. Jake read softly: "'Your Town, your property, yourselves, lie within the grasp of the power whose forbearance you have ungenerously construed into fear, but whose lenity has persisted' . . . Blah blah blah, you are so generous toward us benighted Patriots."

"Look at this part." Tim pointed farther down the page, and read: "'Why, then, will you persist in a ruinous and ill-judged resistance? We hoped that you would recover from the frenzy which has distracted this unhappy country; and we believe the day to be near come when the greater part of this continent will begin to blush at their delusion.'"

"Right, we'll recover and pledge allegiance to His Majesty," Jake muttered. "And they think *we're* deluded?"

"Here." Tim tapped still lower on the page. "'We do now declare that who so ever shall be found, and remain in peace, at his usual place of residence, shall be shielded from any insult, either to his person or his property.'"

"Cower at home and we won't kill you and burn your house," Jake said.

"Yes—only let us overrun your town and all will be well." Tim rubbed his face and sighed. "All right, Mal. What now?"

"Tim, do as you will. But I mean to find out what's happening at my house. I won't have these hellhounds capturing my ferry to use against our people, and besides—I'm worried for Ethan."

"I'll go with you," Tim said.

"Are you sure?"

"Absolutely."

"All right, then. I think we should stay in the woods for now. When we reach my father's property, the Indian corn will hide us until we get to the landing. Maybe from there we'll be able to see where the ferry is."

They proceeded as they had been taught, one covering the other, and had not gone far when Tim, in the lead position, stopped for a suspiciously long time and seemed to be craning his neck, attending to something.

"Come on, Tim, come on," Jake whispered to himself.

Just then, twigs crackled directly behind him. He didn't even have time to be afraid. As he was about to whirl around, he felt the metal of a muzzle on his neck. "You are my prisoner," said the man in guttural accented English.

Jake began to lower his musket, as if to acquiesce. Then he said, "Not yet." Turning as he spoke, he brought his muzzle up sharply under the Hessian's chin. The man's teeth rattled; he howled, recoiling, then lunged forward again. Jake brought the stock down squarely on the Hessian's head and he swooned to the ground.

Now Jake's mind was racing, his blood pumping loudly in his ears. Where had the Hessian come from? If there was one, there were more. . . . Musket fire came from Tim's direction, and Jake turned to see another Hessian fall to the ground.

Jake leapt behind a tree just before another burst of gunfire, and a musket ball glanced off the tree trunk. Peering out, he saw a third Hessian running toward him, bayonet fixed. Jake raised his musket and took shaky aim. But someone else fired before he did, and the Hessian went down.

That was when he realized he and Tim were not the only

Patriots in these woods, for there was no way Tim could have reloaded so quickly.

In this little patch of the war, all was now silent.

"Tim!" Jake called, flattening himself behind the tree again.

"Here, Mal!"

"Are you hurt?"

"No!"

"Who else is with us?" Jake shouted.

No answer. But when Jake peeked again and saw Mr. Rowe hauling himself out of a culvert, he could not believe his eyes.

"You, Mal!" The old man was reloading as he advanced. "Shoot him!"

Jake looked down to see that the Hessian who had declared him prisoner was regaining his senses, trying to roll over. But shoot the man? He was only half conscious, and wholly unarmed. Before Jake could form a reply—in word or action—the Hessian gave a fearsome groan, reached out, and grabbed Jake by the ankle, causing him to lose his footing. As Jake fell, his musket hit the ground and discharged; fortunately, away from his person, but unfortunately, not into the Hessian.

Now Jake was defenseless as the Hessian hefted himself onto hands and knees, reaching for his weapon.

Mr. Rowe planted his feet and blasted away.

The Hessian fell dead of a musket ball to the brain.

Tim ran to Jake and grabbed hold of his arm. "Mal, are you all right?"

"Where did they come from?" Jake asked, feeling dizzy.

Calmly, Mr. Rowe wiped the Hessian's blood from his own face with a shirtsleeve.

"I don't know!" Tim said. "I just turned around and he was behind you!"

"I've no idea how I did that. How I came around and hit that man, no idea. . . ." Jake heard that his voice was high, agitated. His jaw was in a spasm of some sort, his teeth near to chattering. "I had the image, I thought of Arnold, you know the story, of what he did at Ridgefield . . . I cannot believe I did it. How did he not kill me?" Jake knew he was babbling, couldn't seem to stop himself. He felt that if he stopped talking, he would start to cry like a baby.

"Steady, lad." Mr. Rowe placed a hand on Jake's shoulder.

Jake started gulping, again and again; his throat was dry, he was swallowing nothing, but he kept gulping, struggling for air.

"Mal, are you all right?" Tim asked. "Mr. Rowe—what is wrong with him?"

"Sit, boy." Mr. Rowe gently pushed at Jake's shoulder, and he slid slowly down, his back against the tree trunk.

But he was still gulping; he couldn't breathe. He clutched at his throat, panicking.

"Here." Mr. Rowe held his canteen to Jake's lips, and he took a drink: rum and water. "More," Mr. Rowe said, and Jake gratefully obeyed. "That's better."

"Thank you." Jake closed his eyes, tipping his head back against the tree. *This* old daddy knew how to go to war.

"What are you doing here, Mr. Rowe?" Tim asked. "It is dangerous . . . a man of your age, alone . . . you could be killed."

"So could you, boy, so could you. And were you not pleased to see me?"

"Yes, of course, but—"

"I may be too old to march with the militia, but I can still exercise the privileges of war." He withdrew a cartridge from his box, bit off the end, and reloaded. "I choose to fight as I saw the Indians do it, in the French War. Hide and watch. Shoot from cover. Strike and retreat. 'Tis the only way to have a chance, against such numbers. What militia have we here? Fifty men? Most of them unseasoned boys and wizened old men. And they land hundreds to subjugate us." He kicked at the dead Hessian. "Well, you exterminate such barbarians any way possible, I say."

Jake was smiling weakly; he had a mind to hug the old man. "You see, Tim." He closed his eyes. "Here is a man after my own heart."

"Since when?" Mr. Rowe said.

"Since you saved my life," Jake replied, and all three laughed.

"What are you lads doing here, anyhow?" Mr. Rowe asked. "Why are you not on the road with the main body?"

"Mal felt as you do, sir—that we could kill more from cover."

"And we were trying to get to my house, to make sure they didn't capture the ferry. But the ferry is already gone. Do you know what's happened?"

"There's no time to sweeten the truth, boy," Mr. Rowe said with a gentle gruffness. "Your brother Asa is wounded; I know not how. I saw someone paddling him upriver in that dugout of yours—to seek help for him, I imagine."

So Asa *had* thought of the ferry. And who was the someone with him . . . Ethan? "Was he badly hurt, sir?"

"I was close enough neither to see nor ask."

There was no time to dwell on it. "What of the ferry?" Jake asked.

"I don't know."

Jake turned to Tim. "We must keep going. We're almost there."

"Mr. Rowe, you'd better go with us," Tim said.

"For my safety or yours, boy?" As Mr. Rowe spoke, he was removing ammunition from the dead Hessian's cartridge box.

"Your own, sir, of course."

"Pah! I can do more good from my ditch by the road, picking them off as they proceed. Carry on, boys, and Godspeed!" Without another word, he got to his feet and hurried off with a gait that was half hobble, half run.

Jake and Tim moved quickly and silently down to the ferry path, where they hid in the brush to get a good view of the landing. "Look!" Tim pointed; about a quarter mile north, the ferry was adrift in the middle of the river.

"We must get it," Jake said at once.

"How?" Tim asked nervously.

"Swim."

"We?"

Jake looked at him. Tim had made some progress since last year, but it had become clear that he would never be much of a swimmer. "No. You stay on shore and cover me."

Back in the woods, they hadn't gained five rods when Tim, in the lead again, waved Jake ahead and pointed: at his feet was a dead Regular, lying faceup and empty-eyed. A musket ball had torn a ragged hole into his middle; the blood was indistinguishable on his red coat, but bright on the white breeches.

The sight of him caused Jake no sorrow. Kneeling, he checked the man's cartridge box. "Here." He handed Tim two of the four remaining cartridges. Then he saw that the man had a cartridge tin as well; he opened it. It was half full. He looked up and grinned. "Here's a bit of luck, Timo."

Tim just stared, frowning. "He's so young, Mal."

"Then don't look at him." Jake pulled the tin's strap from under the dead man's arm.

"Don't get his blood on you," Tim said.

"His blood? What do I care for his blood?" Jake shot back. "Did you not hear old Rowe say that my brother is shot?" Defiantly, he rubbed his arm across the dead man's wound, staining his own sleeve. "There. That is how much I care for *his* blood."

"All right, Mal, all right." Tim pulled at his arm. "Come. Let's *go*."

When at last they were in line with the ferry—which continued to inch up the river with the tide—the thought occurred to Jake that whoever had set it adrift might also have removed the pole and the oar. So how would he guide the ferry back to the riverbank? They decided to get to the nearest barn and find a rope for towing; Jake would swim with it in hand, fasten it to the ferry, and be hauled in by Tim.

Watching for the enemy, they made their way to Mr. Rowe's barn; finally, they were back on the bank with the rope. Jake divested himself of gun, accoutrements, and shoes. He peeled off first one stocking, then the other—and there was Hannah's sodden letter, plastered to his leg, ruined, the ink staining his skin.

He snatched it away, but Tim asked, "What is that?"

"A letter. From Hannah." He stuffed it into his stocking, and the stocking into his shoe.

"A *letter*, Mal?" Tim's tone was gleeful. "She writes you *letters*?"

"Pipe down," Jake said, wading into the river. Then he dove under and began to swim. The cold water refreshed him, billowing his shirt and riffling his hair. As he stretched his arms ahead of him, brought them back to his sides, he felt the blood and sweat and gunpowder washing away. If only this whole day could be so easily obliterated.

Perhaps in a few hours, though, the British routed, and he in his own bed . . . and tomorrow, Hannah in his arms. But no, don't think such thoughts now; it would be that much more bitter if they did not come true. Just swim, get the ferry: just that one thing, for now, and then the next thing, and then the next.

When he got to the ferry he gripped an edge with both hands and looked around; still no sign of the enemy, though a mile or so to the south, Jake could see their boats in the harbor. Without boarding the ferry he fastened the rope to it and signaled to Tim, then began to push in the direction of Tim's pulling. With the tide to aid them, the task was soon well in hand. They maneuvered the ferry over the little waterfall that emptied into the millrace.

"Do you think they'll come up this far?" Still holding both muskets, Tim hopped on board to give Jake his stockings and shoes. Jake sat to put them on, tucking Hannah's letter into his shoe this time.

"Perhaps."

"Damn!" Tim replied.

It seemed a forceful response to a harmless statement—until Jake looked up to see four red-coated Regulars running directly at them with bayonets fixed. Jake leapt to his feet and reached for his musket, but the men had halted and one said with icy aplomb: "If you make just one more move, we will run you through."

"The game is up, lads—surrender or die," another added.

Jake glanced at Tim.

"Do not think of it," the first soldier said. "Do not even imagine it. Raise your hands over your head."

There would be no Benedict Arnold heroics now. Jake acquiesced.

"Both of you step off the ferry," the second man said. "And you"—nodding at Tim—"lay the weapons at your feet."

Again, Jake obliged . . . but Tim did not move. He said steadily, "I choose death over subjugation."

Jake shot him a panicked look. "No you don't!" Hands still high, he turned to the Regulars, frantically shaking his head: "No! He does not!"

The first man cocked his firelock.

"Tim!" Jake said. "Don't be a fool!"

Tim just stood there, defiant, both hands on both guns.

"Don't shoot him, Benham," the second soldier said. "He's just a boy."

"A boy playing with guns," Benham said evenly, training his on Tim.

"Make your friend surrender the weapons," the second one told Jake.

"Do it, Tim," Jake said. "For God's sake, there are four of them!"

"I don't like it," Tim said through his teeth.

"You need not like it. Just *do* it."

With a sigh and a stubborn shake of his head, Tim laid down the weapons. On signal from Benham, the two silent soldiers ran forward and took possession of the ferry.

"Now," the second man said. "If we let you go, will you be good boys and stay out of it hereafter?"

Jake wanted to say, *Don't call me a boy; you're about three years older than I*. He wanted to say, *No, we will not. We'll find more weapons and kill as many of you as we can*.

But before he could say anything at all, Benham replied, "Let them go? Are you mad, Richards?"

"We've got their weapons and their ammunition. What more can they do? Let's parole them and send them north."

"I shall do no such thing. These wretched Rebels were intent on interfering with the movement of His Majesty's troops. Now they are our prisoners and we are taking them to General Tryon's headquarters. And if you refuse to accompany me, I shall charge you with dereliction of duty."

Richards didn't reply.

"Guard them," Benham ordered Richards, who glumly did as he was bid. Benham cut two lengths from the tow rope and bound first Tim's hands, then Jake's. He cinched the knots far tighter than was needed, but Jake was damned if he'd give Benham the satisfaction of showing pain. He could see by the set of Tim's jaw that he felt the same.

"Now that you are trussed up like *good* little Rebels, we'll present you to the general for disposition." He told the other two soldiers: "Tow the ferry back to the landing." Then he gave Jake and Tim each a nudge with his musket's muzzle. "Proceed before us."

"What are your names?" Richards asked, sounding almost friendly.

Jake's reply was cold: "I can see no good coming from providing that information."

"The general will get it out of you," Benham sneered.

As they walked, Jake realized they were heading back to the cove road; when they reached it, the soldiers led them southward. Where were they going? Jake looked at Tim, who shrugged and shook his head.

After a few minutes, there could no longer be any doubt about the battle's outcome: there were Regulars everywhere, lounging, smoking, making cook fires, drinking, calling out.

"Halloo, Jonathan!"

"Two more Rebels down!"

"Enjoying your holiday, Jonathan?"

"Very much, while I was killing the likes of you," Tim muttered to Jake.

"I've never understood why they think it's so funny to call us Jonathan," Jake mumbled back.

"Quiet, Jonathan!" Benham said, and they couldn't help snickering.

Where the cove road met the ferry road, they were told to halt. A contingent of soldiers and officers stood guard.

"What have you there, soldiers?" one officer asked.

"Prisoners, sir. They were armed. We caught them on the ferry."

"The ferry? Where did it turn up?"

"There is a mill just north of here."

"And what were you boys doing with the ferry?"

Neither one spoke.

"Bring them to General Tryon," the officer said.

"Yes, sir."

But just as they were about to be led away, the officer cried: "Wait!" He yanked the dead Regular's cartridge tin from around Benham's neck. "Where did you get this?"

Benham nodded at Tim. "He had it on his person, sir."

"*I* had it," Jake quickly corrected.

The officer seized Jake and shook him by the arm. "Where did you get it?"

"I took it off a redcoat lying dead in the woods."

Jake saw alarm and grief and anger all register in the officer's eyes. "You killed him?"

"No."

"You lie."

"I've no qualms about taking credit for my kills today," Jake said. "But that one happened to be someone else's handiwork."

"'That one' was my nephew, Rebel."

"Should I be sorry for that?" Jake snapped back. "My brother is gravely wounded. Are you sorry for me?"

The officer stepped closer and deftly gave Jake's ears a painful boxing.

"Little boys who cannot keep their mouths shut must have their ears boxed," the man said evenly. Then, to the soldiers, "Take them away."

To Jake's surprise, the soldiers led them down the ferry road. Where *was* Tryon, anyway? When they reached the path to Jake's house, he was still confused. But as the house came into view and he saw its doors guarded by armed Regulars, it hit him. At once he and Tim turned to look at each other in disbelief.

Jake's home was now Tryon's headquarters.

At the front door, Benham and Richards spoke to a guard, who went inside. Tim was speaking in low tones, but Jake was not hearing his words. He felt numb, unreal, as if this could not be happening. The British had taken over his house and had access to all that was personal. Would they go upstairs, ransack his bedroom? Find Hannah's letters to him? He winced at the thought of these loutish soldiers sitting on his bed, laughing over Hannah's tender words. What of his sisters' room? Would the little girls return to find their clothing turned out of drawers, their dolls and toys destroyed? Or perhaps when the Brits were through with the house, they would burn it.

Suddenly he was distracted by the smell of roasting pig—and by the realization that his mouth was watering. He looked toward the barnyard. Soldiers milled about a pit fire; they must be cooking his father's shoats.

The door was held open, and Jake was granted admission to his own home. Directly he and Tim were guided to the left, where the dining room was full of officers.

There was no mistaking the general. He was well attended, with armed guards behind him and an adjutant at his right hand. A platter of pork was on the table, along with a plate of Sally's bread. Tryon had a napkin tucked under his chin, a mouth full of tender shoat, and a glass of Jake's father's claret in his hand.

"General Tryon, sir, here they are."

"Mmmm." He chewed at leisure, wagging a finger at them, and swallowed. "So you are the naughty boys who were caught on the lower ferry. What were you doing there?"

Neither one spoke.

"Attempting to interfere with the movement of your king's troops, perhaps?"

"He is not *my* king," Tim said.

Tryon picked up another hunk of pork, took a bite, and licked his fingers.

"Of course, we have already captured the Pardee ferry and crossed over to New Haven via the Neck Bridge."

"Was it difficult?" Jake asked. "Subduing fifty militia and all their women and children?" Though anger and hatred welled up in his throat, he was able to keep his voice calm.

Surveying him critically, Tryon rocked back in his chair and propped his muddy boots on the table.

At that Jake's emotions were inflamed beyond all reason, and he snapped, "Kindly remove your filthy feet from my father's dining table, sir."

"Your *father*?" Looking exceedingly delighted by the news, Tryon brought his chair down with dramatic thud. "So you are a Mallery, eh?"

"Jacob Mallery."

Tryon nodded at Tim. "And you?"

"Timothy Morris. My father is Amos."

The general laughed wickedly. "Oh, this *is* rich! The sons of the Sons, right here in my headquarters!" Tryon cupped his fat paws together, forming a vessel. "Do you lads not know that I hold your fate in my hands? And you are not creating a positive impression just now."

"Nor do we care to," Tim said, "as we've no desire to endear ourselves to the man who terrorizes our families."

Tryon turned to his adjutant. "I really *have* found Rebel children to be quite impudent and disrespectful of their elders. Do you not agree? I suppose this is how the parents teach the children in this so-called republic."

"What this republic does not teach, sir, is blind obedience to those unworthy of it," Jake replied.

Tryon's face darkened. "I am no longer amused by these brats." He waved a dismissive hand. "Put them with the other prisoners."

A loud thump sounded beneath the floorboards; Tryon quickly stood. "Is there a cellar in this house?" he demanded of Jake while all around them, men readied their weapons.

Jake didn't answer. Of course there was a cellar, and he had no doubt that its current occupant was Ethan, hiding, afraid.

Damn the little minuteman! Demanding to defend his home, then cowering in the cellar while the British took over the house!

"Find the cellar!" Tryon ordered his men.

"No!" Jake said. "No, let me . . . please. 'Tis my younger brother, I'm sure of it."

"Where is the hatchway, Rebel brat?" Tryon said icily.

"In the larder. Let me call to him, sir, please."

"See how they alter their tunes when they wish our protection?" Tryon kept his eyes fixed on Jake but directed his words to his adjutant. "Offer the cellar's occupant the opportunity to peaceably surrender. If he declines—shoot him."

From the kitchen and pantry came a great commotion; Jake felt as though he would jump right out of his skin. At last a soldier was hauling Ethan into the room, holding his arms behind his back. White-faced and trembling, Ethan looked around the room with wild, frightened eyes. When he saw Jake, a strangled sob escaped him as he tried to say, "Mal . . ."

Jake's disgust and anger melted away. "It's all right, Ethan."

"But they're here. They came. Asa is wounded, cousin Nathan took him—"

"Stop talking," Jake said.

"We didn't know what to do, so we—"

"Ethan! You are in the presence of the enemy!" Jake said sharply.

"Damn you!" Tryon roared, pointing at Jake. "How dare you make so bold? Do you not realize that you are all prisoners?" Tryon was sputtering, his face beet red.

"Sir," Jake said quickly. "He is my brother Ethan. He is only fifteen. He is a student at the college, he is not with the militia."

"He had a weapon, sir," one soldier said.

"Not with the militia, but wielding a weapon?" Tryon said. "That makes him a combatant, which makes him my prisoner."

"Sir, that is my father's fowling piece," Jake said. "He keeps it in the cellar. My brother was frightened, so he went into the cellar. I saw your broadside, sir. Did you not say those who remained at home would be safe?" Tryon appeared to be listening, so Jake hurried on: "I beg of you, sir. I am already your prisoner. Our older brother was gravely wounded. Ethan is the youngest of my father's three sons. Please let him go, he is only fifteen."

Tryon stared him up and down, then stared Ethan up and down. "Ethan, I shall release you."

"Thank you, sir," Ethan said, his voice quavering.

"Tell your sire, if he is yet alive, that your brother is Tryon's prisoner," the general instructed. "Tell him that is the price of his rebellion against his king."

The joke is on you, old man, Jake thought bitterly. *If you wished to punish my sire, you've just released the wrong son.* "Ethan, go directly to Aunt Grannis, do you understand me? Directly."

Ethan bobbed his head up and down. "Yes," he said distractedly. "Yes, Mal . . . but what will happen . . . you . . ."

"I'll be all right," Jake said. "Don't worry."

"How touching," Tryon sneered; then, to his men: "See him
off the property."

See him off the property. Jake was seething. See Ethan off his
own property! As the soldiers led him away, Ethan kept looking
back over his shoulder. Jake tried to comfort him with a smile.

Tryon rocked on the chair's back legs, conspicuously propping
his boots on the table again. "What have you to say to me now,
young Rebel?"

Jake swallowed hard. "Thank you for releasing my brother,
sir."

"Much better. Now *that* is how a Rebel brat should behave," he
told his adjutant. Then he said to the soldiers who had brought
them: "Store them with the other prisoners. A sojourn in the
Sugar House will do them good."

Store them . . . as though he and Tim were a commodity, Jake
thought. But that was war. And Tryon was simply exercising the
privileges of the victor.

Benham and Richards led them back up the ferry path; at the
road, the officer with the dead nephew asked, "Where are you
taking them?"

"With the other prisoners, sir," Benham said.

"No, no. These two belong at the Wallabout."

"The Wallabout, sir? But the prison ships are for maritime
prisoners."

"'But the prison ships are for maritime prisoners,'" the officer mimicked childishly. "Don't presume to instruct me, soldier! They were captured on a ferry, were they not? That makes them maritime prisoners!"

"But, sir," Richards said, "General Tryon said the Sugar House. He said put them with the other prisoners."

"Well, where *is* General Tryon? I don't seem to see him anywhere."

"A prison ship?" Tim asked Jake in a tone of sheer panic.

"General Tryon!" Jake called over his shoulder. "General Tryon!"

"Seize them!" the officer ordered his own men, who pulled them away from Benham and Richards. "Gag them!"

Jake fought in vain as a filthy rag was tightly tied around his mouth; he could sense, but not see, that Tim was being subjected to the same treatment.

As the soldiers dragged them toward the road, Richards rushed up and said in a low voice, "Don't worry, boys. It won't stick. When your families get word, you'll be exchanged."

Jake continued struggling.

"Stop fighting me or I shall make you sorry," his new captor warned.

In reply Jake kicked out at the man, who delivered him a tremendous blow to the back of the head. Jake felt his knees give way, and the ground swelled up and hit him in the face as he lost consciousness.

★ ★ ★

HE WAS SWIMMING, holding his breath underwater, racing from the raft to the rocks, and as he came to the surface to draw breath he heard Tim calling, *Come on, Mal! Come on!* Tilting his head back, he opened his eyes; the sunlight was glimmering through the water, sparkling, beautiful. . . .

"Come on, Mal. Wake up."

Jake gasped and opened his eyes. He was on the beach, but half in the water . . . what was happening? Where was he?

"'Ere lad, y'mate's all right, I toldja 'e'd come round soon as we soaked 'is 'ead."

"Mal? Are you all right?" Tim asked.

Jake groaned, raising his hand to the back of his bruised skull. "Mal?"

"I'm all right," Jake mumbled.

"C'mon, lads, innit t' boat."

"Can't you just let us go?" Tim pleaded.

"C'mon, then, lads, be brave—can't be 'elped," the soldier repeated in his clipped, friendly cockney. "We've got our orders."

"If ya don't go quiet, we'll 'ave to gag y'again," said another. "Ya don't want that, now, do ya?"

Jake, head spinning, could only allow himself to be tumbled into the boat. He was barely aware of his surroundings until they pushed off into the harbor; then he realized they'd been on the beach near Black Rock.

As the cockney soldiers rowed toward the open Sound, the full effect of the British destruction came into sharp focus. All along the East Haven and West Haven shores, homes had been burned, most of them still smoking. Jake scanned both sides of the shore-line for any sign of townspeople, but there were only Regulars and Hessians, British ships and British boats.

When they came into view of Tim's house, nothing remained but blackened timbers. The barn, the smokehouse, the saltworks, all had been burned. Jake looked at Tim; his face was nearly green. But then Jake realized it was not anger or sorrow that had turned him that shade. Tim was gripping the sides of the boat so tightly, his knuckles were white. Peculiar, Jake thought, how even now, Tim's terror of water overcame all other emotions. What in the world would he do with a ship as his prison?

They were rowed far into the Sound, where a brigantine lay at anchor. After the cockneys consulted with the crew, Jake and Tim were taken aboard and put below decks. Still bound, they were made to sit back to back, against a post, then securely roped to it and left alone.

Jake thought of Hannah. He had promised her he would be all right. When she returned home, she would learn that he and Tim were gone. What would she think?

And his brother Asa—dead or dying? And what of his father? Dead? Prisoner, too? And was it true that prisoners would soon be exchanged? After the Battle of Brooklyn, a list of Sugar House prisoners made its way to New Haven. Jake recalled studying the list again and again, searching for Asa's name. Jake imagined Hannah's bright green eyes scanning the list, pictured her wor-riedly biting her lip.

He ran his tongue along his sore palate, thinking of her spider cake. It was the last thing he had eaten. Had he taken a few more bites, perhaps he wouldn't be quite so famished right now. If only there had been time, she would have wrapped some of the cake in paper and put it in his haversack. Or if only he and Tim had thought to eat something when they were making cartridges at his uncle's. He thought of the contents of Mr. Rowe's canteen and almost groaned with longing. He was so parched—would the British ever give them anything to drink?

"Mal?"

"Yes?"

"What if the ship is sunk, with us trussed up this way?"

"We'll both die."

"'Tis nothing to make light of."

"I'm not making light, I'm simply stating the obvious."

"Perhaps it doesn't worry *you* because you can swim well," Tim said peevishly.

Jake felt himself grow impatient. "If the ship sank right now, we would both be in the same boat, so to speak. Neither my swimming skills nor your fear of water would signify."

"You'd have a better chance," Tim continued. "I'd never even be able to—"

"Have you lost your senses, Tim?" Jake interrupted. "With all we've been through today, *this* is your worry? We've killed men and seen our own killed. We both have the stench of blood upon us. Your house was burnt to the timbers. My brother may be dead, and we've no way of knowing whether our fathers are yet alive. My skull is cracked, and it aches worse than anything

I can remember. Now we sit here captured, heading to a prison ship. And your concern is the unlikely event that this ship will sink?"

"I can't help myself. I cannot control it, you've no idea how it feels."

Jake was too tired to carry on. "Timo. Enough. I am sorry, but—enough. I am exhausted beyond all reason and my eyes want closing."

"But what if—"

"Shhhh."

Then there was no sound but the creaking of timbers as the ship bobbed along. Jake had the thought that its gentle rocking would be the only comfort the British were likely to provide, so he ought to take full advantage.

He shut his eyes. Soon he drifted into a state that felt more like stupor than slumber.

AT DAYLIGHT, THE brig dropped anchor. Jake and Tim were hauled up and put into a boat, their arms still tied behind them. The morning was so foggy, Jake couldn't tell where he was, though he was sure it was not far from shore. As they were rowed through the mist, a man-of-war appeared, also at anchor and flying the Union Jack. Jake and Tim were taken on board as scores of other prisoners were brought up from the hold, dragging chains and irons. Some were young, some older; some fleshy, some sinewy; but all were sailors, and all looked tough and strong. Where had they come from? How long had they been kept in that hold?

Standing on deck, Jake leaned toward the man nearest him and began to ask, "Where did you—"

"Quiet, Jonathan!" a crewman shouted, threatening him with an upraised arm. "There will be no communication amongst prisoners!"

Now a man appeared, well dressed, well powdered, well fed. He surveyed the prisoners with a pompous air as he walked before them. "Welcome, Rebels. Welcome to my little fiefdom in the Wallabout Bay." They were in the Wallabout, the infamous bay near Brooklyn where the British kept their prison ships! The last vestige of hope faded from Jake's heart. "Allow me to introduce myself," the man continued. "I am David Sproat, commissary of prisoners, a king's man, a Loyalist—or, as present company might prefer, a Tory, a Refugee. Whatever appellation you may choose, be advised that you wretched Rebels now belong to me, and I shall escort you to your new home."

A hum of grumbling rose from the ranks. "Silence!" Sproat ordered. Then, to the guards, "Release them from their irons." As his order was carried out, he explained, "You see, Rebels, restraints are no longer necessary. You will need your arms to row yourselves to your prison, and if you make even the slightest move to escape, you will simply be shot and tossed into the water. Understood?" Without a pause, he answered himself: "Good. On you get, then—one by one."

Muttering, the prisoners boarded the gondola to which they were directed; Jake and Tim were the last in line.

"Mr. Sproat?" Tim said as they reached his side.

"What is it?"

"Well . . . we should not be here, sir. We are not maritime prisoners."

He looked at them and said with an air of false kindness, "Oh, this is a mistake, then, is it?"

"Yes, sir," Tim said. "We are militiamen. There was a battle at New Haven."

"I am well aware of that."

"We were captured on a ferry. My friend"—Tim jerked a thumb in Jake's direction—"it belongs to his family."

Sproat turned to Jake. "Does your family benefit financially from operation of this ferry?"

"Yes," Jake said, pointedly omitting the "sir."

Back to Tim: "Then I see no difference between it and any other commercial vessel."

Tim began: "But General Tryon said—"

"Never mind. Onto the boat."

Jake began to pass, but Sproat suddenly stopped him by raising his walking stick.

"Come to think of it, there *is* a way out."

"Yes, sir?" Tim asked.

"Renounce your misguided cause and come over to our side."

"Never," Jake said.

Sproat turned to Tim, who only shook his head with grim determination.

"Well, let's give it some time, shall we?" He cackled under his breath. "You'll soon be crying for your home and begging to join us."

Jake and Tim exchanged glances.

"Oh, you doubt me, do you? You'll see. . . . Into the boat, my fine young Rebels!" Sproat crowed, then followed behind them.

The boat was put off, but they were rowing against the tide and made little progress.

"Apply yourselves to the oars, Rebels! I haven't got all day."

With no desire to hasten their arrival, the prisoners—to a man—refused the order without a sound.

"Keep it up, Yankee doodles." Sproat nodded knowingly. "I'll soon fix you."

"I'd like to fix a noose around your neck, you Tory bastard," the man beside Jake muttered, and all within earshot snickered.

All too soon, the boat came around a point and Sproat announced loftily: "Ah, there she is, Rebels—there is the cage for you!"

Slowly, Jake lifted his head. The prison ship rose from the fog, phantomlike, its timbers dark with filth and despair.

"She's called the *Bonhomme*—captured from the French in the last war, no longer seaworthy," Sproat explained in schoolmaster tones. "Fitting, is it not, to use her against Rebels? Just as the French use you Rebels against your king?"

Motion on the upper deck attracted Jake's attention—odd movements, all as one, as though soldiers were on parade. As they rowed closer, he realized it was the prisoners, walking in unison, following some sort of path or pattern. Now one of them noticed the boat and gave a shout, and the prisoners thronged to the ship's rail, some waving hats. As the boat came nearer, they hallooed to the new prisoners:

"Where are you from?"

"Anyone from Groton?"

"What is the news?"

"Anybody from New Jersey?"

Jake stared in horror. These were not men, but skeletons; clad not in clothing, nor even in rags, but in shreds. Their faces were gray, eyes sunken, lips pallid. Their arms, hanging over the ship's rail, were only skin-covered bones.

"Where is the cat that has got all of your tongues?" one prisoner called.

"We should like to catch him and roast him!" yelled another, and a raucous roar of laughter rose up.

The boat came flush with a sort of floating dock on the *Bonhomme*'s larboard side, and the new prisoners were ordered out one by one, onto the dock and up the gangway ladder.

As Jake waited his turn, he took measure of the *Bonhomme*. He knew little about French ships, how they varied from English ones. But she looked like a man-of-war, probably of sixty-four guns. All her portholes had been shut and securely fastened, though two rows of square holes had been cut in her sides. The holes were fitted with crossed iron bars, through which, Jake judged, not much more than a human arm could pass. Well, perhaps a leg, in the case of the emaciated men on her deck— but one leg through an opening did not a free man make. Still, he immediately found himself thinking: *I will escape. I will.*

"You two! Step lively!"

"Mal . . ." Tim stood shakily, trying to steady himself.

"Show them no fear," Jake said.

"But that ladder. . . ."

"I'll be right behind you. Look ahead, not down, while you climb."

Tim hurried up the ladder, and Jake couldn't help but smile at the irony. Here he was, dreading to reach the top; and here was Tim, fearing a fall into water more than he feared boarding a disease-ridden prison ship.

Once on deck, they were directed to climb the accommodation ladder to the upper deck. At the top was a high barricade, at which prisoners waited in a line. As each passed through a doorway, he was asked: "Surname? Christian name? Vessel? Capacity?"

Jake could hear the four questions repeated again and again. In response each new prisoner mumbled his name, the name of the ship on which he'd been captured, and the position he had held on that ship.

Tim was taken in first; Jake tipped his head back to examine the barricade. It was pierced with a multitude of loopholes. What were they for?

"Next!"

Jake walked through the barricade door to find Tim holding his hands over his head as the guards searched him. They then allowed him to advance to the table where one man was asking the questions, another recording the replies as Sproat stood by, looking pleased with himself.

"Surname?"

"Morris."

"Christian name?"

"Timothy."

"Vessel?"

"I am not a maritime prisoner," Tim said.

The man asking the questions turned to Sproat, who snapped at Tim: "Oh, *do* shut up." Then he gestured to Jake, who was now being searched. "Surname?"

"Mallery."

"Christian name?"

"Jacob."

Sproat turned to the registrar: "Just write Mallery ferry, New Haven, for both of them."

And there was an end to the issue.

They were sent through the barricade door on the starboard side; two guards stood at the accommodation ladder that led to the spar deck, where the prisoners congregated.

"Pardon me," Jake said to the guards before descending. "We've had nothing to eat or drink since our capture. When will we—"

"You'll find drinking water in a cistern down there," one of the guards interrupted. "As for food, you'll wait until tomorrow."

"Tomorrow?" Jake repeated.

"Yes. You see, when animals are moved to a new location, they are generally quite agitated," the man said. "But a farmer finds that keeping them without fodder for a day or two does much to resign them to their situation. We've found the same to be true of Rebels."

Laughing heartily at their own joke, the guards nudged Jake

and Tim toward the ladder. On the spar deck, the new prisoners were absorbed into the *Bonhomme*'s grim population. They
gleamed pink beside the veterans.

"Ah, I hate to see new lads come aboard," said a grizzled,
leather-faced man to Jake. "Death has no relish for our skeleton
carcasses, but he'll feast upon your fresh flesh."

"Most grateful for the reassuring welcome." Jake took hold of
Tim's arm and pulled him away, continuing to press through the
throng.

"Horseneck? Anyone from Horseneck?" one prisoner
repeated, grasping each new arm.

"We are from East Haven," Jake said.

"Ah, close enough. Connecticut men!" He clapped them on
the back. "What are your names? I am Fish." He jerked his
thumb at the man beside him. "This is Eels."

Jake grinned. "Not really."

"Indeed, those are our surnames," said Fish, whose pleasant
face was marred by smallpox scars. "Been mates since boyhood.
Went to sea together, and were captured together."

"Same with us," Jake said, gesturing at Tim. "Well, everything
but going to sea together. I'm Jake Mallery; this is Tim Morris."

"Mallery and Morris," Eels repeated. "Surnames suffice on the
Bonhomme, lads. Most men, there's no time for learning more."

"Eels, Eels," Fish scolded. "Enough of that. Come, lads, what
is the news?"

"There was a battle at New Haven—they attacked us on the
east and west shores to get into the city."

"When?" Eels asked.

"Yesterday . . . or was it the day before?"

"We shouldn't even be here," Tim said. "We're not maritime prisoners. You see, Mal's father runs the ferry. We were only trying to keep it from the British."

Why bother to tell it again? Jake thought. *What did these poor wretches care? Even if they did—what could they do?*

"Tryon was sending us to the Sugar House," Tim went on. "It was another officer—he was angry because he thought we killed his nephew, and he—"

Eels cut him off. "It does not signify, Morris. Truth is, it's their game. If they wish to put you on a prison ship, they will do so. You are not the only ones sent here on a whim."

"Well, a soldier told us we would be exchanged," Tim said.

"Exchanged?" Eels laughed bitterly. "No one is exchanged from the *Bonhomme*."

"There are only two things that need concern you at present," Fish added. "Getting into a mess and being inoculated against the smallpox."

Jake had another matter on his mind. "Where is the . . . ?" He looked around, embarrassed.

"The what, boy?"

"You know, the necessary."

"Over by the railing of the hatchway are the tubs," Fish said, pointing. "You will know them by their stink."

"And you . . . in front of everyone?" Jake asked dubiously.

"The first thing you'll learn here is to dispense with all thoughts of modesty," Fish said.

Jake made his way to one of the revolting wooden tubs and

dropped his breeches to relieve himself, his face burning with shame. He kept his head down and did not look up to see whether anyone was paying attention to him.

When he returned to Tim and the others, Eels was saying, "—six men to a mess. The food is cooked every morning and must last you the day. Biscuit and beef, mostly—the meat putrid and the biscuit wormy. Never any fruit or vegetables. . . . You can both mess with us, if you like. We've two vacancies, as two of our mates have gone to shore this week."

"Gone to shore?" Tim repeated. "But you said no one was exchanged."

"Not exchanged, but freed in a way." Fish gestured toward land. "Gone to shore. Dead and buried—over there, near the place called Remsen's Mill. You'll see the sorry particulars soon enough, when you're on the working party."

"What's the working party?" Jake asked.

"A group of prisoners who do chores, including burying the dead," Eels said.

"They force men to do that?"

"Not forced . . . 'tis a privilege," Eels explained. "To be allowed to step onto land, and to give your mates what passes for a decent burial. A privilege," he muttered again.

"I shall never volunteer to bury a man," Tim said.

Eels smiled indulgently. "You'll see, lad. You'll see."

"Does no one escape?" Jake asked, looking toward land. "'Tisn't very far to shore."

"Half a mile," Eels said. "Men have tried. There was an

attempt several weeks ago, in fact. Four men managed to cut a hole in the ship's side with only jackknives. Must have taken months. One night we were awakened by gunfire—that was the first most of us knew of it. The guards had spotted them in the water, sent a boat, and started shooting. . . . A while later they tossed a young man down amongst us, naked and bleeding."

Fish took over as Eels's voice faltered. "It was a lad named Lawrence; we knew him well. He'd been shot in four places, and his hand was nearly severed from the stroke of a cutlass. He said he'd put his hand on the gunwale of their boat, begging for mercy, and that was their response."

"Died within the hour," Eels finished.

"And the others?" Jake asked quietly, after a pause.

"Presumed dead in the water."

"So, lads"—Fish clapped them both on the back—"you'd do well to dispense with any fantasies of escape."

"I couldn't swim a rod, let alone half a mile, whether I was being shot at or not," Tim said with a rueful grin.

But Jake just stared at the water and didn't reply.

They spent the rest of the day with Fish and Eels, learning the workings of the prison and telling one another their stories of battle and capture and of their lives at home. Fish and Eels had gone out with the privateer *Scourge* and were captured after an engagement in the shipping lanes with the British frigate *Maidstone*. They'd been on the *Bonhomme* five months and six days. Eels was married with two young children; Fish was yet a bachelor. Jake was stunned to learn that they were twenty-seven years old—he'd figured them to be at least forty. He wondered what he would look like when he had been here as long as they. *Don't think*, he reminded himself. *Put one foot before the other. Live one minute, then the next.*

Cooking was done only in the morning, so most men ate their meat and oatmeal at that time, and saved the bread—which they called biscuit—for later in the day. Fish and Eels shared theirs with Jake and Tim—a more generous reception, Jake noticed, than many of the other newcomers were getting. The biscuit was more than passing stale and not a little wormy, but after having fasted for—how long? nearly two days?—Jake wolfed his down gratefully.

When Fish observed Tim trying to pick out the worms, he said, "*Eat* the little buggers, Morris! If you extract them, you reduce your rations by half!"

The veteran prisoners within hearing all laughed.

As the sun sank low, Jake separated himself from the others and found a spot alone, where he removed his shoe—and Hannah's ruined letter. It had long since dried, but in drying, all the folded sections stuck completely together, and when Jake tried to open it, it broke apart in little squares. He examined each one thoroughly, trying to decipher any words. Perhaps there would be a *dear* or a *love* or some such endearment that he could keep in his pocket for the duration of this ordeal . . . then anytime he was in need of comfort, he could reach in and hold on to that bit of her, of them.

But it was not to be. Not a single word was legible.

"Are you all right?" Walking up behind Jake, Tim rested a hand on his shoulder.

Jake held up the tattered scraps. "I didn't know I had it in me, Tim. To love this way. And to feel so utterly ashamed of the way I used to treat her."

"Come, Mal. You were not all *that* bad."

"Oh, you don't know half of it. How I taunted her when you were not around." He shook his head. "Vile things, Tim."

"But *why*? I never understood why you treated Hannah that way."

"Nor do I. Hannah has a notion, though. She reckons it was because of the way my father behaves toward me." Jake grinned, quickly casting his eyes heavenward, then giving a shrug.

"How so?"

"She said because my father treated *me* ill, I looked for someone to treat the same. And she was a convenient target—my being so often at your house, her being a servant."

"Maybe she's right. She's a smart girl, Mal."

"Yes, a lot smarter than I am—but don't ever let her know I said it!" They laughed; then Jake grew solemn again. "But now . . . the hardest thing has been proving to her that I'm no longer that person. She can never quite believe my feelings are sincere. Anyhow . . ." Storing the bits of paper in his pocket, he looked around, then pointed. "Uh . . . are those men doing what I think they're doing?"

Tim turned, and they watched with grim fascination as the working party cleaned the foul tubs. "I suppose that is a privilege, too?" Jake asked as they rejoined Fish and Eels.

"We neglected to tell you the *true* privileges of the working party," Fish said. "For one, members are allowed on deck early in the mornings, which, as you'll see after spending a night below, is a luxury not to be taken lightly. Oh, and another trifle: those on the working party receive a half pint of rum each day."

At this Jake's mouth fell open and he looked Fish in the face. "You're joking!"

Fish laughed. "I suspected the rum would favorably impress you, Mallery."

"But surely you're fooling with me."

"Am I fooling with him, Eels?"

"Nay. 'Tis the one shred of comfort the demons provide us," Eels said. "Rum to dull the senses after we bury our countrymen."

"Down, Rebels, down!" A few guards repeated the cry, advancing with their weapons in hand and bayonets fixed. It was time to go between decks, where the prisoners were confined at night.

"Hmm. A half pint of rum would go a long way toward making this place bearable," Jake muttered to Tim as they were herded toward the gratings.

"But is it worth the price?" Tim asked.

"Sign me up, man," Jake said.

Fish sidled over to them and said quietly, "You were wondering about escape, Mal. Perhaps you are curious about mutiny."

"What do you mean?"

He shrugged. "There are hundreds of us, and only a handful

of them. Why do we not overpower them and take their guns?"

"Well, now that you bring it up . . ."

"Look over there." With a toss of his head, Fish gestured behind him.

When Jake turned, he saw the reason for the loopholes in the barricade: musket muzzles stuck out of each one.

"They are there every time the guards come among us. Scores of them, just waiting to put a bloody end to any uprising."

Jake had no time to contemplate this, for they had reached the ladder leading below, and he was overwhelmed by the most repulsive odors yet: things rotting, decaying, dying, dead. . . . He pulled his shirt and neckcloth up over his nose. The smell of his own reeking self was far preferable to these indescribably disgusting vapors.

"You'll get used to it." Fish hit him on the back again . . . then disappeared.

Between decks, any fellowship between old and new was lost as the hierarchy became clear: those who had been here longest headed for their hard-won sleeping places in hammocks and on chests; next came the group that stretched out on the deck, folding thin blankets under their heads; and the new arrivals were lowest, scrambling for whatever meager space was left.

Every time Jake and Tim tried to claim a spot, they were either beaten to it or informed that it belonged to someone else. Before long they found themselves standing in the middle of the deck, stepping awkwardly over cursing heaps of men.

"Damn you, watch where you're going!"

"Get away, boy! Can't a sick man get some peace?"

Jake was so exhausted he lost his balance; recovering it, his foot landed on someone's leg.

"Don't tread on me!" the victim shouted, and all within earshot laughed.

"Best to get some sleep, lads," advised a man lying on his back, looking up at them.

"But how?" Tim asked. "Every inch of the deck is taken."

"That's always the way when there are new arrivals," the man said. "But don't worry, boys, it won't last long. Death kindly makes room for all." With that, he turned on his side and folded his bony hands beneath his cheek.

Looking toward the side of the ship, Jake saw a glimmer of light through one of the air holes. Was it the moon, shining off the water?

"Follow me," he told Tim as he began making his way toward the air holes. If they couldn't lie down, at least they could get a breath of fresh air to sustain them.

But when they reached the starboard planking, men were crowded so thick around the air holes, there was no hope of getting near. At last they found a narrow spot and slid to the deck, sitting with their knees drawn up and backs against the sheathing.

Jake buried his mouth and nose inside his shirt again. If only he had something that held Hannah's scent. If only the letter had not been ruined . . . He thought with longing of what he would be doing right now if he were at home: writing to Hannah, as he had done nearly every night since they had admitted their feelings. He had been surprised at how much pleasure he'd taken in pouring out his thoughts, carefully sealing the letter with wax, slipping it to her the next day.

No chance of putting pen to paper now . . . but then it came to him: he could still write her letters, only they would be in his head. He could talk to Hannah in his mind, and that would keep him sane. Tipping his head back against the timbers, he shut his eyes.

> *Dear Hannah,*
>
> *My boyhood wish has come true at last: I will be living on a ship for a while. I wonder what you are thinking at this moment. Do you know I'm gone, or are you still in Cheshire, thinking we'll soon be together? If you could see my prison you would not believe such a place exists. I know I could never have imagined anything so inhuman. The smell alone is enough to kill a man. How I long to be with you in our secret place amongst the reeds, where we*

"Mal?"

Jake opened his eyes. "Huh?"

"I said, are you scared now?"

"Terrified."

"It feels like a bad dream."

"I've been thinking that ever since the battle began."

"A bad dream that just keeps getting worse."

After another silence, Jake said, "I wonder what we'll be like if we have to stay here as long as Fish and Eels?"

"Mal . . . do you think they'll find out we're here? Our families?"

"I don't know. We'd best not trouble ourselves about it, though. Just take each day as it comes."

"Fish and Eels said we should be inoculated tomorrow. The old prisoners do it for the new, they told me while you were at the—you know, the necessary."

They both laughed quietly over Tim's gentle gibe at Jake's attempt to be modest.

"Asa was inoculated, when he was in the Continentals," Jake said. "He still has the scar from it."

"Did he tell you how it's done?"

"No, and I don't think I care to know."

"First they must find someone who has the pustules on him. Then they scratch your skin raw with a common pin—"

"Thank you, that's quite enough," Jake interrupted.

"—and take some pus from the infected man, then rub it into your wound, which—"

"Tim, did you hear me?" Jake said sharply, and Tim stopped. After a while, in a more complacent tone, Jake said, "It is what it is, and I'll find out soon enough." Tim didn't reply; Jake elbowed his ribs. "The one thing Asa *did* say was that the cure is not half so bad as the sickness."

Tim smiled, but barely. For a long time, they sat without speaking. Despite the ship's gruesome lullaby of groans and curses and coughs and screeches of delirium, Jake found himself growing sleepy.

"I just thought of something funny," Tim said.

"Pray, tell it. I could use a dash of humor."

"*Bonhomme*. Do you know what it means in French?"

"No."

"The common meaning is . . . well, a good-hearted fellow. *Bon* means *good*. And *homme* is *man*. Ironic, isn't it? *Le mal garçon* imprisoned on *le bon homme*."

"We'll get off this hulk, Timo." Jake rested his head on his knees and shut his eyes. "We will."

"You're not thinking about escape, are you?" Tim asked. "After that story . . . ?"

"They say the other three died in the water, but how can they know? I'd never escape without you, though, so we'll have to find a way that doesn't include swimming."

Up on the spar deck, a guard shouted: "All's well!"

"All's well!" another replied from his station.

Jake barely slept at all, thinking of home and plotting revenge, unable to block out the sounds and smells of sick men hacking and soiling themselves and puking, healthy men damning their keepers to hell, and all men tossing and turning in the intense discomfort of dirt and vermin and breath-sucking heat.

"All's well!" the guards insisted upon every hour.

"All's well!"

Prisoner

July 4, 1780

"REBELS! THROW OUT your dead!"

Every morning the guards awakened them with the same stone-hearted order, and every morning Tim greeted Jake with the same grim joke:

"Are you dead yet, Mal?"

"Let me check." Jake slowly stretched an arm. "Not yet."

Few had survived as long as the two of them. Each had his own hammock now, and at night they hung them side by side in a privileged spot near one of the air holes. The rude return to consciousness was yet the hardest part of every day, especially when sleep had been relatively comfortable or when a pleasant dream was interrupted.

The *Bonhomme* creaked as it bobbed with the tide; Jake had come to detest the sound and the motion he once loved. He vowed that when he got off this ship for good, he would never set foot on another.

"Working party!" the guards bellowed.

"Mmmm . . . that's me, isn't it?" Jake mumbled.

"'Tis."

"I'm so tired."

"But think of the rum."

Jake and Tim were no longer allowed on the same working party. Over the entire year, there had been only one successful escape: two burial crew members who were boon companions had gone to shore, then simply disappeared. After that, the keepers forbade close friends from serving together on the working party. It was ridiculous, like most of their edicts; what would prevent two men who were *not* close friends from plotting escape?

Still, Jake often thought that in the case of himself and Tim, it was an effective strategy. Because he was always thinking about escape . . . but he'd never dream of leaving Tim behind.

For a year they had been inseparable, sharing everything: rum, rations, blankets, each illness that came their way, and, once, twenty stripes for stealing moldy bread. Their connection was clear even in the name by which everyone knew them: Malanmorris, as if two were one. They hated being split for working parties, but Jake had pointed out that there was a decided advantage to the arrangement: rum twice as often.

"Working party!"

"All right, all right," Jake mumbled. He swung his legs over the side and let the hammock tumble him onto his feet. On his way to the hatchway ladder, he asked his fellow prisoners, "Dead? Any dead?"

From elsewhere between decks, he could hear others on the working party repeating the same blunt question.

Death had long since failed to hold any mystery, for Jake had come to know it in all its ghastly guises, from violence to pestilence, broken heads to broken hearts. Prisoners perishing from smallpox, from fever and delirium, from the poisonous effects of having their meat cooked in seawater in the copper boiler. Men weakened by disease, then succumbing under winter's bitter cold or summer's suffocating heat. Shot while trying to escape, or wheezing out their last breaths in the night, or expiring on the spar deck in their own bloody excrement.

Jake and Tim had themselves been sick too many times to count, starting with the miserable illness attending the smallpox inoculation, through which Fish and Eels had nursed them. Then had come yellow fever, so called because it yellowed the skin and brought weeks of chills and sweats. Next was a case of what prisoners called "the itch"; it came, some said, from tiny insects crawling under the skin. And there was also the disease known as ship's fever, with its headache, shivering, weakness, and rash.

Those were only the known illnesses. Often you didn't even have a name for the thing that ailed you, but only felt that you might rather be peacefully dead than suffering this way. For a spell, Jake's mouth had been so filled with sores, he could not eat or speak, could hardly even drink. Another time, it was scabs all over his scalp, accompanied by the most torturous itching.

In winter, painful boils had sprouted on his arms and legs,

even on the soles of his feet, making it nearly impossible to move. In spring, his hair had begun to fall out by the handfuls, which so distressed him, he had hacked off the remaining locks with a dull pair of shears.

Once, he was accidentally hit on the forehead with a shovel while on the burial party. With needle and thread, Fish stitched up the cut, but then it became so badly infected Jake had delirious fevers. Each of these ills passed in its time and was replaced by another—sometimes slightly more bearable, sometimes much worse.

But each time he got well, he grew stronger. The same was true of Tim. When they had arrived, Fish and Eels told them to resolve to stay alive for three months. Men who passed that milestone, they said, found it a little easier to elude the Reaper.

Fish and Eels had taught them many other tricks to survival: stay as active as possible, volunteering often for the working party, joining the group that walked the spar deck daily in the intricate pattern designed to make the most of the small space allowed. Insist that your mess cook its meat separately, using its rations of freshwater. Wash yourself and your clothing whenever you could. Take fresh air whenever you could—even in rain, snow, and cold. Trust in God's judgment. Pray for strength.

And do not ever pine for home.

Jake had seen for himself how the homesickness shattered so many young men within weeks or even days of arrival. Unable or unwilling to resign themselves to this place, they yielded to self-pity—the first step toward a quick death.

Jake and Tim had promised each other never to take that path. This was their lot, and they were determined to look always forward, never back. . . .

"Mal, here." Comstock's voice was quavery, but firm. Jake halted; Comstock's messmate Newson had been ill for days. Now he lay still at Comstock's side.

"He has gone?" Jake asked.

Comstock nodded.

Jake sat on his heels and said quietly, "Have you anything for a shroud?"

Comstock offered a thin, shredded blanket.

Jake took it gently from his hand. "I'll cover him with it on deck. You can sew it around him when you come up, all right?"

Comstock nodded again.

"Do you want to help me carry him to the ladder?"

In reply, Comstock struggled to his feet; he lifted his friend underneath the arms while Jake took the legs. "Look out," Jake called over his shoulder, walking backward. "Coming through!" At the ladder, two of his working party mates were already in place, lifting out other corpses.

"Oh, no," Bell moaned. "Not Newson." Newson had been a shipmate of Bell's; Bell was just sixteen, a powder monkey out to sea for the first time, when captured about a month ago. This was his first turn on the working party. Jake had only decided the day before to learn Bell's name, for the pink glow of freedom had faded from the boy's face and he was still alive.

"Newson is no longer amongst us," Jake told him. "Haul up the corpse."

When the job was done, three corpses lay on the gratings, three more shells of former human beings. Jake had known better days and much worse in his three hundred and sixty-three on the *Bonhomme*. Well over a thousand dead, just on this one prison ship, in only one year. But counting would not resurrect them. Best to just move on to another chore.

Next, the working party was split in two. The prized job was to wash down the deck and the gangways where the prisoners were allowed to spend the day. The other group would help the sick to the spar deck, where they would lie in cots for the day unless they were bad enough to be transferred to one of the so-called hospital ships. It was a fate most prisoners resisted; once removed to a hospital ship, few recovered.

Each working party had one prisoner to serve as its commander; the guards gave him the inflated title of boatswain. It was always someone who had been an officer on his captured ship, and this party's boatswain, a man named Hilliard, told Jake and Bell and some others to return between decks and offer assistance to those who needed it.

"Why must *we* be the ones to go below again?" Bell muttered as they walked to the ladder.

"It is always done in turns," Jake said. "Don't worry, I've been here too long to allow any man to take unfair advantage. Come, follow me."

Jake headed first for Cookson, who had been unable to walk these last two days.

"Careful, blast you, lads!" he yelped as Jake and Bell assisted him—his arms around their necks—to the ladder.

"I'm sorry, friend," Jake said. "We're trying to be gentle."

"You're failing miserably!" Cookson returned.

Jake had suffered Cookson's affliction—legs covered with mysterious sores—and he well remembered how painful it was to be moved. Still, he had come to the point where he would rather deal with the dead than the sick. Dead men did not lament, cry, or curse.

"Oh, just leave me here, damn you!" Cookson cried out when he was jolted again.

"No, it will do you good to sit in the sun," Jake said. "Believe me—I had your sores last fall."

"Did you?"

"Yes, so I know you won't die. Well, at least not from that."

Cookson chuckled grudgingly.

"Sit," Jake told him when they reached the ladder. "Hilliard is at the top." Jake and Bell lifted Cookson halfway up until Hilliard reached down and hoisted him the rest of the way.

With Cookson's loud complaints fading away, Jake and Bell waded into the mass of prisoners again, calling: "Sick! Any sick need assistance?"

Walking alone along the starboard side, Jake stopped at the place where the names of all the ship's dead had been carved into her planks and inner sheathing, hacked into the wood with any available tool by grieving messmates and friends. He stood and read the names, row after row. Godfrey Sweet. Stephen Taylor. David Moffit. Thomas Littlejohn. Robert Warnock. On and on went the list, taking no notice of the man's standing in life, whether he had been an officer or a cabin boy, white or black, young or old. Only that he had been here, and died here. Enoch Stillwell. Michael Dupee. Ephraim Henderson. Thomas Abington. Job Knight. Ebenezer Pratt . . .

Jake ran his fingers along hundreds of names and finally found the grooves carved with his own hand:

> MARTIN EELS
> STEPHEN FISH

After thirteen months on board, they had at last succumbed to a scarlet fever epidemic that carried off hundreds within a couple of weeks. The disease began with a sore throat and fever, then progressed to a painful red rash all over the body. In the end Eels had awakened during the night screaming that he was burning up. He had torn off his clothing and run amok, pursued by Jake and Tim until he collapsed and died.

Fish followed soon after; Jake was never really sure whether Fish realized that Eels had gone ahead of him. Fish's death had been quieter and at the same time more desperate. Before lapsing into unconsciousness, he had whispered to Jake: *Stay alive, Mal. Bear witness to what happens here.*

Now Jake had nothing left of Fish but the scar on his forehead and the mark between his thumb and forefinger, perpetually irritated from the smallpox inoculation.

"Mal!" Bell called. "Can you help me here?"

Jake sighed and quickly ran his hand back and forth over his friends' names, as he often did, in memory and for luck.

When at last the chore was finished, twenty-six men lay in bunks on the deck, and Bell asked, "What now?"

"Rations," Jake said, leading the way to the steward's room, toward the aft section of the upper deck.

Behind them, a guard called, "Mallery! How many dead today?"

Without turning, Jake held three fingers above his head as he continued toward the galley. Then, bringing his hand in front of him, he drew in his first and third finger, leaving one remaining. The gesture made Bell laugh, which was Jake's intention.

Every time Jake gestured that way or cursed like a sailor, he couldn't help but think of his father's declaration that life on a privateer would cause him to become "more profane and ungodly than you are at present." He wondered what Father would think of a prison ship's effects upon him. He was, without a doubt, far more profane . . . but also far more godly than he would have thought possible.

It seemed that most prisoners took one of two paths: renouncing the God who had forsaken them, or becoming much closer to Him. Jake had followed the lead of Fish and Eels, whose faith, though shaken at times, had not failed them. They never asked God for favors, Jake had noticed, only for strength.

Jake and Bell parted near the steward's room, each looking for his own mess, all waiting for the nine o'clock bell. Every morning at that hour, the steward and his assistants took their places at a window in the bulkhead. When the steward rang his bell, each mess was called in its turn. A representative from that mess would go to the window and receive the rations.

Six prisoners received the same rations as four men in the British navy. On Sundays and Thursdays, each man got two pounds of beef and a pound of biscuit. On Tuesdays and Fridays, it was a pound of pork, a pound of biscuit, and a pint of oatmeal. On Mondays and Saturdays, a pound of biscuit, a pint of oatmeal, and two ounces of a viscous liquid the British called "sweet oil"— a substance so rancid and foul, no Patriot prisoner could consume it. Wednesdays were the worst : two ounces of suet and one and a half pounds of flour.

At first Jake had thought the rations seemed generous, but he soon learned that most of the food was not edible. And every time the British detected any infraction of the rules, however small, they were quick to put the entire ship on half-rations.

In all the time Jake had been on board, he had never seen a vegetable. On rare occasions, after the prisoners were sent below for the night, the guards would throw some apples down the hatchway. The captives would scramble for them, fighting and grunting like pigs. If you were lucky enough to get one, you hid it on your person and ate it late at night when everyone else was asleep. Jake and Tim had had that sweetest of privileges three times; in a year, three apples shared between them.

"Seven!"

Jake's number was called before he had found his messmates. He waded through the crowd to get to the bulkhead window, where the steward handed out their portion in a wooden bucket.

Today was Tuesday, so there was biscuit and pork; the oatmeal would be ladled out in the galley, where it was presently cooking.

Now he must find his mess quickly in order to get the kettle for cooking their pork, then dash down to the galley under the forecastle. Their number would be called again very soon, and each minute their kettle was not on a hook over the fire meant one less minute of cooking time for their pork.

Pushing through the crowd, he looked for his messmate Meecham, one of the tallest men on board. Meech had been here about three months, an old salt with a shock of white hair who was missing one thumb and many teeth. He was well liked and respected by veterans and newcomers, officers and common prisoners, and Jake had been proud when Meecham asked to be admitted into his and Tim's mess.

"Meech! Meech! Here!" Jake called when he spotted him, and they made a quick and wordless exchange: Jake handed over the mess's biscuit, Meecham gave Jake the kettle, and Jake was off again—but slower, now, to keep the precious freshwater from sloshing out of the kettle.

The galley was about ten feet square. Much of that space was taken up by brickwork enclosing the enormous copper boiler, which was split into two sections: on one side, oatmeal was cooked in freshwater; on the other, meat was boiled in seawater drawn directly from the bay surrounding the disgusting ship. The filth in itself was probably enough to kill a man. But even worse, the salt water had corroded the copper, poisoning those whose meat was cooked in it.

Many of the messes had their own tin kettles. The brickwork around the copper boiler was pierced with hooks and spikes, from which the prisoners were allowed to hang their kettles.

Jostling for position in the forecastle, Jake asked his fellow prisoners, "Did His Majesty call the first group yet?"

"Yes—and he's in a vile mood. You'd better get in there."

The ship's cook, Foucault, was an imperious and mercurial Frenchman who spoke heavily accented English. There were plenty of French prisoners on board—the British hated them even more than they hated the Americans and kept them below decks in an even more wretched state—but no one was sure how or why this particular Frenchman had come to be the *Bonhomme*'s cook.

When in a good humor, Foucault chatted and joked and bent the rules; when feeling low, he was apt to toss French curses and hot cooking implements. "Malle-*ree!*" he shouted when Jake pushed his way into the galley. *"En retard!"* Late.

Jake knew Foucault liked him, but the cook never showed favoritism. If some felt his wrath, all felt his wrath. "I know, I couldn't find Meech with the kettle." He quickly hung it on a free hook and surrendered the bucket, into which Foucault ladled the mess's portion of oatmeal.

In winter, after sleeping with no heat but the warmth of a thousand diseased bodies, everyone crowded the galley for a few precious minutes around the fire. But now, they all deserted the sweating cook and his assistants, preferring to wait in the forecastle.

No more than ten minutes had passed before Foucault shouted, "First group! Remove your rations!"

Jake knew his pork had been over the fire nowhere near long enough, so he took his time, making sure to be the last to retrieve his kettle. Foucault barked, "Second group!" and those messes rushed into the galley. In the confusion Jake slipped the kettle back on the hook, but Foucault caught him and snapped, "Malla-*ree*! Remove your rations!"

"Come, Foucault—'tis nearly raw!"

"Remove, or lose!"

"What's up your arse?" Jake muttered, taking the kettle. When he was at a safe distance, he added, "Foucault you," and a roar of laughter went up from the prisoners awaiting their turns.

On the spar deck he found his messmates and divided the pork and oatmeal among them. Besides himself, Tim, and Meecham, there were Stark and Fortnum, the former an ordinary seaman, the latter a young black man.

As soon as they bit into the meat, all but Tim started in:

"'Tis hardly cooked, Mal!" Stark said.

"Did you even get it over the fire?" Meecham said.

"A man can die from eating raw pork!" Fortnum said.

"Do you not think I know that?" Jake snapped. "Foucault was having one of his foul fits: 'Malla-*wee*! Wee-move yaw wations!'" he mimicked, and his messmates laughed. "So please, feel free to go and reason with him, any one of you."

"No thank you," Stark said.

"I'll pass on that," Meecham said.

"Did I mention I *prefer* pink pork?" Fortnum said, and Jake had to laugh.

Getting to know Fortnum had been a revelation to Jake, for he had never spoken to a black person before—not really. Of course he had exchanged plenty of words with Sally and her family; with Pomp and his boy and the other Negroes on the Morris farm; and with other people's servants, mostly on the ferry. But never on any matters of substance.

On the *Bonhomme*, there was nothing to do except talk—and talking with Fortnum, Jake had been surprised to find that a black man thought and felt much like a white one.

Born into slavery in New York, Fortnum's hopes had soared when the British commandeered the city and announced that slaves would be freed. Soon, though, their motive had become clear: only Patriot-owned slaves would be freed, to punish the Rebels, to deprive them of property. Fortnum told how he and the other Loyalist slaves could only watch in envy as the Patriots' former slaves cavorted around the city, taunting those who had the bad fortune to belong to Tories.

But then Fortnum's master had decided to return to England, selling off all his possessions before he left—including Fortnum and his mother, to different masters. It was the final straw; Fortnum ran away from his new master to join the crew of a privateer . . . and after less than a year at sea, found himself a prisoner on the *Bonhomme*.

At home, Jake had just assumed that Negroes who were treated well were happy; from Fortnum, he had learned there was nothing about being owned that was acceptable to a man. Now Jake counted Fortnum among his best mates on the ship, and he knew that when he had his own household, he would not keep a single servant, white or black, indentured or purchased. He and Hannah and their children would do their own work, and if ever they needed help, they would hire it.

They all sat eating quietly for a while until Tim asked, "Do you know what today is, Mal?"

"One more day that we have survived," Jake replied.

Blithely ignoring the surly edge, Tim continued, "The fourth anniversary of independence. Remember, three years ago on the rocks when you said—"

Jake cut him off: "Independence? What does it mean to me, Tim? To any of us? . . . Today is one day closer to the end of this damned war. That is all."

Their messmates ate in silence, heads down; rarely did Mal or Morris speak a harsh word to each other.

Tim solemnly chewed his half-cooked pork. After a while he said coolly, "You're all for looking forward, always forward. But it helps *me* to talk about happy times, Mal. I am sorry that offends you. I'll keep my thoughts to myself in future." He put his bowl down, stood up, and walked away from the little group.

Jake stole a sidelong look at his mates. Fortnum gave a slight shrug, Stark just continued eating, and Meecham waved him toward Tim.

Taking both their bowls, Jake followed Tim to the spot where he was leaning on the ship's rail. Jake held out Tim's rations and said, "You must be *really* angry to walk off without your food."

Tim didn't even smile.

"Timo . . . I'm sorry. Really. I know it comforts you to talk about home. And some days I can bear it. But today . . . a year in this shite-hole, and sometimes I feel we'll never get off until the working party carries us. . . ."

"'Tis unlike you to talk so," Tim mumbled.

"Working with Bell has me feeling melancholy. I keep thinking of how you and I were, with Fish and Eels. How kind they were to us. And when I was collecting the sick . . . I stopped to find their names."

Tim lifted his head, and they looked at each other. Clasping Jake's shoulder, Tim gave him a brief shake of reassurance. Then, with a grin, he took his bowl back, and they sat on the deck and continued eating.

"The oatmeal is particularly revolting this morning," Tim said with a mouthful.

"Foucault probably pissed in it," Jake answered, and Tim nearly choked laughing.

Jake often wondered why Tim was so eager to talk of home, while he himself avoided the subject. Perhaps it was simply the difference in their temperaments. But perhaps it was because Tim had never had much to complain about. And for Jake, thinking of home sparked guilt over how ungrateful he had been.

He remembered the boy who sat at the ferry landing staring across the harbor, coveting General Arnold's lush estate while considering his own thrifty father a tyrant. The boy who deemed himself *cold and hungry* or *hot and tired* after working a few hours, anticipating a good meal and a comfortable bed. The boy who paddled around the harbor in his own canoe, raking up oysters whenever he wished . . . and thinking that he needed freedom.

Now he could only laugh in the face of that stupid, shallow boy.

Such things were too painful to contemplate; it was much easier to shut them out entirely. The only time he indulged thoughts of home were at night, in his hammock, thinking of Hannah before sleep. He still kept the remnants of her final letter, now no more than shreds from being handled so often. It was the only tangible reminder that home, and she, really did exist.

And he still wrote her letters in his head, telling her his thoughts and feelings—about her, about life, about everything that happened here—and asking her not to forget him, not ever to think he was dead.

Sometimes he had the peculiar notion that only her memories of him were keeping him alive.

"Working party!"

"That's me, isn't it?" Jake said.

"'Tis," Tim replied.

Jake gave his remaining rations to Tim for safekeeping and got to his feet. It was time to take the day's dead to shore. He made his way to the gratings, where several others had already assembled. Comstock had come and gone, sewing the sorry thin shroud around his friend's corpse. It had never ceased to amaze Jake how men would part with their one ragged blanket to keep a friend from being buried without a shroud.

Bell stood awkward and unsure, shifting his weight from one foot to the other. "Go," Jake said, waving him off. "We've enough men for this. Meet us at the boats."

Bell quickly complied, and right away Knight grumbled, "Why did you send him away, Mal? He's strong and healthy— better equipped than most of us for this heavy work."

"Newson was his friend," Jake said. "Let him be. Do you not recall your first time?"

No one answered. Jake lifted one end of Newson, Knight the other.

At the larboard gangway, they trundled the bodies down and onto the waiting boats. To show his gratitude, Bell applied himself strenuously to the oars.

They disembarked at a low wharf on the Brooklyn shore. Jake relished the feel of warm sand beneath his bare feet. Warm sand, firm earth . . . he always felt unsteady and a little giddy, stepping on dry land after being so long on that ship to nowhere.

And he always noticed the colors. On the *Bonhomme*, everything was gray and brown, muddy and dirty. The only patches of color were in the blue sky and the guards' red coats. But on shore, there were vibrant greens and silvery sands, little yellow wildflowers, red-winged starlings, and the bright pink roses that always reminded him of Hannah.

Fish and Eels had taught Jake and Tim to fill their pockets with the wild roses' berrylike fruit whenever they had the chance. The firm, tart hips stayed on the bushes until late in the fall, and the men stored them like apples in winter. Those who managed to lay in a supply avoided the hideous scurvy, which caused the gums to swell and bleed, the skin and hair to dry out, and such pain in the knees that young men walked as if they were grandfathers.

Jake thought often of how he would tease Hannah when he got home: *Every time I saw wild roses, I thought of you—and scurvy.*

He pushed his feet repeatedly under the sand as he crossed the beach to the hut that held shovels and wheelbarrows. The prisoners placed the corpses in barrows, and then the morbid procession of bodies and barrows, guards and gravediggers, started toward the sandy bank that served as a cemetery.

On the way, they passed the white stucco house of the miller Remsen. Jake snapped his head around quickly, and sure enough: the face, a girl's, drew away from the blue-shuttered window, the curtain slid back into place. Jake smiled. It was a little game he played when he was in the burial party—trying to catch her peeking from that window.

From his first days on the *Bonhomme* he had heard about Remsen's daughter. It was said that even though her family were Tories, she had sympathy for the Patriot prisoners and was keeping count of the bodies buried on shore. The story was told that she had once come out to bring the working party fresh bread, but the guards had warned her away, and then her father had stormed out of the house and pulled her back indoors.

As the group approached the sandy bank, the stench of death grew ever stronger. Jake had become so accustomed to it, he generally did not even smell it; today, though, his senses were heightened due to Bell's presence. He also noticed a sight to which he had grown jaded: decaying arms, feet, and elbows sticking out of the sand.

"There, Rebels!" One of the guards pointed out a fresh stretch of sand, then all the others encircled the burial crew, keeping their distance but standing with muskets at the ready.

Bell stood, staring at a hand that reached up from the ground, as if seeking help.

Jake put a shovel into Bell's hand and said, "Dig."

"Oh God," Bell muttered. "What is that?"

"Exactly what it appears to be. Dig, please."

"I can't do it."

"Bell, do you believe in God?"

"Of course."

"Then you believe their souls are with Him now?"

"Yes."

"'Dust thou art and unto dust shalt thou return.' Keep that in mind always." For emphasis, he thrust his own shovel into the sand and repeated: "Dig."

Bell obeyed, and Jake set to work. But he could not help thinking of his own first burial day: the horror, the anger, the desperation—and afterward, the numbing rum.

The sound of retching brought him back to the present; he turned to see Bell on hands and knees, puking his morning rations into the sand.

"You're going to regret that, man," Jake said.

"This is inhuman; this is madness." Bell's voice was high and desperate.

"Get up, Bell."

204 * PAT RACCIO HUGHES

"Look at them." Bell nodded toward their captors. "The bastards, they don't want to see, they won't even come close."

"Uh, they will if we don't get back to work."

Hilliard approached and said firmly, "Now, son, I know it is your first time, but you've got to toughen up. If you don't get back to work, those damned guards will be all over us."

"Yes, sir," Bell said right away, struggling to his feet.

"I wish *I* were an officer," Jake said, and Bell managed a smile.

After a while, a guard ambled over and said crisply, "That is enough, Rebels. Put them in."

Without a word, the party obeyed, then covered the corpses with sand.

"Enough," the guard said again. "March." He led them away, and the prisoners fell in, surrounded by guards who continued to keep a distance.

As they left the burial site, Jake was greedy for fresh air. He breathed so fast and so deep, he felt light-headed. A peculiar sound came from behind him. The wind in the reeds? No, a sort of steady whine . . . It was Bell.

"Stop," Jake said over his shoulder.

"I cannot."

"*Stop.*"

"Newson was like a father to me," Bell blubbered. "To see him discarded as though—"

Jake caught hold of his arm with a lobster grip. "You do *not* let them see you weep," he whispered, shaking Bell angrily. "*Ever.* Understand?"

Bell nodded. He quickly brushed his hand across his eyes, gulped, snuffled, and walked on.

"Here." Jake elbowed him. "See that patch of grass?"

"Yes."

"When we get to it, do as I do."

"All right."

Without breaking stride, Jake bent down and pulled up a chunk of emerald grass. "Did you get one?" he asked Bell a moment later.

"Yes."

"Keep it in your pocket. Tonight, take it out and hold it to your nose. It will help you sleep." He inhaled deeply of his bit of earth, then slid it into his pocket. Another lesson from Fish and Eels, when they had taken him and Tim on their first burial party. *A little piece of home*, Eels had said. *It will give you immeasurable comfort.* At first Jake had been skeptical, but he had quickly learned how sweet indeed it was to smell dirt and grass all night instead of death and disease, to have a bit of solid ground to hold on to. He had kept his swatch until it had disintegrated and had never since returned from shore without one.

Again passing the miller's house, Jake spotted the fleeting face in the window, an orchid flash of gown. Did she recognize him, after all these times? He used to imagine being able to slip her a note with his and Tim's names on it, asking her to somehow contact their families . . . but that fantasy had ended long ago.

Back at the hut, the prisoners returned the burial instruments, then attempted to loiter on the beach. But the guards barked, "Don't tarry, Rebels! To the boats! To the boats!"

Rowing side by side with Bell, Jake fixed his eyes on the disappearing colors. "Are you all right?" he asked Bell.

"I don't think I can bear it," was the somber reply.

"Yes, you can," Jake said. "You will."

THE *BONHOMME* HAD a regular crew of officers and seamen, but also a guard of about thirty soldiers, composed of regiments stationed at Brooklyn. Three groups took turns of a week at a time: British, Hessians, and the green-coated Loyalist Refugees. The Hessians generally were the kindest, probably because they had nothing at stake in this war. One young Hessian had told Jake and Tim in broken English that he and many of his friends were not in it by choice; they'd been conscripted, even kidnapped, by their own government, which didn't let them keep the bounties paid by the British. When it was Hessians in charge of the burial party, they often let the prisoners stay at the landing place for thirty minutes or more, even allowing them to bathe. Hessian guards sometimes smuggled contraband to prisoners: candles, tobacco, tea.

Most of the British guards were cold and unsympathetic, but the prisoners expected nothing else. They were two sides at war; they were supposed to hate each other. Besides, some of them were tolerable, and had even been known to relax a rule now and again.

It was especially galling to the Patriots when the despised

Refugees were placed in authority over them, for the Refugees were aggressively cruel. With humiliation and taunts, they missed no opportunity to lord their elevated status over their former countrymen and subjected them to the lash over the slightest infraction. It was Refugees who whipped Jake and Tim for pilfering rotten bread.

So it did not bode well when, late on the morning of the 4th, green coats arrived to take the place of the British guards.

While the prisoners were still grumbling over that development, someone called out, "Fresh meat!" It meant that new prisoners were coming aboard, escorted by the ghoul Sproat. Scores of men rushed to the railing, calling out the usual greetings, but Jake had long since grown weary of the sight of apprehensive captives making their slow way up the larboard gangway.

Besides, he hated new arrivals. Surviving here day to day, with no mirror to enlighten him, he could delude himself into thinking he looked the same as when he was captured: hale, handsome, and vibrant. But in the pitying, horrified faces of new prisoners, he had to confront the grim reality.

"Roll call!" the commander's adjutant shouted from the barricade door. "Assemble for roll call, Rebels!"

When roll call was announced, prisoners were required to stand at something resembling attention. As each man was called, he stepped forward to be recognized, repeating his name. A mark was made in the registry, and he was told to "pass," or return among his comrades.

By now, Jake's and Tim's names were high atop the registry;

they made their way forward, where Sproat was standing with Captain Larson, the *Bonhomme*'s short, fat commander, called Lardarse by his prisoners.

"Mallery," Jake said.

"Pass," said the adjutant.

"Morris."

"Pass."

"You two? Yet alive?" Sproat asked jovially. It was not the first time Sproat had reacquainted himself with them, generally calling them "the boys from the ferry." He seemed to think their situation was a wonderful joke. "Have the pair of you signed a contract with the devil?"

Before Jake could think of a response, Tim said with mock innocence: "Us, sir? I thought I saw *your* name at the bottom of Lucifer's parchment."

Sproat's face curdled, and Jake and all other prisoners in the vicinity ducked their heads to laugh. As Jake and Tim moved toward the back of the group—their preferred spot for Lardarse's speeches—Tim's witticism preceded them, and each man gave him a pat on the back or a word of approval. Jake was always proud of Tim's dignified defiance, but never more than at times like this. While Jake in a similar situation would have preened and crowed, Tim simply smiled with compressed lips and gave a slight nod to each compliment.

"Quiet, Rebels!" the commander's mates bellowed. "Be seated and let us have quiet, your commander is about to speak!"

"Here we go," Jake muttered to Tim, rolling his eyes.

Lanphier, a relative newcomer and self-styled renegade, came to sit beside Jake.

"Refugees to guard us on the Fourth!" he muttered. "It is intolerable."

"Intolerable?" Jake laughed bitterly, shaking his head. "You haven't been here long enough to know the meaning of the word."

"Silence, Jonathan!" a guard called to them from his position at the ship's rail.

As the talking and mumbling died down, Lardarse paced pompously before the prisoners and began the familiar harangue: "Just look at the pathetic lot of you." He surveyed them as if repulsed by the sight. "Mere skeletons, barely clothed, living here like animals, dying by degrees . . . and for what? For whom? Does anyone care for you, attempt to secure your release? I guarantee the answer is no. Washington will not trade you for Regulars or Hessians. He says that would give advantage to the enemy, for you are mostly private sailors. Congress says you are not *their* responsibility. Meanwhile, you all rot away, stubbornly sticking to your so-called cause whilst your countrymen abandon it." He paused for dramatic effect. "I repeat: they abandon it. Now, segregated as you are, you certainly have no way of knowing about the Continental mutiny. So allow me to enlighten you."

Jake did not so much as blink, and he sensed that Tim, beside him, also remained still as an Indian. But all around them, prisoners muttered disbelief to one another.

"You doubt me, Rebels? But it is true! . . . And lest you believe yourselves to be the only hungry Patriots, consider the plight of the Continental soldiers: starving to death because your local farmers will not provide them with food. Freedom? Liberty? No, your farmers care only for their pocketbooks. And your General Washington? So sympathetic was he to the plight of his troops, he hanged two of the starving ringleaders."

Now the buzzing of the captives reached a crescendo, and Jake wished they would keep quiet and stop granting Lardarse the satisfaction he was seeking.

The commander pitched his voice above theirs to continue: "I am not finished, Rebels! Not finished giving you all the war news! We have succeeded in our goal of capturing your port of Charleston in South Carolina. Patriot losses: fifty-four hundred men and four ships. 'Tis your worst defeat of the war . . . thus far. And as your pathetic rebellion falls apart, you diseased fools forfeit your wretched lives every day in unspeakable misery." He gestured at the green coats. "Look at your countrymen, do they look as though they are starving? Join these loyal Americans, Jonathan! You will be whisked off this hulk right now, today, provided with hearty fare, clothed, allowed to rest in the shade on solid ground. Why suffer longer when you could be living in comfort and esteem in the service of your good king, who would welcome you back with open arms? Now, who will come forward to accept this generous offer?"

Not a man moved or made a sound.

"You are fools, the lot of you! You will die here, you know that! No one is looking for you, no one cares. . . ."

Jake stopped listening. He had heard this tirade dozens of

times; never had he seen a single prisoner capitulate. Most men, he knew, felt as he and Tim did: to stand up and walk off the *Bonhomme* in shame, before all your fellow prisoners, would be worse than death.

When Lardarse stopped talking, the prisoners got to their feet and the ruddy newcomers were sent among them.

"Who is from New Jersey?"

"What news have you?"

"Any Philadelphia men?"

And this time, a new question: "They said there's been mutiny—is it true?"

"'Tis. Connecticut troops led an insurrection in New Jersey because they've been starving."

Connecticut troops? In a mutiny? Jake and Tim looked at each other, then moved closer to listen.

"The farmers care only for their own pockets," the man continued. "They try to sell the soldiers food, but the soldiers have no money."

"Then they were not lying."

"No."

"Levi?" Tim had taken one of the ruddy newcomers by the arm.

"Yes?" The young man looked puzzled—and repulsed by Tim's touch.

Tim released him and pressed his hand to his own chest. "Tim," he said.

Still Levi stared. "I'm sorry?"

"Tim Morris. From East Haven."

"Tim?" the newcomer repeated, suspicious, skeptical.

"Yes."

Whoever this Levi was, Jake hated him for not recognizing Tim, for shirking his touch. *You'll soon see*, he thought. *You'll either be dead, or you will see.*

"Oh! You're alive!" Levi said. "I'm sorry . . . I . . . I didn't know you, Tim."

"That's all right; I am much altered, I know. How did you end up here?"

"I went out on the crew of a privateer, the *Prudence*," Levi said. "We were captured a few days ago."

"Levi, this is my friend Mal. Have you ever met?"

"I think not," Jake said.

Levi held out his hand; Jake refused it, holding up both palms in front of him, taking a step back.

"Mal!" Tim scolded.

"I don't want to contaminate you," Jake said pointedly, looking Levi in the face. "But I will say that I'm sorry to make your acquaintance, as it results from your grievous misfortune."

Levi gave a gracious nod.

"You'll mess with us, Levi," Tim said. "Mal and I will help you with everything."

Jake wasn't ready to be so generous; hadn't this outlander better prove himself worthy? "Tim, we should check with our messmates first," he said. "Perhaps they have other ideas."

"Of course," Tim agreed, but he looked askance at Jake. "Of

course, we must ask the others. . . . But tell me, Levi. Can you give me any news of my family? Have you seen my mother?"

Straightaway, Jake's heart began to pound. His family! Of course, that was how Tim knew Levi. And if Levi could provide news of Tim's family, maybe he could also provide news of Hannah!

"I did see your mother, a number of months ago. She came to Branford to visit with mine."

"Uh . . . how do you two know each other?" Jake ventured.

"Our mothers were childhood companions," Tim told him; then, to Levi: "Was she well? And my father?"

"Hannah," Jake said under his breath.

"All seemed well," Levi said. "At least, your mother was not in mourning . . . except for you, of course."

"Do they think I'm dead? Do they know I am here?"

"They believed you'd been taken prisoner; that is all."

Jake nudged Tim. *"Hannah,"* he repeated.

"Oh! Yes!" Tim looked at Jake, as though surprised he had forgotten. He turned back to Levi and explained, "Hannah . . . our indentured girl. I'm certain you don't know her, but possibly mother mentioned her in some way?"

"Indentured girl?" Levi seemed puzzled as to why Tim would be inquiring after a servant; Jake hated him anew.

"Hannah is more a sister than a servant," Tim said. "She and Mal and I grew up together."

"Oh. Well, there *was* something. After your mother left, my mother told our girl that the Morrises' girl had left the family and now Mrs. Morris had no help in the kitchen. Would that be the girl?"

"We have no other kitchen help," Tim said, his voice much lower. "Hannah is the one."

"Left." Jake felt light-headed, nauseated. "Where would she go?"

"Levi, can you recall anything more?" Tim asked.

"My mother was speaking to our girl as though in warning," Levi said. "I was trying to listen at the door. I had the impression of something improper, that perhaps she had run off with a man."

"Noah!" Jake blurted. He slapped the back of one hand against the palm of the other. "Damn!"

"You don't know that, Mal," Tim said quietly.

"Who else would it be? Noah returns, all prinked out in his Continental uniform, and she'd have long forgotten about me!"

"Mal . . ."

"Damn him! Damn them both!" He stalked off and found a spot where he could be alone, leaning over the ship's rail and staring down at the brackish bay.

The Morrises' girl had left the family. . . . We have no other kitchen help, Hannah is the one. With the words echoing in his head, Jake's thoughts raced over the day before the battle, when he and Hannah had met in the reeds. . . .

"Mal." Tim had come to stand beside him, and rested a hand on his shoulder. "Things might not be as they seem. Levi said only that it was his *impression*."

Jake made a sound of derision. "And he pulled that impression from the north wind?"

Tim didn't reply.

"Think of it, Timo. No news of us in ages . . . then Noah returns, free of his bonds, just as her indenture is up. Noah, who never called her names or treated her with contempt."

"But those days were past. When you two stood together and told me, in our kitchen . . . it was clear how you felt about each other."

"Yes. But do you know what she said just the day before?"

Tim shook his head.

"She said sometimes she was certain I was playing a cruel joke on her. She said she would ask herself how a boy who hated her so much could now claim to love her."

"Oh," Tim said, his voice low. Then, after a silence: "I *am* sorry, Mal."

But Jake didn't care to be an object of pity. Shaking Tim off, he warned, "Do *not* patronize me."

"That's not my intent."

"When did he hear this, anyhow?" Jake asked irritably. "Does he say?"

"He's not certain."

"Well, when did he go out with the *Prudence*? Is he certain about that?"

"'Tis not his fault, Mal. We asked him."

"Oh, damn it, Tim, just let me be, would you?" Jake moved farther down the rail, and Tim did not follow.

Desperation weighted him like an anchor. Hannah was all he had been living for, his *When I get home* . . . Now he was ruined, completely undone. He ought to just fling himself over the railing and end this misery. *Do it*, he told himself: *If you throw one leg over, pride will force the other to follow. Then they will shoot you, and it will finally be done.*

But he could not bring himself to it. If he allowed the enemy to kill him, for whatever reason, they would be the victors. He reached into his pocket and withdrew the worn shreds of Hannah's letter—and tossed them overboard instead. They flew about like moths before landing in the murky water.

"Mal." It was Lanphier, whispering at his ear.

"What?" Jake snapped.

"We are going to celebrate the Fourth with liberty songs. Are you with us?" Jake slowly turned his head; Lanphier flashed a wicked grin. "It will drive the damned Refugees mad. Will you sing?"

Jake's reply was a grim smile.

"Stay where you are for now," Lanphier said. "On signal, we'll start with 'God Save Our States.'"

Perfect way to nettle the cork-brained Refugee guards on the 4th of July—singing a Patriot song to the tune of "God Save the King"! On an ordinary day, Jake would have been the one to come up with an idea of this sort. But today was no ordinary day.

As prisoners all over the spar deck began to sing, he joined in:

> *"God save the thirteen states,*
> *Long rule the United States,*
> *God save our states!*
> *Make us victorious*

Happy and glorious,
No tyrants over us,
God save our states!"

Happy and glorious, Jake thought. *There is a joke on me. No matter what happens on this ship, in this war,* I *will never be happy.*

More prisoners joined in as the singing grew louder with the second verse:

"O, Lord, thy gifts in store
We pray on Congress pour
To guide our States.
May union bless our land,
While we, with heart and hand,
Our mutual rights defend
God save our states!"

"All right, Rebels, that is enough of that," one of the Refugees called when the song was finished.

"Yes, we've indulged your silly ditty; now let us have silence," another added.

Surely if she had run off with Noah, they were married by now. Think of Hannah—so concerned about what was proper, what was lawful—running off without getting married! Had she confessed to Noah what she had done with Jake? The idea of her with Noah that way was enough to drive him mad. *'Tis of a young apprentice who went to court his dear* . . . Yes, it was just such antics that had driven her back to him. He could easily picture Noah returning and learning of their attachment: *Hannah, you must be joking. That blackguard? He does not love you, he could never love you! Don't you remember the way he spoke to you, and that profane song of his?* . . . Jake squeezed his eyes shut and turned his attention back to the singing.

His fellow captives were on to "Independence Song." Perhaps if he sang even louder, he could drown out the sound of his own thoughts:

> *"George of Great Britain, no more shall he reign.*
> *With unlimited sway o'er these free states again*
> *On Heaven alone dependent we'll be*
> *But from all earthly tyrants we mean to be free!"*

"Leave off, Mal." Fortnum came up beside him and laid a hand on his shoulder. "Tim says you had a bad shock—"

Jake shrugged him off.

"—but aggravating the Refugees is not the way to—"

"Let me be, Fortnum!" Jake snapped. "I've been on this goddamned tub a lot longer than you have. I know how to take care of myself!"

Fortnum opened his mouth to reply, changed his mind, and walked away.

"Now let us have 'Invitation to the Refugees'!" Lanphier called.

"Come, gentlemen Tories, firm, loyal, and true,
Here are axes and shovels, and something to do!
For the sake of our king,
Come labor and sing.
You left all you had for his honor and glory,
And he will remember the suffering Tory—"

All at once there was great scuffling as the guards formed up in a line, leveling their muskets and advancing on the prisoners. "Down, Rebels, down!" came the order.

The prisoners left off singing and began to protest:

"What?"

"There are yet hours of daylight!"

"Frightened of a few little songs, are you?"

"This is your warning, Jonathan!" came the reply. "Get below!"

Jake looked up at the barricade; muskets poked through every loophole.

"Oh, see how brave they are!"

"Ready to fire on unarmed men!"

"Refugee swine!"

"Damned whoresons!"

Jake was among those at the front, where the space between guard and guarded was rapidly diminishing. The Refugees shouted above the insults, "Get below, Rebels! Below! Now! . . . Down, Jonathan! Down! . . . At once! You are warned!"

Many prisoners obeyed, but those in the front ranks were

unwilling to comply. They stood their ground, pouring curses on the Refugees until the ominous crack of a warning shot was heard, and Jake looked up to see a smoking musket pointed in the air.

With prisoners and guards shouting and pushing and chaos threatening, the Refugees drove them back at bayonet point until they descended between decks, and the gratings clanged shut behind the last man.

The obedient prisoners reproached the defiant ones:

"Now see what you've done!"

"Gone and had us shut up in this hole hours before usual!"

"You cannot best them, don't you know that yet?"

"There are different ways of besting them," Jake replied.

Tim was standing behind him, looking grave. "Mal . . . stop this," he said with quiet firmness.

Jake ignored him and shouted, "Come lads!" Climbing the ladder, he began to chant: "United American States! United American States!" He banged rhythmically on the hatchway door. "United American States! United American States!"

"United American States!" Lanphier and the other insurgents crowded around Jake at the bottom of the ladder. "United American States!" As more and more joined in, the chant swelled to a roar. Jake had never heard so much noise between decks; the very timbers of the hulk seemed to vibrate with the sound. A feeling welled up in his throat: excitement, anticipation . . . pride.

Now Tim was on the ladder behind him, tugging at his sleeve, shouting over the din, "Come away, Mal. Stop this!"

Jake shook him off. "Let me be."

"They will not tolerate much more!"

"Get away from me, Tim!"

"United American States! United American States!"

All at once the hatch was flung open, and in a blinding box of light the Refugees descended, howling like wild animals, swinging cutlasses and wielding bayonets. Jake tumbled backward, hitting his head on the deck. The Refugees' livid curses and insults mingled with the prisoners' screams of pain. All was chaos, with men falling, flailing, and as Jake tried to scramble to his feet, he was knocked down again and several more trampled him, grinding his face into the filthy deck.

With no hope of regaining his footing, he tried to protect his head with his arms as the multitude swarmed around and over him, and he managed to crawl away from the fray just as the guards halted their attack, backed up to the hatchway, and ascended.

"Now have you had enough, you damned Rebels?" one of the Refugees yelled down. "If not, you are welcome to continue your frolic!" He slammed the gratings with a crash and threw the bolt back into place, plunging the prisoners into darkness.

Jake realized that somehow, he had avoided being cut. But his face was slick with liquid; what could it be but blood? "Tim!" he shouted. "Where are you?" He staggered blindly, tripping over the moaning, cursing throng. "Tim!"

"Mal! Over here! Hurry!" It was Fortnum, his voice filled with horror.

"No," Jake mumbled, turning all around. "No . . . Tim!"

"He's hurt! Over here, Mal!"

"Where? I can't see!"

Someone grabbed Jake by the arm and pulled him toward the air holes, which drew in the daylight. First he saw Fortnum, sitting on the deck, his countenance stricken; next he saw the most dreadful sight of his life: Tim, slumped against Fortnum, covered with blood, the bones of his head and face laid bare by the cutlass. Jake could discern the curved shape of the steel blade, from the bottom of Tim's chin to the top of his skull.

"Oh, God." Jake dropped to his knees, cupping the uninjured side of Tim's face in his hand. "Oh, God, no."

"Is it bad, Mal?" Tim closed his eyes and swallowed hard. "It *feels* bad."

"There's a lot of blood, but I think . . . it's just on the surface," Jake said. "You know how it is, when one's head is cut, there's always a great deal of blood. Remember? When Fish stitched up my head?"

Tim managed a grin. "Mal, you never *were* much good at lying."

A sob caught in Jake's throat. . . . Why hadn't he come away from the hatchway? Why hadn't Tim listened and left him alone? "Start over," he mumbled, shutting his eyes, rocking back and forth. "Do it over, do it over . . . start again. Please, God. Start again."

"Is there any water?" Tim asked.

"I'll find some," Fortnum said quickly. "Here, Mal—you hold him."

When Jake slid down to the deck to take Fortnum's place, he saw Levi standing over them, looking aghast—Levi, the cause of it all. "Get away," Jake said. "Please, just get away from us."

"Come." Bell was there, too. He took Levi by the arm. "Help me collect some water."

"Cutlass," Tim mumbled. "Why is it called a cut-*lass* when it's generally used to cut *lads*?"

"Shhh, save your breath." Meecham was beside them, kneeling on the deck.

"I am so thirsty," Tim repeated.

"Water!" Jake yelled wildly. "Has no one any water?"

Silently, the offers came: scant rations of hoarded water, a cup for Tim to drink from, a ragged neckcloth to wipe the blood, folded blankets for pillows.

Meecham wetted the neckcloth and began to dab at Tim's wounds.

"Meech! Don't!" Tim screamed.

"Leave him alone!" Jake shouted, lashing out at Meecham. "Don't touch him!"

Tim kicked out in agony, writhing.

"Someone help him!" Jake screamed wildly. "Goddamn you Refugee bastards, you did this! He is dying! Help him!"

Meecham touched his arm, saying in a low, firm tone: "Stop it, Mal—you're frightening him."

"It's all right, Meech." Tim was breathing fast, as though he'd just run a race. "I know I'm dying. . . ."

"No," Jake moaned. "No, no, this is not happening . . . this is my fault. . . ."

"You are not to blame," Tim said.

"Of course I am. You told me to come away, I didn't listen. . . ."

Tim tried to raise himself up, his eyes widening as he said with agitation, "Please, Mal—don't blame yourself."

"This is not the time, Mal," Meecham whispered. "Let him go in peace."

"Never mind, Tim." Jake soothed him back down. His wounds were gruesome in the extreme, but Jake forced himself to look. It seemed only fair. What could he do to help Tim, to comfort him? His mind raced. . . . "Rum," he muttered. He was owed a pint but had been driven below before the hour at which the steward generally paid up. Still, he knew others often hoarded their rations. "Rum!" he shouted. "Who has rum?"

There was a lot of mumbling, but no one came forward. Jake knew what they were thinking: why waste rum on a dying man? He knew because, God help him, he had at times harbored the same sentiment. His ration of rum often seemed the only thing between himself and madness. The reluctance was not surprising, but it enraged him nonetheless.

"Morris has been on this hellhole for a solid year!" he screamed. "Will no man honor that?"

"Mal," Tim said. "Mal . . . don't worry."

Now Meecham got to his feet. "We will have rum for Morris!" he called, his voice cracking. "I'll kill any man who holds out!"

One by one, the men came: "He can have this."

"It isn't much, but he's welcome to it."

"Here is some."

"Give him mine."

Jake held a cup to his lips, and Tim drank gratefully. "That's good," he said. "More."

Jake fed him a prodigious amount of rum until at last Tim slumped back against him, looking decidedly languid. Jake felt giddy with relief. For sure, he thought, Tim would now be at peace. . . .

Then he remembered the bit of earth in his pocket. Shifting his burden, he withdrew it carefully. "Here, Tim, look what I got today on the working party." He held the tuft under Tim's nose.

"Thanks, Mal. Put it in my hand, I want to hold it."

Jake complied.

Tim held the little patch of earth on his chest, working it between his fingers. "I'm in no pain now, you know."

"You oughtn't to be," Jake said with forced cheer. "You had more rum than I've ever drunk of an evening in my life."

"Enough to kill a mere mortal, then," Tim struggled to say, and Jake laughed for him.

Tim closed his eyes. *This is where it ends*, Jake thought. Tim would fall asleep, his life would ebb with the loss of blood, and he would pass quietly to the other side. . . .

And for a while, Tim did sleep. But he woke screaming in agony, then descended into a terrified delirium in which his worst fear became real.

"Help me, Mal! I'm drowning!" He flailed about, as if in the water, reaching up.

"I'm right here," Jake said, grasping his hand. "You are not drowning."

But Tim pulled away, gasping and thrashing. "Stop fooling, Mal!" he shouted. "Pull me in!"

"Tim, you're not in the water! You're on the *Bonhomme*!"

"Mal, stop it! I can't swim! Help me!"

Jake turned to his messmates in despair. "What can I do? What should I say?"

"Tell him what he wants to hear," Fortnum whispered.

Jake put himself two years back, paddling the dugout beside Tim. "I won't let you drown, Tim, I swear it," he said. "I'm right here. Only grab on to the dugout, I won't let you drown. You can do it, Tim, I know you can. . . ."

The words seemed to calm him; his breaths grew more shallow and regular until he fell into a restless unconsciousness. Jake's chest ached so much that he felt, truly, his heart would break.

Then came the cry from the spar deck: "All is well!"

"All is well!"

It was the final straw; Jake could bear no more. "All is well?" he screamed. "All is well, you goddamned Refugee bastards?"

Among his fellow prisoners, a profound silence fell.

"You bastards, do you think you are men because you slaughter helpless prisoners with your damned cutlasses? This is Jake Mallery and I say you'd better not ever let me off this damned ship, because I swear I'll kill every last Refugee coward I see!"

"Mal . . . enough!" Meecham whispered fiercely. "They will have their revenge on you!"

"What more can they do to me, Meech? What more?" Jake said, and he succumbed, at last, to defeated weeping.

He did not care who heard him, who saw him, or what anyone thought of him.

Meecham and Fortnum and Stark tried to comfort him, but he pushed them angrily away. No one else dared approach.

Jake could not believe that Tim's life was ending, and in such a manner, in filth and pain, darkness and despair. He thought of Tim taking his stand on the ferry, holding two muskets and saying, *I choose death over subjugation.* But Jake had not allowed him to have that noble death; he'd thought it was so important to stay alive. Now, after a year of fighting together every day for survival, buoying each other up through illness and despair, he would have to carve Tim's name into the sheathing with all the others. He had refused to let Tim die on a hero's terms, but instead killed Tim himself for a few liberty songs, for the satisfaction of a little defiance . . . all because of Hannah. And he hated her, now, because of what he had done to Tim. Because he had killed his best friend in the world for the love of one faithless girl.

His mother's words came back to him with a vengeance: *You must not be so impetuous. Learn to be less selfish. To consider others.* And Mother said, *Own your fault, Jacob.* Yes, he would own his fault. Tim was dying, and it was his fault.

Despite everything he'd been through in the past year, he had learned nothing.

At last he could weep no more. His chest heaved with each subsiding sob, and for a long, long time, he sat and stared at nothing, feeling vacant, obliterated. The smell of blood was so strong he could taste it—rusted metal in his mouth. His clothes, soaked with blood, stuck to his skin. Tim's breaths were slow and shallow now; Jake heard the rattle that meant the end was near.

But to his surprise, Tim tipped his head back, opened his eyes, looked directly into Jake's, and said clearly, "Don't tell my mother."

Don't tell her what? Jake thought. *That you died? That I killed you? That you spent your last hours in unspeakable horror, slowly bleeding to death while your inhuman captors crowed that all was well?*

"I won't, Timo," he only replied. "I won't."

Tim smiled the way he often did at Jake, a smile somewhere between amused and bemused. He reached up, touched Jake's face with trembling fingers, and said, "*Bon homme*." Then he shut his eyes and breathed his last.

AT SUNRISE, THE guards called, "Rebels! Throw out your dead!"

Jake clutched Tim to his chest, shielding Tim's face from their fellow prisoners. "He is not," he murmured. "He is not, he is not." He repeated the words again and again until his messmates pried his fingers from the corpse.

Patriot

July 4, 1781

"JAKE! ARE YOU sick?"

His mother was calling to him, from the kitchen. Breakfast. The pleasant smell of oyster stew filled the room. He must get up, do his chores. But his bed was so blissfully comfortable. He buried his head beneath the pillow. Just another minute or two, then he would dress and go down. *Don't wake up*, he told himself. *Keep your eyes closed and you'll fall right back to sleep.*

"Jake!"

Jake? No, not his mother. Oyster stew in summer? Not his bed, not his room. *Don't wake up. . . .* But now he heard them talking just below.

"He must be sick," Mrs. Pickett murmured. "Go and see what ails him."

"He is only weary," Mr. Pickett replied. "Let him sleep a while longer."

"But what if he is sick again?"

"I'm all right," Jake called sleepily. "I'll be down in a minute."

There was no answer but the sound of chairs scraping the floor as the Picketts took their places at the table.

Why had they let him sleep so late in haying time? In the loft of the tiny springhouse, his bed was a straw mattress on the plank floor. He had a pillow, a worn sheet, and a tattered quilt. The springhouse roof was sloped tight to his sleeping spot; sometimes, thrashing in a *Bonhomme* nightmare, he banged his head hard on the ceiling. And now that it was summer, the loft was often exceedingly hot, especially in the evening.

But every day upon waking, Jake said a prayer of thanks for this place. To be able to sleep, alone, in cleanliness and silence; to be surrounded by the sounds of wind rustling through trees and birds singing; to have solid ground beneath him; to smell food cooking instead of the sickening stench of the *Bonhomme*—all were extravagant blessings.

Also each morning, he felt anew his guilt and shame that Tim would never again experience these ordinary joys; that he had escaped and was doing nothing for the poor wretches who remained behind; that he was living a lie here on Long Island, taking charity and comfort from the same enemy he had vowed to kill while Tim lay dying in his arms.

Jake rolled over and sat up, slowly, his bones and muscles still achy from the *Bonhomme*'s privations. He put on clothing that did not belong to him: first stockings, then breeches. He tucked the shirt he was wearing into the breeches, buttoned them, tied them at the knees, and slid his feet into battered shoes. He scratched at the constant itch on his face.

Each time he felt the beard stubble on his cheeks, he was surprised by it. For he still thought of himself as the boy who had run headlong into battle two years ago, brash and terrified, defiant and ignorant. War had kidnapped him on that road to Black Rock, and he wasn't sure he would ever be ransomed.

He had spent a solid year on the *Bonhomme* pretending things would eventually be set right—as if he and Tim would be scooped up from that living hell and deposited right back on the ferry, at the point of capture.

But after Tim's death, he had sunk into the most crushing despair, speaking to no one, hating everyone on the ship—and off. He hated Hannah for betraying him. He hated his father for not trying to find him. He hated Ethan for being freed; with Ethan a prisoner, Father would have crossed the River Styx to save them. He hated the dead Regular for carrying a cartridge tin, and the dead Regular's uncle for avenging his death. He hated old Mr. Rowe for the costly lesson on looting the dead. He hated every guard, even the Hessians, but especially the Refugees, and imagined himself finding the one who had killed Tim and subjecting that man to a similarly horrible death. He even hated his fellow captives for witnessing his downfall—and for being kind to him in the face of it.

Most of all, Jake had hated himself. Every night he'd prayed to be among the dead in the morning, and every morning he'd cursed himself for being yet alive—and unable to find the courage to end his own life.

Then came the October afternoon when the British had made their gleeful announcement: General Arnold was a traitor.

Jake didn't believe it, at first. Surely this was just another foolish attempt to coerce the prisoners into renouncing the Patriot cause. But the details sounded all too real. Arnold, then in command of West Point, was deeply in debt, and his pride had been wounded by the earlier accusations against him. He had approached John André, a British captain in Philadelphia, with a plan: Arnold would turn over West Point for the sum of 20,000 pounds. The plan was foiled, and André was caught. . . . But not Arnold.

André was hanged.

Arnold was made a British general.

Arnold a British general! Arnold, the hater of Loyalists, the hero of Saratoga, had turned Judas, selling out for money because he was feeling slighted? It seemed impossible, until new prisoners arrived and confirmed the news. *With leaders like Arnold, the door will finally shut on your pathetic rebellion!* the British crowed. *Your precious Washington, your Jefferson, Franklin, and all the rest will be hanged! May as well save yourselves, boys!*

Some prisoners were so disheartened that they took the oath on the spot, and were heartily congratulated by the British, fed, clothed, and removed from the *Bonhomme*. But the news had had the opposite effect on Jake, serving to rouse him out of his torpor.

After fifteen months of death for breakfast and degradation for supper, he would be damned if he'd go truckling to the British now.

Instead, he decided to escape—even if it meant being killed in the process. Let Arnold live and be despised. Jake might sink to the bottom of the Wallabout Bay, but that was better than joining the British, or letting them continue to kill him by degrees on this rotting hulk.

So he and four others came up with a plan. Beneath the forecastle was a necessary room for the ship's guards that generally remained locked and in disuse. One man was certain he could pick the lock while standing in line for morning rations, then readjust it so that it seemed intact. Late in the afternoon, the five would slip into the necessary and remain there when the orders were given to go below for the night. After dark, when the pacing guard was at the far end of the spar deck, they would sneak out and leap overboard.

On the day of a moonless night, they decided it was time. When word came that the lock had been dealt with, their spirits and confidence soared. Later, they'd crowded into the stinking necessary and stood still as Indians, scarcely daring to breathe, for hours. Just as planned, they'd cascaded over the ship's rail when the guard was at the far end of the deck.

But moments after they hit the frigid water, the alarm bell sounded and the shooting began. *Any moment now*, Jake thought, *I'll be hit, and I'll either die right off, or slowly bleed to death and sink to the bottom of this filthy bay*. Chaos surrounded him—men screaming in pain and shouting in fear, the flash of muskets lighting the night. Jake panicked, and forgot what to do.

Then all at once he heard Tim's voice, excited, encouraging: *Come on, Mal! Swim!* And though it was dark as pitch and the shore so distant, he *saw* Tim, beckoning to him from the rocks.

Underwater, Mal! Tim called. *Swim underwater, and they won't see you!* Jake took a deep breath and submerged himself, as far down as he could go, stretching his arms ahead of him, pushing the water behind with all his focus and concentration, stretch, push, stretch, push. . . .

By the time he reached shore, the shooting had stopped, and all was quiet. He knew he had to continue, but he could only lie on the sand, trying not to gasp for breath. That was when the girl had knelt beside him, whispering, *Come quickly. Come with me.* In his dreamlike state he realized she was Remsen's daughter. *You must get up*, she insisted. *You must come.* She shook him vigorously by his shoulders, refusing his pleas to leave him there. *No, come with me, you must, come now*, she said, tugging at him, as if she would move him herself, and finally he struggled to his knees and began to crawl in the direction upon which she was insisting. *No, stand, on your feet, you must*, she continued in the most peremptory manner until at last he got up, and she with her arms around him helped him into a barn, where she covered him with hay while he shivered violently. *The others?* he asked. And she said, *I've seen no others.* Jake was too sick and exhausted to protest as she efficiently removed his clothes and rubbed him dry with a towel. She then wrapped him in blankets, fed him rum and water, and hid him beneath the hay again. *You're safe*, she said. *Don't move. Sleep. I'll be back in the morning.*

For days the girl had tried to feed him, to strengthen him, but everything kept coming back up, and he had felt so helpless and ashamed to have her cleaning him again and again. One night she had brought him a pair of shoes and said, *You must go, I am afraid for you if I keep you here longer. I shall pray for you.* He thanked her; she said she only wished she could have done more; and they parted, never having asked each other's names.

Jake had walked eastward all night for many nights, desperate to put distance between himself and the Wallabout. Remsen's daughter had told him how to avoid the British garrisons. During the day he hid in woods and ditches, covering himself with brush while he slept. As he pushed himself farther and faster, he grew weaker and sicker. Then the fever came on, and he knew from his strange thoughts and visions that he was tumbling into delirium. Still, he was lucid enough to realize he must stay far from dwellings, so that his shouts and babbling would not be heard. He made his way deep into a field of harvested corn before collapsing, and as he drifted away in the darkness, he thought: *This is where I'll die. But at least I'm on solid ground. At least I am free....*

"Jake!"

Mrs. Pickett's voice brought him back to the present.

"Are you sure you are well?" she asked, weary but gentle, from the bottom of the ladder again.

"Yes, ma'am. Just coming now." Jake made his way down the ladder. "Good morning," he said, taking his seat. Mr. Pickett's shirt was wet with perspiration. "Why did you not wake me, sir?"

"I told Mrs. Pickett you worked enough for two men yesterday."

"That was yesterday," Jake mumbled. "Why should I sleep while you work?"

"You don't seem yourself this morning, Jake. Is everything all right?" Mrs. Pickett spoke with such warmth, he could scarcely bear it.

"Of course." He picked up his spoon and began to eat.

"I don't think he should work today, William," Mrs. Pickett said.

"Perhaps you should go back to bed, Jake," Mr. Pickett agreed.

"I'm fine," Jake said. "I'll do my share."

"You've done more than your share, boy," Mr. Pickett said. "We don't want you getting sick again."

"I'm all *right*." Jake heard the edge in his voice; he lifted his head just in time to see Mr. and Mrs. Pickett giving each other a significant glance. "The stew is very good, ma'am," he said softly. "Thank you."

"Oh, you're welcome, dear," Mrs. Pickett said, reaching over to pat his hand.

But instead of feeling comforted, it only made Jake angry. He quickly finished eating, stood, and nodded to Mr. Pickett. "I'll meet you out there." He took his hat from a peg by the door, and once outside jammed it onto his head. He went to the tool-box, retrieved a scythe, and swung it forcefully before him as he walked to the hay field.

Mr. Pickett should have awakened him earlier. Stupid old man. The whole point of starting at daybreak was that it was easier to cut the grass while the dew was still on. Now the grass was dry, the sun beating down. Old Refugee idiot and his silly wife . . . taking him in, a stranger, having no idea who he was, nursing him back to health anyway and sharing what little they had for these last seven months.

Of his first weeks with the Picketts, Jake had only hazy memories: Mr. Pickett finding him in the field, carrying him over his shoulder, like a sack of grain, into the springhouse. Jake on a pallet before the fire, wrapped in blankets, sure that he was dying. Mrs. Pickett tending to him night and day, spoon-feeding him crackers soaked in wine and sugar water, the only thing he was able to keep down. At last he began to recover, and they began to ask questions. He had spun a tale about being a Tory orphan, pursued by vengeful Patriots. They believed it. Stupid Refugees, how could they be so naive?

In the partially mowed field, Jake began a new row, swinging his scythe more gently now, right to left, leaving broad windrows in his wake. The smell of the fresh-cut grass, the rhythm of the work, the flashing of the scythe in the sun all had a calming effect upon him.

Now Mr. Pickett resumed work in his own row, moving in his slow, stooped way, and seeming, as always, older than his years. Jake paused, removed his hat, and ran his shirtsleeve over his sweating face. Mr. Pickett looked up, gave him a mild smile, and returned to his work.

Jake sighed deeply. He had no reason to be angry with them. Only himself.

He put his hat back on and began mowing again.

Like Jake on the *Bonhomme*, the Picketts rarely spoke of the past, only of what was happening today, what might occur tomorrow. Jake knew but little about their life before the war. They'd had three children, all around Jake's age, and they, too, were from Connecticut, near Danbury. After 1776, they'd had to flee to Long Island. A son and daughter had died of some sort of illness. The other son was with a Loyalist regiment in the South and had not been heard from in more than a year. . . .

Jake and Mr. Pickett had been working for a while when Mr. Landon hailed them, walking from the farmhouse on this land. He and his family were among the dozen or so Refugees who lived there; Mr. Pickett often said he would rather be alone in the tiny springhouse than in the large farmhouse with so many strangers. Everyone on the property farmed the land and shared the barn.

After greetings, Mr. Landon said, "Well, I'm afraid I have some distressing news."

"Oh?" Mr. Pickett asked, frowning.

"The Rebels are going to try to recapture New York."

News? Jake thought ruefully. *More like a figment of Washington's imagination.* For five years now, recapturing New York had been nothing but a Patriot fantasy.

"The Rebels have been recapturing New York ever since it was taken," Mr. Pickett said lightly.

"Yes, but have they ever marched five thousand troops across Connecticut to undertake the job?"

Mr. Pickett's eyes went wide.

His pulse racing, Jake asked, "Where did they get five thousand troops?"

"The damned French. The soldiers are all frogs, under an officer called Rochambeau. He landed at Newport and has just completed his march. I hear Washington plans to join them."

"Where did you hear this, Landon?" Mr. Pickett asked.

"The traders are at the tavern."

Mr. Pickett waved his hand in disgust. "Those lying Rebels will say anything. Tell me no more, Landon. Take no offense, but I must get back to work. Good day." With a curt nod, he returned to his mowing.

"He means nothing by it, sir," Jake stammered.

"Of course not," Mr. Landon said. "I should have known better than to mention them to him. Good day, Jake."

"Good day, sir."

Mr. Landon walked away, and Jake also went back to his task.

The traders crossed the Sound in skiffs and whaleboats, Tory to Rebel and Rebel to Tory, helping one another by exchanging goods. Mr. Pickett thought it was disgraceful and would have no part of it.

When Jake had first learned of the practice, he'd decided that when he was well enough he would to seek out some traders and ask to be taken home. But as he grew stronger, he also grew more comfortable with the Picketts. He felt warm and secure in their care—peaceful, content. And what was there to go home to? Facing a life without Hannah? Having to tell Tim's parents how he had died?

So he had put it off. Just a few more days. Just another week. Maybe next month . . .

"We'll hear their cannon tonight."

Jake looked up. "What?"

Mr. Pickett gestured north. "The Rebels. Today is their damned holiday."

"Yes." Jake suddenly felt very dizzy; he rubbed his forehead. "Yes, I know."

"Son, are you sure you're all right?"

"I'm just . . . I feel a bit . . . off. Maybe if I—"

"Sit," Mr. Pickett said firmly. "I'll get you a drink."

Sitting on the ground would be too hard on his knees—both going down and getting up again. Another reminder of the *Bonhomme*. But if he didn't sit down he would fall down. So he made his way to a tree stump, sat, and leaned forward with elbows on knees, forehead against the heels of his hands.

Mr. Pickett approached with the water jug. When he leaned down to give it to Jake, the scythe was still dangling from his wrist by a cord. Jake's eye caught the flash of metal—but instead of the curve of the scythe, he saw the curve of a cutlass.

"No!" he shouted, throwing his arms up to guard his face. He fell backward off the stump and found himself cowering on the ground; then, realizing with horror what he had done, he struggled to his feet.

"What is it, son?" Mr. Pickett asked, patting his shoulder.

"Nothing, nothing . . . I'm sorry . . . I . . ."

"Here. Drink this."

The words put Jake in mind of old Mr. Rowe on the day of the battle, offering his canteen of rum and water. And as he drank he felt so dispirited, so heavy at heart, that his head dropped, and a deep intake of breath escaped him with a sound like a sigh or a sob.

"You are going back to the springhouse," Mr. Pickett said firmly. "You need to lie down for a spell."

"But it might rain this afternoon," Jake protested. "We must get the hay in."

"Your health is more important. Come." Mr. Pickett took him by the arm, and Jake allowed himself to be led toward the springhouse.

When Mrs. Pickett saw them coming she left off weeding her garden and rushed toward them, calling, "Is he all right? Jake, are you ill?"

"I'm fine," Jake said. "It's nothing."

Lying Rebels . . .

"Go up and rest for a while," Mr. Pickett said, leading him indoors.

"No, I . . . I want to speak with you. I have something to say."

Mrs. Pickett patted his back. "It can wait until later."

Today is their damned holiday. . . . He had to tell them. It was time.

"No, it can wait no longer. Please. Sit down." He took his own place at the table, and they did the same without a word. Their worried looks made him feel ashamed. How could he have deceived these good people for seven long months? He looked down at the table and began, haltingly. "I am . . . I have . . . I am not"—he shook his head—"not who you think. I *do* have a home, and a family, just across the Sound. I am . . . I am—"

"Rebel." Mr. Pickett spat out the hated word.

Jake raised his head quickly and met Mr. Pickett's gaze. "Patriot."

"Traitor!" the man shouted.

"American!" Jake returned, just as loud.

Mr. Pickett slammed his fist on the table. "Damn you! How dare you! Am I not American? Is Mrs. Pickett not American?" He stood and leaned forward, narrowing his eyes. "You come to our place of refuge—partake of our generosity—passing yourself off as one of us when you are nothing but a damned *Rebel*?"

Jake felt himself trembling with anger as he stared back at Mr. Pickett.

"Who are you?" Mr. Pickett demanded. "Why are you here?"

Mrs. Pickett took her husband's arm and said quietly, "He is a boy who needed our help. That is all."

Mr. Pickett sat, then repeated his question: "Who . . . are . . . you?"

"I am Jake Mallery. From East Haven. My father is Isaac. He was in the Rebellion from the start. He is in the Sons of Liberty, he—"

"Sons of violence," Mr. Pickett interrupted.

Jake took a measured breath, then went on: "I was in the militia when the British raided New Haven. I fought in the battle, two years ago tomorrow. I was captured with my friend, Tim Morris. They called us maritime prisoners, because we were defending my father's ferry. They put us on a prison ship, the *Bonhomme*, in Wallabout Bay."

The sympathy in Mrs. Pickett's sharp gasp gave Jake the courage to lift his eyes to hers. But when he saw the tears streaming down her cheeks, he quickly ducked his head again.

"I was a prisoner for one year, three months, and twenty-six days. On the second of November, I escaped . . . swam to shore. I was helped by someone who found me. This person concealed me until it was no longer safe, then sent me away. I traveled by night and hid by day, living on the food people put out for their animals. I kept walking east . . . thinking I'd be able to get across the Sound, somehow, and reach home. But then I got sick . . . and you found me"—he nodded toward Mr. Pickett—"and brought me here. I told you I was a Tory so that I would be safe amongst you."

"Among your enemy," Mr. Pickett said.

"Yes, sir," Jake admitted. "I thought I would continue on, when I regained my strength. Disappear one day, and never have to tell you the truth. But I grew so fond of you both." He looked up briefly at Mrs. Pickett. "My own mother died several years ago. And you"—he turned to Mr. Pickett—"were kinder to me than ever my own father was, and treated me . . ." His voice trailed off.

Mrs. Pickett said softly, "Go on, Jake."

"I felt I had no reason to go home. There was a girl . . . Hannah. We planned to marry. But I learned from a new prisoner that she'd run off with another boy, and I was shattered. It was exactly one year ago . . . the Fourth, so some of us decided to sing liberty songs. We had Refugee guards that day. They were always the hardest on us. I'm sorry to say it, but it's true. They kept telling us to stop singing, but we kept going.

"They drove us between decks at bayonet point. We kept singing. I was pounding on the hatch, leading the others in a chant. Tim kept trying to call me back, but I wouldn't listen. While he was climbing the ladder to pull me away, the guards opened the hatch and attacked with their cutlasses. Tim—"

He cut himself off; he had no choice. Stop speaking or weep like a child. For a long time, they all sat in silence. Then Jake went on: "I held him as he died. It was all my fault. So how could I go home? How could I face his family? They adored him. His parents . . . Tim was their only son. How could I tell those people I had caused his death? I no longer cared about Patriot and Tory. The war was nothing to me anymore, and I just wanted to forget everything. But today it has all come back to me. It's a year since Tim died. Two years since the battle. And"—he gave Mr. Pickett a weak, rueful smile—"it's our damned holiday. And that *does* matter to me. I *am* a Patriot, whatever that means, exactly. I feel . . . so low for deceiving you. You have done everything for me, and I am so sorry for it, lying to you all this time."

"You have nothing to apologize for, Jake," Mrs. Pickett said, in tears.

But Mr. Pickett snapped, "Nothing but your cause." Then he pushed his chair back noisily and stomped out of the springhouse, slamming the door.

That's the end of it, Jake thought. Mr. Pickett would go to the authorities and report that he had been inadvertently harboring a Rebel. Then back to a prison ship Jake would go.

He turned to Mrs. Pickett. "Do you hate me now?"

She gave him a rueful smile. "I used up my allotment of hatred long ago, Jake. And even if I had any left, I would not vent it on an innocent boy."

"I'll be nineteen in September," Jake said. "I don't believe I'm considered a boy any longer. And I feel far from innocent."

"Well, hatred follows from blame, dear," she replied. "And I do not blame you."

Jake could no longer bear to look into those soft, sad eyes. He pushed his chair back, stood, and walked slowly to the door, where he stopped. "I won't run away," he said. "Tell Mr. Pickett I've gone back to work."

"But my husband said you felt ill. You should lie down."

"I feel better now," he said, and he closed the door behind him.

WITH HIS RAKE, Jake spread the cut grass so that it would dry in the sun. He worked methodically, even gratefully, mindful that this could be his last time out in the sunshine for . . . well, maybe forever. Mr. Pickett was probably on his way to the British garrison at Lloyd's Neck. He'd return with some soldiers, who would take Jake into custody. To the Sugar House? Back to the Wallabout? Or maybe . . . an admitted Patriot, behind enemy lines in civilian clothing—perhaps the British would hang him for a spy, as they did Hale. But he felt eerily at peace—not panicked, only curious. As if it did not concern him.

He'd expected Mr. Pickett would be away for a long time, so he was startled to hear footsteps a short while later. Turning quickly, he saw that Mr. Pickett was alone.

"Will you turn me in?" he asked, raking faster.

For reply, Mr. Pickett put his hand on the rake's handle, to stop its motion. Then he said slowly, "Will, Elizabeth, and Thomas."

"Your children," Jake said quietly.

He nodded. "I can name them only in order of their ages, for I certainly could not place one before another in their significance to their mother and me." He cleared his throat and continued: "We lived a peaceful life, loved each other and our country. We were satisfied. But when your so-called leaders began this rebellion, forcing their radical views of 'independence' and 'liberty' on every American, I stood with those who chose to say: *You do not speak for me.* I did not, I *do* not, believe that violence and war should solve our problems with the British government—*our* government, Jake. Our government, even though we live across an ocean. But Franklin, Adams, Jefferson, and the whole lot— they took it upon themselves to speak for us all: *We must have independence! We must have war!*

"Those of us who did not agree were called traitors, inimicals. *We* the traitors, when *they* were the ones inciting treasonous civil war! When *they* were the ones causing all the mayhem and bloodshed! So I spoke up, Jake. I told anyone who would listen, just as I tell you now: it is far easier to start a war than to work at solving the problems that lead to one. For having the audacity to hold that opinion, I was tarred and feathered in front of my family and my neighbors. Tell me, young Patriot—is *that* what you call liberty?"

Jake recalled Mr. Chandler's nakedness and shame, his trembling, his fear . . . was that how it had been for Mr. Pickett? He shut his eyes against the image.

"And I said Parliament *did* indeed have the right to tax us!" Mr. Pickett's voice was shaking. "I believe that yet today!"

"But why, sir?" Jake asked.

"You're too young to recall the Seven Years War, but I fought in it. Did your father?"

"Yes, sir, he did. The French War, he called it."

"Yes—the French War. Our war against the French, to drive them off our continent. And then *your* side invited them back here, fighting side by side with our conquered enemy—to conquer us! As for taxes: we accepted our king's protection in a war that proved to be very long and very costly. If a country accepts protection, should it not pay the price?"

"No taxation without representation," Jake mumbled.

"Ah." Mr. Pickett nodded slowly. "I see you've learned to spout their specious mottos. But I don't recall our complaining when we were accepting Britain's troops and money. Do you?"

"You know I'm too young to remember," Jake said. "I'm sorry for interrupting, sir. Go on, please."

"Will was eighteen when the news came of your Declaration of Independence. He joined the Queen's Rangers at once, and went off to stand against Washington and Congress. At the time, I was so proud of him for defending his beliefs. I understand now that his fury was fed by mine. I doubt that he's alive, but I hold out hope, for my good wife's sake.

"Then, in '77, your government kidnapped Thomas and me and charged us with recruiting our neighbors for Loyalist regiments. It was true, of course. The so-called Patriots had started a civil war and were recruiting men for *their* cause. Why, then, didn't *we* have the right to protect ourselves and our beliefs? But in the name of liberty, and without a trial, we were imprisoned underground at New-gate and threatened with execution. It seems standing up for oneself is a capital offense in your young republic. Now I ask you, Jake: Which is worse? Reign by king or reign of terror?"

Mr. Pickett paused, as though waiting for a reply, but Jake said nothing. "Several months later, Thomas died in my arms, of smallpox, after suffering the most excruciating agonies, which were left unattended by our jailers. He was seventeen years old."

It was a long time before Mr. Pickett was able to continue. "Like you with your friend, I felt I was to blame for Thomas's death. After all, I had drawn him into this war, just as I drew Will. And also like you, I eventually escaped, after witnessing more inhumanity and death than I would have thought possible for one man to bear. But I dared not return home, for fear of the Patriots. I made my way to Glastonbury, where I had friends, and learned that my wife and daughter had fled to Long Island. I was smuggled through Rebel country to join them. All through the journey I dreaded having to tell Mrs. Pickett that we had lost Thomas. But when I arrived, I found out what she had been dreading to tell *me*: we had also lost our girl, who had taken ill over the winter and died, longing for her brothers and me."

Jake, averting his eyes from Mr. Pickett's stricken face, leaned on his rake and stared out over the hay field.

"The Rebels will win, Jake—I know that now. The British have ill-managed this war from the start, with their foppish, incompetent generals like that imbecile Howe, far more interested in whoring than fighting. And they have badly misjudged us Loyalists—disregarded us, almost entirely. As if we don't know our own country, our own countrymen! The Regulars insult us, steal from us, accuse us of base motives. They threw Mrs. Pickett and me out of three dwellings near Lloyd's Neck before we came to this location, simply to be as far from them as possible.

"And when it is over, they'll abandon us to our fate. One day a Rebel will return here to reclaim his farm—then where will Mrs. Pickett and I go? I've been declared dead by the Rebel government, all my property seized. I shall never see my home again; my family is destroyed. God alone knows what's to become of my good wife and me."

After a long silence, Mr. Pickett sighed deeply. "Now then, my young Patriot . . . come along. It is time."

"You're turning me in, sir?" Jake asked impassively.

"No, Jake. You are going home."

"Home?" He shook his head, feeling panicked. "No! I'll stay with you—can't I?"

"Your family, your father . . . perhaps your relations have not always been warm, but he is longing for you."

"He cares nothing for me. He has my brothers and sisters."

"You're wrong. I know it."

Jake thought of his father's words in the fort—*Steady, Jacob, God nerves the soldier's hand*—and of Father offering his last cartridge with trembling fingers.

"And your brothers and sisters," Mr. Pickett went on, "I'm sure they all pray for you and miss you."

"But Tim's family." He shut his eyes against the thought. "How can I tell them?"

"It is not your fault," Mr. Pickett said firmly. "What you did . . . it was an impulsive act, born from pain and anger."

"Yes, well, my mother always warned me about my temper and selfishness. If I had listened, Tim would be alive. He should have lived, and I should have died, and I shall never get over that."

"Jake . . . don't you think I feel the same about Thomas? He was my child. How could I have dragged him into my war, and why had he to die instead of me? Perhaps you never *will* get over Tim's death. I know I'll never get over Thomas's. But you must face up to it. And you owe it to Tim's family to let them know what happened to him."

Jake said nothing, then slowly nodded agreement.

"You survived that hell for a reason, Jake. As did I. Now it is our task before God to find out why."

"But . . . home? Now? How will I get there?"

"You'll ask the traders."

"No." Jake shook his head firmly. "I feel the same as you about them, sir. I'll have no part of it."

"This one time, we must both make an exception." Mr. Pickett gave him a wink. "I'll borrow Landon's cart and take you to the tavern."

"But . . . why must it be now? Can't I stay a while longer?"

"Jake." Mr. Pickett fixed his eyes on him. "The traders are here now, and it's the Fourth of July. You are a Patriot. You must go home." He laid a hand on Jake's back to urge him in the direction of the springhouse.

"Mrs. Pickett," Jake called as they came into view of the little garden, where she was weeding her vegetable patch. She stood and looked, expectantly, in their direction.

"I'll tell her," Mr. Pickett said. "You get your things together, then say good-bye."

Get your things together. Jake went inside and climbed up to the tiny loft. What things? He had come here with nothing but the rags in which he'd escaped and the battered shoes from Remsen's daughter. When he'd recovered enough to walk outside, Mrs. Pickett had given him the clothes he was wearing: osnaburg breeches, checked blue shirt. He took them off, folded them, and placed them on the bed.

When she had returned him his clothes from the *Bonhomme*, carefully laundered and mended, Jake had stuffed them beneath his mattress, wishing never to see them again. But now he pulled them out and put them on. On the *Bonhomme*, they had hung from his scarecrow frame; he had put on some weight since then. Jake took a final look around the loft and descended the ladder for the last time.

He walked around the damp springhouse that had been both a healing home and another kind of prison—a prison of the spirit.

Here was the fireplace that had given him such comfort in sickness. But when he warmed himself in winter, he was plagued by images of his fellow captives convulsed with shivering on the *Bonhomme*, and Tim's rotting arm sticking out of frozen sand.

Here was the little table where he had been so grateful for simple meals. But every time he sat down to eat, he thought of his messmates lining up for moldy meat, wormy bread, and gray oatmeal.

And there was the mattress Mr. and Mrs. Pickett shared . . . whenever he looked at it, whenever he observed the old couple's tender care of each other, he was reminded of all that he would never have with Hannah. Would he ever be able to love another? Would anyone ever be able to love him, hideous as he now was?

He picked up Mrs. Pickett's cracked hand mirror and slowly raised it. Facing himself was a frightening exercise, for the young man who stared back was barely recognizable: visage thin and sallow; sunken, red-rimmed eyes; stitch-scarred forehead. His hair was still short and brittle, and it never had regained its chestnut sheen. His cheeks and chin were dark with stubble; he shaved only occasionally, due to the painful remnants of a *Bonhomme* rash.

Home. He was going home. But who would know him when he got there?

WHEN JAKE STEPPED out of doors, Mrs. Pickett came forward and embraced him warmly. Then she held him at arm's length, appraising him head to toe, and said: "You are leaving us just as you came to us."

"It seems right. And besides . . . when Will comes home, having his own clothes might be a comfort to him."

At that her eyes filled up, and she blotted them with a corner of her apron.

"I am sorry," Jake said. "I only—"

"Thank you, Jake," she interrupted, and he understood her meaning: *Thank you for having faith in my faith.*

Mr. Pickett drove up in the borrowed cart and hailed Jake from the road.

"You knew all along, didn't you?" Jake asked Mrs. Pickett.

Her answer was in her gentle smile. "God led you to us, dear," she said. "He knew we needed one another. Now He is leading you home. And if He sees fit, we'll be together again, one day, under happier circumstances."

"I can scarcely speak." His shaky voice proved his words. "I'm so grateful to you both, so humbled. . . ."

Mrs. Pickett embraced him once more. "God bless you, dear," she said, then rushed inside.

Jake walked to the road and climbed up beside Mr. Pickett on the seat of the cart.

"My wife will miss you a great deal," he said as they set off.

"And I her," Jake replied. He added hesitantly: "And you as well."

After a pause, Mr. Pickett said, "All this time we have been under the same roof, not knowing we had shared so much."

"I *am* sorry I lied, sir. But living with you and Mrs. Pickett has changed my sentiments about those I called enemies. I hope the same will hold for you."

"Yes," was all Mr. Pickett said, quietly.

For a while, they rode in silence, Jake mulling over all that Mr. Pickett had said about the war and the Patriot leaders. He had never heard such things before. He'd never thought of the Tories as being against war; they were only against independence, toad-eaters for old King George. They were cowards, Jake's sire had always said: they feared change, so they bowed to royalty. All the spirited people, Father said, were in the Rebellion.

But now Jake thought of Mr. Pickett's words . . . *It is far easier to start a war than to work at solving the problems that lead to one.* Thomas Jefferson and Benjamin Franklin, John Adams and Thomas Paine and the others, Jake had no doubt they ate good meals every day and slept in comfort every night. It was all very well for such men to promote war as the answer to grievances. They were not the ones who went to battle, who suffered in captivity, who witnessed the deaths of their friends. They were not the ones who lost their lives.

All very well for Patrick Henry to say "give me liberty or give me death" while addressing Virginia statesmen in powder and ruffles. What did he know of life in the Wallabout, where there was no liberty, yet every prisoner was desperately trying to outwit death?

Jake remembered Dan's indignant words so long ago: *Perhaps you needn't call yourself a Patriot, spouting such Tory garbage.* He wondered what Dan was doing now, whether his ideas had changed at all.

"You're awfully quiet," Mr. Pickett said at last.

"I was thinking about the day one of my friends nearly accused me of being a Tory."

"You!"

"'Tis just as you said about your sons, sir. I called myself a

Patriot because that's what we were in my family, what all my friends were. But I didn't really believe we would win. I sang the songs and drank the toasts, but . . . I'd no interest in joining the Continentals. I suppose all I really wanted was for the war not to interfere with me. And then there was the battle. Watching the British boats land on my home beach, suddenly it was all real. It *meant* something. When Tim and I were captured, I found that my home was made Tryon's headquarters. We were taken to him."

"To Tryon himself?"

"Yes. I met him. He was drinking my father's claret, eating my father's shoat, and propping his damned muddy boots on my father's table."

"Tryon," Mr. Pickett said with a dismissive wave. "Another fool."

"Then on the *Bonhomme* . . . with the British and the Refugees pounding it into our heads every day that we were damned Rebels, and that was the reason for our suffering . . . how could one help but identify oneself with the cause? I *must* be a Patriot, do you see? How else could I justify it to myself, sir, everything that's happened? How could I ever admit that I have lost so much for anything but a worthy cause?"

"Just so, Jake," Mr. Pickett said, slowly nodding. "Just how I felt at New-gate. I'm a far more ardent Loyalist than I was at the beginning of all this, when I was simply expressing my opinion. Hardship and heartache bind a man to his cause."

After that they stayed silent until they reached the little port on the Sound. Mr. Pickett halted near the entrance to the King's Arms.

"Can't you let me stay?" Jake asked. "Just for a while longer? We have so much more to talk about."

"We understand each other, Jake. That is all that matters."

After a silence, Jake asked, "But what'll I do when I get inside? I'll feel ridiculous, marching in there and—"

"Simply ask for the traders, present yourself to them, say who you are and that you've escaped from a prison ship, and tell them you wish to go home."

Jake had the sensation of being an overgrown boy. This was a relatively simple thing he must do, and yet . . . it threatened to overwhelm him. But then he realized why.

Once he made this move, he would not be able to undo it. For two years, he'd been apart from the world—imprisoned and then sequestered—and now he was returning to face all the hurts and uncertainties that had weighed so heavily upon him.

When he arrived in East Haven, he would be starting an entirely new life. An adult life. Without Tim, without Hannah, without a clue as to how he would fare.

No wonder he felt overwhelmed.

"Go, Jake." Mr. Pickett's tone was gruff. "I must get back to work."

"Will you wait?" Jake asked. "In case I—"

"No," Mr. Pickett interrupted. "You will get down, and I shall drive away, and you will be on your own. That is all."

Jake nodded. They shook hands, then Mr. Pickett gripped his shoulder.

"Thank you," Jake said.

"Go with God, Jake."

"And you, sir." Jake jumped to the ground.

"Wait." Mr. Pickett removed his jacket and held it out to Jake. "Take this."

"No, sir." Jake raised his hands to refuse. "I couldn't."

"I cannot send you home in just a shirt and breeches. Please. Take it."

Jake smiled and obeyed. "Thank you." He put the jacket on, adjusted it, and gave Mr. Pickett an expectant look. Mr. Pickett gave a satisfied nod, clucked to the horse, and drove away. Jake walked confidently toward the King's Arms. "Good morning, I am Jake Mallery," he mumbled to himself. "I am from East Haven, and I wondered if—"

The door opened, and two men burst out, laughing raucously, ignoring him thoroughly. Were these the traders? Leaving already?

"Pardon me," he called. "Are you—?"

"No!" one man shouted back without turning.

"Inside!" the other advised briskly.

As Jake's eyes adjusted from the glaring sun to the dark tavern, he could see nothing but vague forms. He headed for the barmaid, who was drawing ale from a keg. "Excuse me," he said, keeping his voice low. "But can you tell me . . . which are the traders?"

She laughed. "Which traders are you wanting? The ones from Norwalk, the ones from Horseneck, or the ones from East Haven?"

"East Haven?" The floor seemed to give way beneath him. He

gripped the edge of the bar. "There are East Haven men here? That . . . that is where I'm from!" he babbled.

"Well, you can deliver their ale, by way of getting acquainted." She pushed two brimming mugs toward him; the sight made Jake's mouth water, but he had neither coin nor currency, British or American. "Those two over in the corner."

"Thank you. Yes, thank you." The men had their backs to him. Who were they? He picked up the mugs and took a deep breath. Jake felt certain he would know them. He'd known everyone in East Haven, when he left; he doubted there had been many new residents in wartime. Would they be friends of his father's, or Uncle Luddington's—the fathers of any of his friends? Silas and his crowd? Wouldn't that be a joke! Well, whoever they were, Jake hoped they were friendly.

He reached around one of them to put the glasses on the table, then said, "Pardon me, gentlemen. I'm told—"

Annoyed at the intrusion, they turned slightly, and Jake was struck dumb.

The gentlemen were Caleb and Gideon.

Both stared at him, puzzled, expectant. "Yes?" Gideon asked impatiently.

"What is it?" Caleb snapped.

Jake opened his mouth, but no sound came out.

"Oh, God! Mal!" Gideon leapt to his feet and flung his arms about Jake's neck. "Mal, dear God!"

"Gid," Caleb said in a low, embarrassed tone. "Um—that's not Mal."

"*Hell* it isn't!" Gideon pushed Jake's face right up to Caleb's.

As the light of recognition ignited in Caleb's eyes, Jake said, "Today's the Fourth. Care to race at swimming?"

Caleb gave a burst of a laugh and seized Jake in a violent embrace. "My God! How did you . . . how could you . . . what are you doing here?"

"I might ask the same of you two."

"Except that we haven't been gone for two years and given up for dead!"

Gideon pulled Jake onto the bench beside him, draping an arm across his shoulders. "I can't believe it. Look at you! *Where* have you been?"

Caleb was examining him carefully. "Drink," he said, pushing his mug of ale toward Jake and signaling to the barmaid for another.

"Thanks," Jake said, and drank down half the mug's contents.

"He *is* like a cormorant—remember, Cay?" Gideon said. "You never know where he'll pop up!"

"Ethan told everyone about Tryon. He said you and Tim were taken prisoner," Caleb said. "But when the list came back, you two were not on it. Captain Morris went to New York under a flag and appealed to Tryon. He claimed to have no knowledge of your whereabouts."

"We were put on a prison ship."

"A *prison* ship!"

"The *Bonhomme*. After Tryon sent us away, another officer said we were maritime prisoners, because we were attempting to defend the ferry." He shook his head. "He was out for revenge, because he thought I killed his nephew."

The barmaid brought Caleb's drink.

"And Tim?" Gideon asked, his tone low.

Jake cast his eyes down. "You know if he were yet alive, we would be together."

"Yes."

"And we *were* together, until the very last."

Gideon raised his glass. "A bumper to our Tim, fine Patriot and dear friend."

"Hear, hear," Caleb said.

"Tim," was all Jake could say, his voice breaking.

They touched their glasses and drank. Jake spent the next few moments gulping back tears and rubbing at his eyes with the back of his hand while Gideon patted his shoulder.

"He died on the ship, Mal?" Caleb asked at length.

"Yes." One day he would tell them everything, but Tim's family deserved to be the first to hear it. Jake cleared his throat and steeled himself to ask: "What of my brother Asa? Dead?"

"No, quite alive," Caleb said.

Jake looked up, surprised. "*Is* he? Oh, I thought sure. . . ."

"He was very bad—shot in the chest. He'd a long convalescence, but he's well now."

"My father?"

"Also wounded, but also better," Caleb said.

"Wounded? Where?"

"At Black Rock, I believe, was it not, Gid?"

"I meant . . . where on his person."

"Oh." Caleb grinned, embarrassed. "In his leg. He walks with a limp and a cane, but he's as cantankerous as ever he was."

"It's funny, but . . . I never worried about him," Jake said, shaking his head. "Not really. I told Tim the day of the battle, my father would survive if the whole town perished."

"Mal—he's done everything to try to find you," Gideon said quietly.

"*My* father?" Jake asked.

"Yes. As soon as he was able, he joined Tim's father in searching for you. All their inquiries turned up nothing."

"How did you come to be on Long Island?" Caleb asked.

"I escaped. By swimming. A few months after Tim died. I meant to make my way home, but . . . I couldn't. I can't explain now, but I have been . . . playing Tory, I suppose. Living with a Refugee couple near here. They cared for me when I was ill—it was only today that I admitted who I was. Odd, isn't it, Gid? You were forced from here, and they were forced from Connecticut. Now here we meet."

Gideon smiled uneasily.

"A neighbor knew there were some traders here. Little did I expect—"

"Hmm. Nor would we have, a year ago," Caleb said, seeming embarrassed. "We started as raiders, and then became traders."

Jake gave them a puzzled look; Gideon shrugged. "I called our boat the *Revenge*, because I said I was coming back to get what was rightfully mine. But we found the people here in straits just as bad as ours. So we began to trade. They have British goods we need. We have produce they need."

"Dan—is he involved?" Jake asked.

"Dan is with the Continentals," Caleb said. "After the battle, he had a tough time of it. There were accusations—people said the British had received intelligence about East Haven through Mr. Chandler. You *know* Dan couldn't bear that—so he went with the army, to prove to everyone that he was the hottest Patriot."

"Dan would *not* be pleased with Caleb and me," Gideon said.

"Nor is Washington," Caleb admitted.

"But this war has dragged on so long. And no one is harmed by what we do, Mal," Gideon added apologetically. "'Tis only people helping each other. It has nothing to do with the armies."

Jake didn't reply. When he was on the *Bonhomme*, such comments would have enraged him. But now he felt torn. On the one hand, what his friends said was probably true. On the other . . . Caleb and Gideon were in the bloom of health, sitting here with great mugs of ale before them. There were thousands of prisoners and soldiers who would count as luxuries the things everyone at home thought of as necessities. What would those men say about trading with the enemy?

And yet . . . he himself had been *living* with the enemy, so who was he to judge?

"Mal?" Gideon asked. "Are you angry with us?"

Jake replied with another question: "How is Ethan? Still at college?"

"After the battle, he stayed at home to help your father," Caleb said.

"And my little sisters?"

"Not so little anymore . . . especially Lorana. You won't recognize her. She has become quite a beauty."

Jake sat back in his chair, smiling. It would be good to see his sisters and Ethan. Perhaps his homecoming would be better than he'd thought. "So . . . how did you two fare the day of the battle?"

"I returned with the Mount Carmel men," Gideon said. "We joined the detachment on the cove road but were driven back. Then we did what we could by shooting at them from cover."

"I was at the Point, then Beacon Hill," Caleb said. "Captured, then paroled. But where did you and Tim go? Everyone was looking for you at Beacon Hill—including your sire."

Jake told how he and Tim had heard the British talking about capturing the ferry and decided to try to defend it. He told of the Hessians in the woods, and how his old nemesis, Mr. Rowe, had saved his life. "I should have thought he'd have explained about Tim and me. He knew where we were headed."

"I imagine he would have," Caleb said, "had he made it through the battle."

"*What?* He was killed?"

"James Chidsey saw it happen. He'd already been taken prisoner when the Regulars found Mr. Rowe in a culvert by the road. They said, 'What are you doing, you old fool, firing on His Majesty's troops?' Mr. Rowe said, 'I am exercising the privileges of war!'"

Jake smiled, remembering: the exact words Rowe had said to him and Tim.

"The British said, 'If we let you go, will you do it again?' And Mr. Rowe said, 'Nothing more likely! I rather think I should!'"

"They asked him to surrender himself," Gideon said. "Instead, he raised his gun to shoot."

"Here's to old Rowe," Jake said, raising his glass.

"Old Rowe," his friends repeated; they all drank.

"Of course you've heard about Arnold," Caleb said.

"I hope you'll be kind enough not to torment me about it," Jake replied.

"At least not for a week or two," Gideon said, and they laughed.

"You must admit, though: without Arnold, the cause would have been lost years ago."

"Can you believe him? *Still* defending that traitor scum!" Caleb said to Gideon, who just shook his head, grinning.

Jake shrugged. "I'm not excusing him, nor can I fathom his behavior. But Arnold was the lifeblood of this rebellion for years. You cannot take that away from him."

"Well, don't expect me to drink a toast to *him*," Gideon grumbled.

"Nor me," Jake answered, and they all sat silent.

Then Jake saw Gideon signal to Caleb, who said tentatively, "Mal . . . did you have any news of home at all?"

"Only what was conveyed to us by new prisoners. Men would come aboard and everyone would ask—" He grimaced at the memory, waved his hand and took another drink. "How many homes were burned? Have people rebuilt?"

Again, Caleb and Gideon darted each other a look. Jake leaned forward, pointing at them. "Why *do* you two keep doing that? Is something wrong? Are you keeping something from me?"

His friends paused, then leaned across the table to whisper to each other.

"What is it?" Jake shook Gideon by the arm. "Tell me. Is it bad?"

"There's someone you haven't asked about, Mal," Caleb mumbled.

"There are many people I haven't asked about. But who . . . oh—not *Lydia*? You don't think I still—"

"Hannah," Caleb interrupted.

Quickly, Jake averted his eyes. "You know about *that*?"

"Um . . . the whole town knows, Mal," Gideon said.

"Oh." Just when he had started to look forward to returning, here was a new and better reason to stay away. But he dug down for the old bravado, and said jauntily, "Ah, well. What's done is done. I was a fool to care for her. And to anyone who snickers, I'll be happy to admit that . . . after I pound him senseless."

His friends stared at him, but they didn't laugh or even smile.

"What?" Jake asked, frowning.

"What *are* you talking about?" Caleb asked.

"I know what happened. A new prisoner came on board who knows Tim's family." Jake ran his finger around the rim of his mug. "We asked about her. He told us."

Gideon and Caleb gave each other a look of puzzlement, then Gideon said, "What, exactly, *did* he tell you?"

"About her running off with Noah. I feel like such a—"

"Mal," Gideon interrupted, and Jake looked up at his serious face.

Caleb, too, stared with a sober countenance. "That's not the way of it. Not at all."

Jake shook his head, confused. *"What?"*

Reaching across the table, Caleb gripped Jake's arm. "She's got your child, Mal. A little boy. She calls him Jake."

Jake pulled violently away, glaring fiercely. Damn Caleb, to taunt him this way after all he'd been through, as if they were still children bantering on Five Mile Point!

But Caleb wasn't laughing, and now Gideon said, "He's not playing, Mal. Hannah *did* go away—for her lying-in. The Morrises sent her to stay with Mrs. Morris's sister. It's got nothing to do with Noah; he's still in Continental service, as far as we know."

"But . . . but . . ." Jake propped his elbows on the table and held his head in both hands, casting his memory back. Levi had spoken of something improper. It was Jake who had supplied Noah's name. Now it turned out her only impropriety was the one she'd committed with Jake . . . the one that had got her with his child. And she'd had to face the consequences alone. "Did she . . . how did she . . . ?"

Gently, Gideon laid a hand on his back. "Hannah refused to say who the father was, right up until the birth. But the midwife said she named you."

Jake squeezed his eyes shut. She'd kept their secret all through her pregnancy, hoping not to tarnish his name. At such times it was the midwife's duty to find out who the father was, for he

must be made to support the child. Poor Hannah, all alone, inter-
rogated at the height of her labors; what pain and desperation she
must have felt to give in and name him at last. And all this time
he'd been thinking the worst of her, hating her from the depths
of the *Bonhomme* and wishing he were dead.

"Captain Morris told your father," Gideon went on. "He
refused to believe it, but Ethan had found some letters in your
bedroom. He showed them to your father."

Jake felt himself begin to tremble.

"Your father went to visit Hannah," Caleb said. "And the next
thing we knew, she and the babe were living at your house."

"Mal, are you hearing this?" Gideon asked.

Jake opened his mouth, but instead of a reply all he heard was
a sharp, deep gasp, as when a person comes to the surface after
being underwater too long.

"Is he all right?" he heard Caleb say.

"I'm not sure."

"I'll get him something stronger."

"Mal?" Gideon asked as Caleb hurried away. "Are you all
right? This is *good* news, no? You're pleased, are you not?"

Jake nodded, but he still could not speak.

Caleb put a draught of rum into his hand. "Drink it, Mal."

"Is he upset?"

"No, he's glad. He's just . . ."

Jake drank the rum down, then raised his eyes to his friends.
They both grinned broadly; Caleb shook him by the shoulders.
"You have a son!"

"And a fine one, Mal," Gideon said warmly.

"They're all mad for him, at your house."

"Your sisters carry him everywhere."

"And your father is forever dandling him on his knee."

"My father?" Jake thought he sounded as though he were strangling.

"You've never seen an old daddy make such a fool of himself over a baby."

"*My* father?" Jake only repeated, and his friends laughed. "And Hannah?"

"She's well," Gideon said. "She's just like one of the family."

"She has always believed you were alive," Caleb said.

"If anyone dares to say 'Mal was,' she flies at them."

"It's too much." Jake struggled to his feet, casting his eyes all around. Where was the door? He had to get out of here. He was drowning, suffocating—he would die if he didn't get out of this tavern now. He bolted for the door and ran around the side of the building, leaning on the wall, breathing hard and fast. This could not be real. . . .

No, this wasn't real, because Hannah had run away with Noah, and it had hurt Jake so badly that he'd sung the liberty songs to make the guards angry. He wouldn't stop even when Tim begged him to, and that was why Tim had died: because Hannah had run away with Noah. And after he'd escaped he had hidden away with the Picketts because there was nothing to go home to except confessing his shame to Tim's family.

But now Caleb and Gideon said he had a son, and Hannah loved him still, and the only thing that had not changed was that

Tim was dead and it was Jake's fault, and it had happened for no reason at all.

Hannah loved him still, and they had a little boy. That was the reason Jake had survived . . . but why did Tim have to die?

He felt he could not bear this pain. His body heaved with sobs as he pictured Tim, bleeding to death in the *Bonhomme*'s filth, looking up at him, the wan smile, the fingers on Jake's face: *Bon homme*. And in the morning when Jake's messmates wrested the body from his tight grasp, the damned Refugee guards would not allow him to bury Tim because he'd just been to shore the previous day. . . .

Caleb and Gideon joined him, one on each side, lending support without speaking. Standing there with these boys, his friends—these men, so kind and solicitous, yet so hopelessly ignorant—Jake realized he was not like them anymore, nor would he ever be again. He was like Tim and Fish and Eels and Meecham and Fortnum and Bell and all those he had left on the *Bonhomme* and buried in the Wallabout. He was like Mr. and Mrs. Pickett and Thomas and Will and Elizabeth and Remsen's daughter and everyone else who had been touched by this war in a way Caleb, and even Gideon, would never understand.

"You don't know," was all he said, at last. "You don't know."

"All will be well," Gideon said, and he wrapped an arm around Jake's neck. "Let's go home."

THE *REVENGE* WAS a small fishing skiff with a single lugsail. When they had rowed off the beach, Caleb hoisted the sail and set the tack. Gideon sat at the tiller and took hold of the sheet;

Jake sat fore. Once under sail his friends tried to tell him all about Hannah and the baby, who was just now learning to walk. But Jake would not be engaged.

"Don't you want to hear about your child?" Caleb asked.

"No. I want to find out for myself."

"Are you all right, Mal?" Gideon said.

"Yes," was his only reply, and then they were quiet.

The wind was in their favor, and soon they were running with it. Jake leaned on the bow and looked toward home. Thought brought on thought as he relived the day's events. He felt as if he were floating, unreal, ghostly . . . anxious to arrive, yet grateful for every second of the crossing.

He was desperate to see Hannah, and at the same time dreaded meeting her eyes. *She has always believed you are alive.* But what if she gave him the same blank stare as Caleb? What if she was repulsed by his appearance?

And how had she changed in two years? How must she have felt when she realized she was pregnant, not knowing where he was or whether he would return? He thought of how his cruel song had come true: *Till her belly grew up to her chin and her spirits fell down to her heels . . .* And of course she carried on with that solemn dignity of hers, protecting his name even though her own was dragged through the mud. He wished he could have been with her when she had their child. He thought of his own mother, so ill during those times. The image of Hannah giving birth afraid and alone raked at his heart.

How could he have been so quick to believe that she had

forsaken him? It seemed impossible now, unimaginable—but then, so did the *Bonhomme*.

That was the only explanation for it: away from her for a year, struggling for survival, he had lost sight of her. Now he would never doubt her again. He would spend the rest of his life show-ing her that he loved her, taking care of her and their son. A son. He had a son called Jake—that was enough to content him with being Mal forever.

All at once it occurred to him that they were in the open Sound in broad daylight, and turning to his friends he asked, "Is it not dangerous? Making the trip by day?"

Gideon and Caleb exchanged a look and burst out laughing.

"What is *that* supposed to mean?" Jake said.

"Only, we know what we're doing," Gideon assured.

"You're losing speed, Gid," Jake told him. "You're sailing too close to the wind."

Gideon jerked his head toward Jake and said to Caleb, "Listen to him. As if I haven't done this countless times!"

"Some things will never change," Caleb replied, shaking his head.

"You're pinching, I tell you," Jake said. "Free a little."

"Go back to your private reverie, will you?" Gideon advised, but he took the advice, and before long they were sailing full and bye.

Jake shut his eyes and turned his face to the sun. Soon he would be teaching his own son to sail, to swim, to rake oysters and tend the ferry. When he was small, who had taught him all those things? He could not remember. Surely it was Asa, never his father.

His father . . . it must have been a trial for him, religious and strict as he was, to learn about Hannah and the baby. It was hard to imagine the old man traveling to Stonington to see her, hard to picture poor Hannah telling him face-to-face. But his sire had stood by her, accepting, no, loving their child. *Your father . . . He is longing for you.* Jake thought of the Picketts, longing for their dead and missing children, imprisoned on Long Island with their memories of life before the war. From now on, Jake knew, things would be different between his father and him.

The sun was nearly touching the water by the time Jake spotted East Rock and West Rock in the distance. It reminded him of Tim, the morning of the battle, saying, *Come no farther, damned British scoundrels, we have guard over those who live here. . . .*

Now Jake was returning alone, with the full knowledge of what that meant, to Tim's family and to himself. The night of Tim's death had left a permanent scar, no less than the stitches on his forehead or the inoculation mark on his hand. And it was only right that he should bear that scar, but he understood now that the only men responsible for Tim's death were the ones who killed him.

He would confide all of it to Hannah—Tim's terrified delirium, his searing pain, his haunting words: *Don't tell my mother*— and she would help him decide what to say to Tim's parents. Hannah would understand, for she had fought in wars all her life: the war of a child orphaned young, of indentured servitude, of an unmarried woman alone with her burden.

Jake's eyes scanned the horizon, back and forth, again and again until he said, "Is that the Point? I think I see the Point!"

"It won't be much longer," Caleb replied.

Jake's throat felt dry, his palms wet. Who would see him first? How would he react? What would happen next, and next, and next? When would the Morrises have to learn that Tim was dead? When would he see Hannah and their child? What did the baby look like? How would the child respond when he found himself in the arms of his father, a stranger? Jake's skin was crawling with anxiety, he could not sit still. . . . He kicked off his shoes, stripped off his stockings, and said, "I'll swim to the rocks."

"*What?*" Caleb said.

In response, Jake flung himself into the Sound.

"Mal!"

"Are you mad?"

"'Tis half a mile yet!"

The water was already taking its soothing effect. He was not worried about the distance; if he could swim from the *Bonhomme* to shore on a frigid night, in his depleted state, with shots ringing all around him, he could surely swim home now.

There was no need to dive under, for he was not racing and he didn't need to hide. It felt good to swim on the surface, with the setting sun reflecting off the Sound and onto his face.

You are leaving us just as you came to us, Mrs. Pickett had said, but that was not quite right. Inside, he was a different person.

Not changed, but changing. Not healed, but healing.

Home would be a new place, a place where he was husband and father . . . a place without his dearest friend, without boyhood, without resentment of his father, without childish idolatry of an arrogant military man.

I used up my allotment of hatred, Mrs. Pickett had said, and Jake thought, *Yes, that is how I want to be*. He imagined the cool, clear Sound washing away his anger and bitterness, his fear and shame and pain.

He had grown up on a prison ship, and he had survived. Now he vowed to himself that he would honor Fish's final request by telling the story of those who had perished. They had sacrificed all in the name of this thing called liberty, and it should never be forgotten.

Jake stretched his arms in front of him, pushed the water aside, stretched ahead again. Stretch, push, stretch, push; with every stroke, he felt stronger, more capable. The shore was very close now. He sensed it in the temperature of the water, in the screeches of gathering gulls, in the sound of waves lapping against land.

For him the war was over, no matter how it might end. And when he reached up and touched the warm red rock of home, he finally knew how it felt to be free.

Author's Note

★

APPROXIMATELY 11,500 AMERICANS died on British prison ships anchored in New York's Wallabout Bay, near what is now the Brooklyn Navy Yard. By comparison, the estimated American death toll for all Revolutionary War battles combined is only about 4,500. At the war's end, the prison ships were sunk to the bottom of the bay. Regrettably, our national photo album of the Revolution consists only of a few snapshots: Washington crossing the Delaware, Paul Revere on his horse, winter at Valley Forge, a handful of Patriots tossing tea into Boston Harbor. The prison ship martyrs' ordeal has been all but forgotten.

In 1808, the prisoners' bones were disinterred from their makeshift graves near Remsen's Mill and given a proper burial in a nearby tomb. Another hundred years passed before the Prison Ship Martyrs Monument was built in Brooklyn's Fort Greene Park, and the remains were reinterred in a crypt on that hallowed ground.

While it would be impossible to list all the sources that informed my knowledge of the people and events in this book, I want to mention two standouts: *The British Invasion of New Haven, Connecticut*, by Charles Hervey Townshend, and Captain Thomas Dring's memoir *Recollections of the Jersey Prison-Ship*, edited by Albert Greene. I owe a particular debt to Captain Dring's remarkable document, which details the brutal treatment he and other American prisoners endured, including a deadly attack by Loyalist guards for singing patriotic songs on the Fourth of July (1782). Some of the quoted matter in the "Prisoner" section of this book comes direct from Dring's account.

Readers often ask authors of historical fiction whether the people in our novels "really existed" and if events "really happened." Jake Mallery is based on a real boy named Jesse Mallery, an ancestor of my husband, Samuel Mallory Hughes (the name's spelling was changed in the nineteenth century). At age sixteen, Jesse, along with his father, Isaac, and his brother Asa, fought in the Battle of New Haven on July 5, 1779. The Morris family is modeled on that of Captain Amos Morris, whose home still stands as the historic Pardee-Morris House in East Haven, Connecticut. (My husband is also a descendant of the Pardees, whose ferry and family are mentioned in the book.)

According to a typewritten Mallory family history—which I discovered as we were cleaning out my husband's childhood home in Pennsylvania—Jesse was at the Morris home just before the British attacked: "Jesse Mallery and his friend were there, and when they saw the British coming, said 'Let us get another mug of cider,' which they did, and as the British came into the back door, they ran out of the front door down the lane [to Black Rock], bullets whistling around their heads as they ran." With that colorful account, this book was born.

In researching the people of the era—about whom I had known almost nothing—I found them to be remarkably human, not at all the wooden caricatures of perfection that are often paraded before us. By the time of the Revolution, many American teenagers were surprisingly similar to their present-day counterparts. Foreign visitors commented on their independent spirit— and their smart mouths. They annoyed their neighbors, they sneaked out at night, they partied. Young men like Jesse Mallery grabbed one more cup of hard cider before rushing out the door to fight the British. And despite the inexplicable myth that our forebears universally practiced sexual abstinence before marriage, premarital pregnancy was, indeed, far from uncommon.

Finally, what about the character of Hannah? I know that some readers will ask. Jesse Mallery did in fact marry a girl named Hannah, but as far as I know she was an indentured servant only in my imagination. According to East Haven's Congregational Church records, Jesse Mallery and Hannah Rowe, both eighteen, were married in 1781. The marriage appears in the church records during the latter part of the year, although the date is not specified; the couple's first child was born in March 1782. Jesse and Hannah raised a total of seven children, lived into their sixties, and are buried side by side in New Haven's Union Cemetery.

Lowell School
1640 Kalmia Road, NW
Washington, DC 20012